FAIL

TO THE

CHIEF

A NOVEL OF
POLITICAL SATIRE
(MAYBE)

FAIL
TO THE
CHIEF

A NOVEL OF
POLITICAL SATIRE
(MAYBE)

V.R. CRAFT

LIFFEY
PRESS
an imprint of
OGHMA CREATIVE MEDIA

OGHMA
CREATIVE MEDIA

Liffey Press
An imprint of Oghma Creative Media, Inc.
2401 Beth Lane, Bentonville, Arkansas 72712

Library of Congress Cataloging-in-Publication Data

Names: Craft, V.R., author.
Title: Fail to the Chief/V.R. Craft.
Description: Second Edition. | Bentonville: Liffey, 2019.
Identifiers: LCCN: 2018952667 | ISBN: 978-1-63373-474-6 (hardcover) | ISBN: 978-1-63373-475-3 (trade paperback) | ISBN: 978-1-63373-191-2 (eBook)
Subjects: | BISAC: FICTION/Satire | FICTION/Political | FICTION/Humorous
LC record available at: https://lccn.loc.gov/2018952667

Liffey Press trade paperback edition January, 2019

Cover & Interior Design by Casey W. Cowan
Editing by Gil Miller

"All the world's a stage,
And all the men and
women merely players."

—William Shakespeare,
As You Like It, Act II, Scene VII

1

"TEN SECONDS!" BRYAN'S PRODUCER, Shanda, shrieked, which was completely unnecessary because he had no less than three assistants flashing ten fingers each at him. At his first reporting job in Nowhereville, Oklahoma, he'd been lucky if anyone in the control room was awake enough at five a.m. to turn his mic on, let alone cue him. The camera ops were usually asleep in their chairs behind the camera.

But after ten years, he'd finally made it to the big leagues, hosting what was sure to be the most popular prime-time reality show in history.

Shanda continued her shrill countdown. She didn't have a regular voice, at least not one he'd ever heard her use. *"Five, four, three, two...."*

The network's choice of insipid theme songs boomed into his IFB, the tiny device in his ear that allowed him to hear both the network... and Shanda. While the show's slate flashed on the monitor beneath Bryan's camera, he adjusted his tie for the millionth time, then gave up and stood, hands sweaty as they gripped his mic. He had another clipped to his lapel and dozens more surrounded the set, but the producers wanted him to have something to do with his hands.

"Standby!" Shanda shouted in his ear as the music faded and the pink-haired camera op raised her hand in Bryan's direction. He popped up on the monitor and she pointed at him.

"*Cue!*" Shanda screamed, and he made a mental note to adjust his IFB volume as soon as they rolled the first package.

"Hello, and welcome to a night that will change all our lives forever," he read off the prompter. The script was corny as hell, but every time he complained Shanda told him he got paid to look good in a $5,000 suit, not write his own lines. "As you know, there have been many popular reality shows, but none with the serious impact of what you are going to see tonight. Contrary to the rumors you may have read on social media, this show is *not* a joke. It is legally binding, and the winner *will* get the job. I'm your host Bryan Seafoam, and *this* is your next *American President.*

"Now, the contestants" —he waved behind him at the green screen. On the monitor, it looked like all ten contenders were seated behind him in a U-shaped auditorium— "have been briefed on and agreed to the rules, but we'll go over them again for you folks at home."

Also unnecessary, given the huge amount of publicity the show had received in the last few months, but something the producers made him do, anyway.

Bryan moved off the set, walking slowly and keeping his head turned to the side so the camera op could follow him. She kept pace with him, the big black eye of the camera never straying from his face as she steered the enormous rolling tripod with one foot, pushing off the floor with the other, like a kid riding a skateboard.

"Many of you had questions about how this presidential election would work." Bryan ambled down the red carpeted hallway and through a large archway, chosen because there was ample room for the cameras to follow him. "As you probably know, due to rising concerns about a number of problems—campaign spending, the fact that more Americans vote for the worst-rated reality show than vote for president, and the disastrous voter fraud scandal of two years ago—Congress proposed the Twenty-eighth Amendment, more commonly known as the By the People, For the People Act, to completely overhaul our election system. When it was ratified, it repealed the Twelfth Amendment, which had given us our electoral system since 1804."

Through the archway, he walked to the center of the room and sat at a large, intricately carved wooden desk. A sea of blue carpet spread out around him, interrupted only by the fifteen-foot diameter seal of the United States. Each room in this building—the candidates' home until they were voted off—was an exact replica of a room in the White House. He was in the "Oval Office," which was built to scale larger than the real thing's 816 square feet, in order to accommodate all ten contestants, plus cameras, crew members, aides, and assistants.

"The By the People, For the People Act did away with our old system of electing a president. The ten contestants you see filing in right now" —he paused while the control room cut away from him to show the suited men and women marching into the room— "will live in this building until they are voted off the show. They will eat, sleep, and work here, unless directed to leave for a competition. They will be recorded twenty-four seven, and viewers are encouraged to log onto the Candidate Cam—the address is on your screen there, or you can visit our website and follow the link—to watch our live feed.

"After each episode, we'll open up the website for voting. When you vote, you'll be asked to enter your voter registration number, password, and answer three secret questions you chose when registering—also a requirement of the By the People, For the People Act—and you will not be able to vote more than once. Online voting will remain open for exactly thirty minutes, and results will be announced at the end of *American President: Aftermath,* which will air immediately after this show.

"The Candidate Cams will be live twenty-four seven, and will be archived, as will our live show. So that you can make an informed decision, you can go back and watch anything any candidate does at any time during this competition. If you are looking for a particular piece of video, our website archives come with an interactive assistant, Artie, who can help you find what you'd like to watch.

"No, there will not be an election day this year. There will be no traditional campaigning or voting. The person who receives the least votes after each voting episode will be eliminated, and the last candidate standing will be your next *American President*. The second runner-up will be vice president, and the person in third place will be Secretary of State. All other cabinet positions will be appointed using the existing guidelines.

"The inauguration process has also changed. On our final voting night, the winner will be announced and the inauguration will happen immediately, in a three-hour, star-studded spectacle." Bryan suppressed a wince. He'd tried to talk Shanda out of it, pointing out *star-studded spectacle* sounded like a magic act in Vegas, but as usual, she didn't care about his opinion. "Now, let's meet the contestants!"

He breathed a sigh of relief as Shanda shrieked *"Clear!"* and the monitor rolled a lengthy package introducing the candidates. As pre-recorded bullshit flooded the screen, he looked at the actual people, glad-handing and beaming false smiles at each other. Senators, congress-people, governors, people who were just rich and bored—all about to get a big surprise.

The package ended and Shanda shouted *"Cue!"* in his ear, just seconds after he remembered to turn down the volume on his mic pack. He got up, walked around the desk, and marched straight into the crowd of candidates. They all shut up and stepped aside, faux smiles tattooed on their faces.

"Thank you all for agreeing to participate in this historic occasion." He gestured to the rows of red-and-white striped couches to either side of the group. "Please have a seat, and I'll explain your first challenge."

The presidential hopefuls looked first at the couches, then each other. Leave it to the leaders of our country to waste an hour analyzing who sits where and who's next to who and what will NASCAR dads think if I sit next to a member of the other party?

"Sit directly behind where you're standing," Bryan said. "We need to move quickly, as you have limited time for your first assignment. You'll see why in a moment."

Reluctantly, the candidates sat, stiff as statues. Bryan turned and walked back toward the desk, stopping at the end of the couches. He was directly between Phil Willard, a Californian who had been in Congress longer than Bryan had been on Twitter, and Sara Finnegan, a former tech CEO who claimed her business expertise would help fix the country's economic problems.

"Now, as you all know, the By the People, For the People Act says that all challenges must be selected by the voters. So in the previous weeks, we opened up our Facebook page to suggestions, and compiled a list of the ones with the most likes. Then we distributed the list to all of you" —he swept a hand backward, toward the candidates— "and asked which challenges you'd most like to participate in. We will be using the twenty challenges that were least popular among your group."

"What?" Willard sputtered, slapping the knees of his jeans, which he wore every day with a suit jacket and tie, to show the people of his state he was just like them. Just richer and more powerful.

"Why *did* you ask our opinions?" demanded Martin Morganstern, a former Wall Street banker and current senator from New York who, like Finnegan, claimed he could fix the economy if elected.

"We asked which assignments you wanted to see, not which ones you hoped to avoid," Bryan explained. "Obviously those are the ones that stand the best chance of making you look less like your carefully-crafted images and more like yourselves. By doing those challenges, we believe we'll get a more accurate representation of what you're all really like.

"Now, let's get started. This first challenge was number three on the list of top twenty competitions you didn't want to do." Bryan walked over to the desk and picked up a six-inch binder. "Your assignment will be to balance the Congressional budget. Those of you who have served in Congress may be familiar with this process, but you'll be doing things a little differently today. You will not have the option of shutting down the government if you can't agree. You will arrive at a balanced budget within the next twelve hours, or you will all be disqualified."

"Outrageous!" Milton Buckshaw was the morbidly obese, booming-voiced governor of Texas, known more for his bluster than his accomplishments. "You can't expect us to do in twelve hours what Congress can't do in two months."

"And you can't disqualify *all* of us." Sara Finnegan stared daggers at Bryan. "Who's going to run this country if you disqualify every single candidate running for president?"

Bryan smiled. Out of the corner of his eye, he saw the prompter on the nearest camera blink, a sure sign the network's automaton, Artie, had updated it with an answer to the question she'd asked. It was a reasonably accurate program, but he didn't need a script to handle this one. In fact, he'd been waiting for someone to ask.

"That won't be a problem, Ms. Finnegan. You lot are just the A team. We've got a B team ready to go if you all wash out by episode two. There's also a C team."

The candidates gawked at him.

"This is exactly why I voted against the By the People, For the People Act," said Fred Haverty, an Ohio senator who had earned an early advantage in the presidential race by naming every one of his mistresses before the press could dig them up, thus, in his words, proving he was honest. "This country could wind up being run by someone who didn't even make the first cut."

"We were all top contenders in our parties before the act passed." Buckshaw yanked his belt buckle up higher on his massive midsection. "What did you do, ask the cleaning staff at your hotel if they'd like to run for president?"

"Yeah, I'd like to know who's on this B team," Willard said.

"All sorts of people who have wanted to be president at least as long as you all have. In some cases, much longer." Bryan leaned against the carved desk and scratched his head, trying to look deep in thought. *ACT NATURAL AND TRY TO SOUND LIKE YOU'RE ADLIBBING*, prompted the prompter. "Let's see, several people from the Green Party, besides the one who made it onto the A team" —he nodded at Bob Fuller, who was only on the show because Shanda thought adding a "no-chancer" would make things more interesting— "a bunch of Libertarians, Kanye West, some guy named Ross Perot who says he's been running since before my parents were born, guy who goes by the name of Joe the Plumber—"

"This is ridiculous!" Buckshaw hefted his considerable girth off the couch, causing Finnegan and Willard to scramble for higher ground. Rumor had it he was in talks with the network to appear on the next season of *Lose the Lard* if he didn't win this show. "You can't possibly think one of those clowns would make a better president than one of *us.*"

"It's not up to me." Bryan flashed the smile he used to reserve for people who had just been voted off *Sing Your Heart Out* and weren't going quietly. "These are the rules the network decided on, all approved by the American people through Facebook polls."

"Then the American voter is failing to grasp the gravity of this situation," Haverty said. "Surely the voters didn't think some guy with a plumbing show would be better equipped to run our country than me."

"I think the American voter is tired of taking crap from politicians." He was supposed to sound like he was adlibbing. "The idea is not to elect an inexperienced unknown, but to force all of you to do the job Congress keeps failing to do. So if you think anyone in this room would make a better president than Joe the Plumber—who does not have a TV show by the way—then I suggest you all work together and balance that budget. Because if you don't, you're proving that you care more about your own egos than you do about America having a capable leader."

With that, he walked off the set, leaving the candidates squabbling in the background.

2

THAT WAS A BIG risk, but it worked." Shanda chased him down the hall to his dressing room, her six-inch stilettos drilling tiny round marks in the red carpet. "Twitter's blowing up, and there are more comments about you than the candidates. Someone even started a hashtag called **voteforseafoam**."

Bryan groaned and collapsed into his makeup chair. "Did you explain that I'm not running and I have no interest in the job? Or that I'm not even old enough to be president?"

"Of course not. Everyone with any sense knows that, and we want the hashtag to trend. But don't worry, the candidates will start getting some attention soon." Shanda put a hand out to stop the camera operator at the door. "Stay." She slammed the door in his face.

"Oh, I wasn't worried about them." Bryan grabbed the jar of baby wipes he kept on his dressing table and scraped the first three layers of makeup off his face. President was the last thing he wanted to be. After starting his career in television with the goal of reporting serious exposés about the problems of society, he instead wound up interviewing actors, singers, jugglers, and people trying to fit in skinny jeans. What he really wanted was a job with no bullshit, but that would mean no politics... and no television.

"You need to be watching what the candidates do so you can ask them about it when you pop back in later." Shanda turned on the TV that filled almost an entire wall, tuned to a live feed of the Oval Office where the candidates were attempting to balance the budget. "We have you scheduled to check in with them in four hours. I'm hoping we have multiple hashtags trending by then."

"Sounds great." Four hours sounded like a great opportunity to take a nap. It was going to be a long night, and if anything exciting happened, he could find out on Twitter when he woke up.

"We're hoping to get some good soundbites out of that." Shanda shook her head at the screen, where Willard yelled something about spending money on a program to reduce greenhouse gases by putting charcoal underwear on dairy cows.

"Does the National Institute of Health really need five hundred thousand dollars to determine why people make poor decisions when drunk?" Buckshaw shot back.

Shanda snickered. "That's just the tip of the iceberg. They'll be at each other's throats in an hour. But even if they're not, I've got interns digging up dirt on every one of them."

"You know I hate doing that. I'm not a hard-hitting investigative reporter." Not now, anyway. Not since he gave up real journalism to host reality competitions. "And I thought this was going to be a serious show."

"This is whatever kind of show gets us ratings, and I'm not asking you to investigate anything—I've got people doing the hard part for you."

He leaned back and closed his eyes, but he still saw the bright lights of the set playing on the inside of his lids. "Okay, but just try to stay away from tacky tabloid crap."

"It's all tacky tabloid crap. Guess what? We're digging into the candidates' internet browser history." He couldn't see it, but he knew Shanda's bright red lips were curved into a smile by the sound of her voice—somewhat less ear-splitting than usual. "While they're arguing about cow farts, we're going through the laptops in their rooms—and before you ask, yes, we can. Their contract stipulates they have no privacy expectations while on this show and we can access their rooms and luggage at any time for security or publicity reasons. Now rest up, we've got a long night ahead."

3

AT MIDNIGHT, SHANDA'S SCREAMING woke him from a nap on the sofa in his dressing room. He fumbled for his tie while assistants hauled him from the couch to the makeup chair.

"Have you been watching the feeds?" Shanda barreled past the makeup artists and waved a tablet in his face.

He blinked, struggling to focus through the haze of not-enough sleep in his eyes. "I guess I nodded off. What happened?"

"They're ripping each other to shreds." She tapped the screen with a red, white, and blue striped nail, and a live feed rolled.

One of the makeup people slammed Bryan back into his seat as he leaned forward to watch the video, and the other jabbed an eyeliner pencil in his face. "Look up at the ceiling."

"That's okay, I'll turn up the sound," Shanda said.

Did that mean she was going to stop talking?

But some of the voices on the recording were almost as shrill as Shanda's.

"I will never agree to that deal." Buckshaw's voice got louder with each word. "You will not cut funding to my state's economic recovery plan—"

"So if you're elected president, you're only going to act in the interest of your own home state, just like you are now?" Sara Finnegan's voice cut him off as the makeup artist released Bryan and he bounced out of his chair.

Shanda shoved the tablet into his hand.

"That's entirely different. As a member of Congress—"

"As a fellow member of Congress, I'd like to talk about the funding we've given Texas two years in a row," Haverty's smooth voice cut in as Bryan hurried down the hall, Shanda running after him.

"Yes, let's talk about that. Is it true you used the money to commission a seventy-five-thousand-dollar statue of yourself to be built and displayed at the state capital?" Morganstern asked.

Bryan froze the video and walked into the Oval Office, which now looked more like a federal disaster area, just in time to see Willard paste a surprised look on his face. Unfortunately, he did that by dropping his jaw and leaning his head back, a move that made his turkey neck look much worse. The world of social media was going to have a field day with that as a GIF.

"That is not true at all. You see, I dedicated that money to beautifying the capital, to create jobs. A committee voted to—"

"A committee you appointed," Finnegan cut in.

"Not at all! I made a few recommendations, but—"

"And created about ten jobs, most of which went to your friends and supporters, and all of which will evaporate with the federal funding you so desperately want to keep." Haverty straightened his navy tie. "Well, *I* will never vote for *that*. Never!"

"Jump in any time now." Shanda was still out in the hallway, but her voice was an ever-present intruder in his ear, thanks to the IFB.

"Why don't we take a moment and recap where we are?" Bryan asked as loudly as he could without making his mic pop, and the arguing died down to a dull roar.

"Yes, Senator Foster here is making his stand over a pork barrel for the state of Iowa." Finnegan smoothed her frozen brown bob and stepped next to Bryan, apparently trying to make sure the cameras focused on her.

"An *actual* pork barrel," said Ronald Chump, the multi-trillionaire who'd decided to run for office only after being told he couldn't direct-purchase the

White House. He tried to sue, claiming he legally owned it anyway because he'd paid more than the building was worth in taxes, but after his lawsuit was kicked out he gave up and threw his hat in the ring.

"I will not allow Congress to cut funding to my state's hog farmers." Joe Foster raked a hand through what was left of his graying brown hair. "We produce more pork than any other state in this beautiful country."

"And receive more of it, too," Buckshaw said. "That subsidy will cost almost twenty million."

"That money is for the farmers who produce our food, not an indulgent statue," Foster shot back.

"Jump in now," Shanda said.

"Let's back up a second." Bryan consulted his tablet, where reminder messages from Shanda and the show's computerized research assistant—yet another Artie application—peppered the screen. "To start, I'd like to remind all of you that the federal budget this year is capped at four point five trillion—"

"Which isn't *nearly* enough to dispense all the pork my fellow members of Congress want," Buckshaw cut him off. "When I'm president, I'll put a stop to that by introducing a bill—"

"Hang on there, Congressman." Bryan held up his free hand. "First, I need to point out that revenues for this year are only four point three trillion."

Although it was November 1st in Washington D.C., he was sure he heard crickets chirping over the ensuing silence.

"Of course, this has never been a requirement before, but don't you think you should at least try to stick to four point three trillion?" Bryan asked after ten seconds of the candidates' staring like he had two heads.

"Well, we could do that with my planned bill to eliminate pork barrels," Buckshaw said. "It would—"

"It could be done if we subsidized hog farmers and stopped spending so much on health care," Foster groused.

"We already cut funding from ten billion to five billion," snapped Willard. "Leaving millions with less coverage than last year. I promise if I'm elected—"

"You'll raise taxes to pay for more bloated federal programs." Chump marched over to Bryan and jabbed a finger at his chest. "Now listen here, young man, you've got to put a stop to this silly competition so I can fix the budget myself."

"Yeah, this doesn't work that way." Bryan waved his hands over his head. "Time out!"

All the candidates returned to their what-is-wrong-with-him stare.

"Time out? Can't you see we have work to do?" Haverty demanded.

"Of course, but the By the People, For the People Act clearly states the voters will be able to give candidates feedback in real time. None of you want to miss an opportunity to gain votes later, do you?"

"I always want feedback from my constituents." Morganstern adjusted a diamond cufflink on the sleeve of his Saks suit.

"Mr. Morganstern, you haven't been elected anything yet. You don't have constituents, but we need to move on." Bryan tapped his tablet and the giant green screen that formed the "window" of the Oval Office dissolved into a display of the show's Twitter feed. "Artie, the computer program that performs all our research and assists viewers with the video archives, gathered the suggestions on social media marked **#ihaveanidea** that had the most likes, shares, and retweets."

"This should be brilliant," Finnegan mumbled under her breath.

"Go after her," Shanda screeched in Bryan's ear.

"I'm sorry, what was that? Would you care to say it a little louder?" Ronda Harper elbowed Bryan out of the way to stand next to Finnegan.

He breathed a sigh of relief. At least now he didn't have to play the bad guy. Although it was sort of supposed to be his job now, and he had *wanted* it to be his job for a very long time, it might hurt his career at this point. After years of being the nice guy who handed tissues to crying contestants, he couldn't suddenly start calling people on their bullshit. If he did, TV commentators would slam him for "trying to be a real reporter all of a sudden," and his fans would hate him for being mean to the contestants. Some days he wished he'd never given up real journalism to host TV shows, even if the pay was a lot better.

Finnegan cleared her throat. "I believe our time would be better spent continuing to work on the problem. I don't think favorite tweets will provide a solution we economic experts haven't arrived at in four hours."

"We economic experts? Didn't your company go bankrupt shortly after you bailed out with a golden parachute?" Ronda turned to face the camera and flashed her unnaturally white teeth. "I worked my way up from a job waiting tables to—"

"Using your husband's reputation to get yourself elected to Congress?"

"What a sexist thing to say. This is why it's important that *I* be president, because you'll set women's rights back fifty years."

"We don't have time for this." Bryan tapped the tablet again. "Here are the suggestions. Number one comes from Avery L. on Facebook, and it says, and I quote, 'We spent almost ten million in taxpayer money last year for upkeep on the White House, including half a million on flowers alone, and almost three million on annual holiday decorations. Is all that really necessary? I mean, how many flowers do you really need in a ginormous mansion? Couldn't you cut that spending down to five million?'"

"That sounds like the fiscally responsible thing to do." Morganstern straightened his tie and turned to face the nearest camera. "When I was the head of Cheatham Bank, the largest banking group in the country, I made sure we didn't waste money on unimportant things like decorations, or paid vacations for employees. I even limited the amount of money we spent on toilet paper each month. If the employees ran out, they just had to find another solution. It prevented them from wasting paper."

"Actually, according to an exposé into your inhumane HR practices, it just caused them to use more expensive printer paper for, ah, alternative purposes." Haverty stepped between Morganstern and the camera. "I understand some also used the widely-distributed company newsletter with your picture on every cover."

"Yes, and I installed security cameras to catch every employee who took that newsletter to the bathroom, and I fired every last one of them."

"Perhaps now would be a good time to hear your plan for job creation," Haverty shot back.

Bob Fuller stopped twisting his hemp necklace around his fingers long enough to groan. "I hope you at least printed that newsletter on *recycled* paper."

Morganstern made a sound that was somewhere between a grunt and a chuckle. "Hmmph. Of course not, recycled paper costs twice as much, and it's used."

"We don't have time for that right now." Bryan waved his hands in the air again. "Everyone in favor of reducing the White House's budget by the proposed amount, raise your hand, and our computer program will compile a list of those for and opposed, which will be posted on all our social media feeds."

The candidates awkwardly stood with their hands in the air for sixty seconds, while a commercial for a headache reliever played on the nearest monitor, followed by one for a prescription anxiety medication.

"And we're back," Bryan said after Shanda's cue. "The results of the candidates' vote on our first social media suggestion are in. It looks like the majority is in favor of reducing the White House's decorations budget. That gets you five million closer to balancing the budget."

"We still need to get rid of that appropriation for the hog farmers," Harper said. "Obesity is such a big problem in this country, and it's costing taxpayers—"

"Are you making fun of my weight?" Buckshaw yelled.

"We'll have to go to the next suggestion now. Once we're done with these you can go back to discussing other items." Bryan pressed the arrow on his tablet and read the next question, wondering what the candidates were going to fight about next. "And this one's from Tiffany in Las Vegas. **#ihaveanidea** Bryan Seafoam, you're so sexy, you can enter my Oval Office any time and'— oh, uh, this one's, ah, not for the candidates."

He stabbed at the tablet, trying to advance to the next suggestion. Artie couldn't filter out propositions from female fans? What a crappy app.

"Who was supposed to check the most-shared #ihaveanidea?" Shanda screeched in his ear. She was supposed to kill her mic when talking to anyone other than Bryan, but she never remembered.

"This is just another example of the country's declining morals," said Bob Brumley, the Republican last-placer who managed to make every campaign issue about his religious views. "Our country needs to get back to conservative Christian values, which I talk about in my book, *I Vote God's Shares....*"

Bryan tuned him out as he continued to pound the arrow on his tablet. Why wouldn't the screen change? Great, the tablet was frozen. Just what he needed.

"What are you doing?" Shanda yelled, and this time she was *definitely* talking to him. *"Move off that suggestion now."*

"I'm sorry, we seem to be having technical difficulties," he said, hoping she'd take the hint. "Why don't we take a look at the candidates' rooms while we get the rest of those suggestions ready?"

"Cut to one of the Candidate Cams!" Shanda shouted.

4

WELL, THANKS SO MUCH to our investigative crew for providing that in-depth analysis of Senator Haverty's nightstand drawer. Who would have thought a guy with twenty mistresses wouldn't have a single condom hidden in there? Let's hope there's one in his wallet. Now, back to the suggestions for the candidates." Bryan turned to read directly off the monitor behind him, since one of the production assistants had snatched his tablet and run away. Shanda now controlled which suggestions appeared to the viewing audience.

"Okay, our next idea comes from Bob in Kansas via Facebook. 'Congressman Foster, you suggested earlier that you could balance the budget by providing more subsidies to hog farmers at the expense of the health care budget. Have you considered the country wouldn't need as much expensive health care if maybe we didn't eat so much bacon?'"

Foster leaned forward and squinted through his round-rimmed glasses at first Bryan, then the monitor, then Bryan again. "And just what do you think would happen to the economy if we all stopped eating bacon?"

Bryan shrugged. "It's Bob's question, but why don't you tell us what you think would happen?"

"It'll be an economic disaster—and not just for the people of *my* state." Foster glared at Buckshaw. "Hog farming is a pretty big deal down in Texas, too. Not to mention dozens of other states. Tens of thousands of people will lose their jobs, wind up on public assistance—"

"Which we can pay for with the money we save on subsidizing triple bypasses." Fuller loosened his green tie and settled back on the striped couch, propping his Birkenstock-clad feet on the glass-topped coffee table. Gnarly toes poked out, and Bryan wished Fuller was one of those idiots who wore socks with sandals. "Anyway, all those out-of-work farmers can start growing kale."

Both Buckshaw and Foster stared at him with similar looks of horror.

"You think we're going to grow *kale* down in *Texas?*" Buckshaw sputtered.

"For starters." Fuller shrugged. "But not for long. Once we legalize marijuana nationwide, that'll be the biggest crop in every state."

So that was Fuller's plan. No wonder he looked so smug, sitting quietly on the sofa and smiling at all the other candidates. He was going after the stoner vote.

"More declining morals." Bob Brumley shook his head. "In my book, I detail God's plan for those who dabble in these illicit—"

He was cut off by the sound of a screeching alarm. All the candidates stopped and looked around the set.

"Nothing to worry about." Bryan turned away from the monitor and smiled at the contestants. "That's just to let us know our time is up for this segment. You have a little more than eight hours left to settle the budget problem. Oh, but don't worry—the suggestions will continue rotating on that screen in case you need some ideas. Best of luck to you all."

They were going to need it if they didn't somehow balance the budget by six o'clock tomorrow.

5

BRYAN SNUCK A FEW more hours of sleep in his dressing room, then checked on the candidates around nine. They yelled at each other over coffee, donuts, and, in Foster's case, bacon, which he'd demanded the kitchen send up to prove he wasn't abandoning Iowa.

Shanda gestured for Bryan to join her off set, and he left the candidates squabbling. "They're no closer to a resolution. Leave them to their imminent failure. The segment planned for later will go much better if we have the B team on standby."

Bryan watched the feeds and periodically popped in throughout the day, as tempers got shorter and arguments longer. Just after noon, Foster and Fuller almost came to blows over the farm subsidy.

"That appropriation is the last thing keeping us from getting below five trillion." Fuller was now barefoot, had taken off the green tie, and rolled up his shirt sleeves. "We've already cut funding for White House holiday decorations, a badminton court for the prisoners at Guantanamo, studying the effects of cocaine on the sex drive of Japanese quail... there's nothing left but the farm subsidy."

"That bill is keeping thousands of farmers in business, and you want the whole country to eat kale? We'll starve to death, I tell you. Not everyone can stand to eat kale."

"Do you realize if we can't agree on this we may never balance the budget?" Finnegan asked. "What if we just cut the farm bill in half?"

"Won't get us below five trillion, and we *still* have so much spending to cut." Willard scratched his head. "There's got to be something we can all agree on."

"My state needs the full subsidy." Foster slammed his fist down on the table, splashing coffee onto the glass surface. He absently grabbed the nearest piece of cloth and dabbed at the spill.

The nearest piece of cloth was a green tie.

"Let go of it." Fuller snatched back his tie. "This is a genuine hemp tie dyed with all-natural—"

"Oh, dry up, it's just a tie. Can I get you a Kleenex or would that make you cry more about the tree?" Willard asked.

"How would you like it if I used your tie to wipe my nose instead?" Fuller grabbed Willard's tie, and Willard grabbed Fuller by the collar. Show aides rushed in to pry the two apart before one of them could take a swing at the other.

"It's just like a debate without time limits or rules," Shanda said in Bryan's ear, as he stepped between the two men and the two very large, well, bouncers.

Bryan pictured himself covering this as one of the hundreds of reporters straining at the doors downstairs. Would he wish he was here right now if he was one of them? Yes, he probably would.

Right now, he wished he was downstairs, still doing the job of a journalist, digging up dirt and confronting politicians about their lies, instead of breaking up fights and soothing hurt feelings with platitudes.

"We need to stop this," Finnegan yelled. "In two hours, Joe the Plumber is getting my job. Or one of your jobs. One of our jobs, uh...."

"She has a point." Haverty shoved the almost-empty donut box toward Buckshaw. "Let's reduce funding for your state's recovery to three million. It's not getting cut off completely, and then if we reduce health care just a little more...."

"Now, if we all stopped eating beef and ate more vegetables, we'd have much lower health care costs," Fuller said. "We could reduce health spending and actually provide more care to the people who still needed it."

"Please." Haverty rolled his eyes. "Let's limit ourselves to things Americans will actually do. They will buy burgers, they're not going to buy kale."

"So you agree with me?" A grin split Buckshaw's tired face, and he stepped closer to the senator.

"Of course not." Haverty took a sip of coffee and made a face. "That's cold. Ah, what I was saying, Governor, is that Americans care about health care and burgers, but they'd be okay with cutting funding for discretionary funds."

"We already cut the flower fund, what more do you want?" Buckshaw waved his hand around the room. "Should we stop repainting the White House, too? Let it start to look shabby? Stop funding museums and libraries and other cultural centers of importance? Maybe we don't need a defense budget, should we cut our spending on that?"

"That's your cue. Interrupt them," Shanda said.

Bryan's voice boomed from the room's loudspeakers. "Would now be a good time to see what Americans think you should do to balance the budget?"

"Last night would have been a good time to hear that," Ronda mumbled.

"Well, we wanted to give people the chance to watch the debate and respond as you decide what you're cutting." Bryan turned to the large monitor covering the window of the Oval Office and Shanda popped up a poll—she still didn't trust him with the tablet.

He pointed to the first graph. "As you can see, Americans want to eat their burgers and get subsidized health care for their quadruple bypasses afterward. Support for cutting both funds is extremely low, only fifteen and eighteen percent, respectively. Support for cutting defense funding and Social Security is even lower, and those are the three biggest categories on the budget. But don't worry, our viewers have some alternatives reductions you can make."

"Well, let's hear it." Chump thumped his hand on the coffee table. "I need to get on with fixing this budget myself."

The other candidates shrugged and a few bobbed their heads in a slightly-better-than-noncommittal way. It was clear no one thought the viewers would have a good suggestion.

Bryan nodded to the screen and Shanda advanced to the next slide.

"This is the most favorited, liked, shared, and retweeted suggestion on all forms of social media." Bryan paused for dramatic effect. The candidates did that thing where they smiled because they knew they were on TV but the irritation was creeping into the corners of their eyes because they hadn't slept. "Okay, so this one is from Joe in Florida—no relation to Joe the Plumber" —no one laughed— "and Joe says, 'I know how to save more than a hundred million dollars from the budget, giving you money to fund both health care, and recovery in Texas, without cutting defense spending or Social Security.'"

"This better be good," Harper muttered.

Bryan jumped back in before another argument could start. "'All you have to do is vote to get rid of your salaries, which shouldn't be hard since almost all of you are independently wealthy, and are still allowed to make income off your stocks and other investments. There are five hundred twenty-five members of Congress, all making at least one hundred seventy-four thousand dollars a year since the last time you voted to give yourselves raises. The Speaker and majority and minority leaders make a little more. Then get rid of the ten-thousand-dollar subsidy you all get for health insurance, since you can all afford to buy that yourself, too. Oh, one more thing—you all get forty thousand dollars a year just for furniture in your offices. I gotta tell you, you guys are getting ripped off! You should slash that to two thousand dollars each. That's more than enough to buy brand new furniture at a discount store. And the president, whichever one of you that is, doesn't need a salary, either, cuz that's also always a rich person who doesn't need the money.' And that's what Joe in Florida thinks you should do to solve the budget problem."

There was absolute silence for about five seconds. The sound of crickets returned to the room.

Then all hell broke loose.

It started with a loud bray of laughter from Buckshaw. "You want us to work for free? The people who are running our great country?"

"Well, Joe isn't wrong that most of you—all of you standing in this room in fact—have multiple other income sources. Your book, *Poor Boy from Texas*, is on the *New York Times* bestseller list, isn't it, Congressman Buckshaw?" Bryan asked.

"Well, I, well, that's not the point. You're asking us to cut off the salary for all of Congress."

"I see no problem with it," Morganstern said. "This country needs a return to fiscal responsibility. When I was CEO of Cheatham Bank, I cut wasteful spending, even limiting the number of Post-its employees were allowed to use in a work shift."

"I'm in favor of it." Chump straightened his shoulders and raised his chin in the direction of the nearest camera. "When Congress works for me, they can work for free. Hey, how's that for a campaign slogan?"

"Do you even understand how the branches of government work?" Ronda Harper asked him.

"I think cutting Congressional salaries is a good idea." Haverty changed the subject back to the budget. "I make enough money off my investments to keep an apartment for all my mistresses. I will happily vote yes if it allows us all to stay in the race."

"Well, all but one of you—and no, I can't give you numbers on that." Bryan smiled. Every one of these people had assistants running programs to guess based on social media chatter. "It might affect how you settle this issue. You will all get results after the vote in a few hours, of course, assuming you agree to balance the budget. I'll let you think on that."

"I can live off the vegetables in my garden," Fuller said as Bryan started to walk away.

"Oh, one last thing." Bryan paused and turned back around to face the candidates. "I almost forgot. You remember the B team? They're waiting in a building down the road, and they've been watching our live feeds, along with the rest of America. A few minutes ago, all ten of them signed a resolution saying they'd vote to zero out Congressional salaries as well as the other spending cuts proposed by Joe in Florida, if another resolution couldn't be reached. Just thought you should know."

6

TWENTY MINUTES BEFORE SEVEN, the candidates voted for the salary slash, while **#don'tpaycongress** hit the top of the trending list.

When the show went live at seven, Bryan spent the next hour interviewing the candidates about their "decision-making process." Holding the mic and nodding like he cared, he pictured himself opening the floodgates for a torrential stream of bullshit.

"I knew I had to do what was best for this country."

"I couldn't put my own financial needs ahead of my constituents' needs for a capable leader."

"I mean, Kanye West? And people think voting for the Green Party is crazy?"

"I just couldn't see handing this thing over to the B team. I mean, if *we* couldn't handle balancing the budget, how could they?"

"At the end of the day, I know God will take care of all my needs, because, like I say in my book, I vote his shares."

"When I was CEO of Hewitt Computers, I cut the salaries of ten thousand workers to save my company. I have no problem cutting the salaries of Congress."

"What she means is that she had no problem reducing the wages of people who made less than fifty thousand dollars annually, while her own salary of half a million a year went untouched, but she's willing to cut Congressional salaries to stay in the race a *few* minutes longer."

Bryan was relieved when, at exactly 7:55, he had to cut them all off so the American people could vote. Most of the next hour, devoted to *American President: Aftermath*, was spent replaying highlights from the budget deliberations and encouraging viewers to explore the many hours of video on the show's website. As the boring bullshit played on, he kept his face set in a pleasant expression. He had no right to hate his job, even if it was the exact opposite of everything he'd ever wanted to do.

At 8:55, he told the audience voting had closed and the person leaving the show tonight would be announced... right after this next break.

At 8:56, an aide flanked by two members of the National Guard delivered an envelope to his desk in the Oval Office. The candidates all stopped squabbling long enough to stare and slobber. Three more minutes with these people, then he could go home, sleep in his own bed, and forget for a few hours that he was a Kleenex-provider and a hand-holder and a part-time therapist, not a journalist.

"Cue!" Shanda shouted, and his head popped up on the monitor below the camera.

"Welcome back, American voters. I'm your host Bryan Seafoam, and this is the moment you've all been waiting for. Inside *this* envelope" —he waved it in the air— "are the results of tonight's vote."

He paused for effect as the camera panned across the rows of candidates, sitting neatly on the striped couches. Each one went for a look of cool confidence, and each one failed miserably.

Except for Bob Fuller, who looked like he'd just smoked a joint, probably because he had.

"Okay, announce it now," Shanda screeched in his ear.

"All right, the name of the person who received the lowest number of votes and will be leaving our show tonight is...." He paused for the drumroll, which was stupid but Shanda thought was a brilliant idea. "Phil Willard, I'm sorry your run has ended so early. Let's see the most shared comments from people explaining why they didn't vote for you."

He gestured for the long-time congressman to join him at the desk. Willard stopped to shake the hand of every other candidate, then sat in the chair across from Bryan for his exit interview, looking about as comfortable as the guy in the diarrhea medication commercial that had aired during the previous break.

Bryan waved at the huge TV screen behind him, and Shanda advanced through the comments, which mainly focused on Willard being the last person to agree to cut Congressional salaries, despite the fact that he was both rich and had been collecting a salary in Congress longer than some other representatives had been alive.

Willard cleared his throat. "While I'm deeply disappointed that the American public isn't educated enough to grasp my economic recovery plan, I am at least relieved the next person running this country won't be a plumber or pop star. But don't worry, I'll be back in four years, and this time maybe I'll rap my recovery plan so the masses can understand it."

That was going to be another viral GIF on social media.

"Remember, the Candidate Cams are live twenty-four seven, so you can watch your favorite candidate sleep... or whatever else they choose to do in the Lincoln Bedroom replicas they've all been assigned." Bryan kept the fake smile plastered on his face. Just one more minute. "Tomorrow morning we'll present the candidates with another challenge, this one lasting for a week before you vote again. You won't want to miss this!"

7

IT WAS JUST AFTER eleven when Bryan walked into his Beverly Hills mansion. The housekeeper had gone home hours ago, so he tossed his coat in the general direction of the hall closet and trudged up the marble staircase. Once in his bedroom, he dumped his phone and keys on the bedside table, yanked off the tuxedo jacket, and flung it as far away as he could. The rest of the stiff, uncomfortable suit followed. He felt a little guilty about making a mess for the maid, but at the moment, he felt a lot worse about wearing that ridiculous outfit. It reminded him of everything that was wrong with his life.

Too tired to deal with showering, he flopped down on the bed in his underwear. The thought occurred to him that he really should get under the covers, but he lacked the will to move just then.

Why should he? The mattress was thirteen inches of memory foam, the sheets and blankets all 1,000-thread count Egyptian cotton. The bed in his Nowhereville apartment had been a million-year-old pile of stained polyester and long-broken spring coils that squeaked and protruded in painful places every time he moved.

He was almost asleep when the phone rang. Why didn't he put that damn thing on silent? Slapping his hand around on the bedside table, he eventually located the device and pulled it close to his face, finally forcing himself to open his eyes.

It was Shanda. Of course it was. He was tempted to ignore her call and put the phone on silent. But what if something shocking had happened on the Candidate Cams and he was needed back on set? Not that he wanted to go back there, but if he ignored Shanda over something important like that, she'd probably demand he sleep in one of the Lincoln bedrooms on set.

"Hello?" He hoped she wasn't calling to say he needed to go back to the White House right now.

"I have great news. We've finalized the list of correspondents to help with the next assignment—and it's exactly the group we wanted."

By we she meant her, because possible candidates had not been discussed with him. Rubbing sleep out of his eyes, he tried to remember what the next challenge was. Oh, right, the candidates would all be going to different venues, and he couldn't visit all nine places in one day for an appreciable amount of time, so the show would add reporters to help with the coverage.

"Um, that's great. Can you tell me about it in the morning?" Unless Foster was screwing a prostitute in a pig costume, he wasn't going back to that building for anything tonight. Why was Shanda calling him about this *now*? Didn't she ever fucking sleep?

"We just finalized the deal and I wanted to prepare you."

"Prepare me? For... what?"

"Well, we have some really great people. There's Valencia Mills, you know, from Are You the Next Instagram Queen? *And before that she hosted* GIFS Gone Wild *for a couple seasons?"*

"Mm-hmm." Maybe he'd just go to sleep with her talking. She'd never notice.

"And Jeremy Hayden from Who Wants to Marry a Gay Millionaire—"

"Mmm."

"And Barnaby Wilkerson, host of Strip Club Idol, *that show on Skinemax?"*

He was almost asleep. By the time she was done talking—

"There's just one more—Joanne Jameson from NNN—you know, National News Network, for those people who actually watch serious news all day? Anyway, she told us you worked together in Oklahoma. I didn't even know they had TVs out there."

Joanne?

Bryan's eyes popped open. Damnit, he should have asked which TV personalities were being considered, something he might have done if he hadn't been so busy with interviews and promo shoots and radio shows and TV shows and all the other things he had to do to promote *American President.*

"Bryan? Are you still there?"

"Uh, yeah. Yes, we had TVs in Oklahoma. I worked at a TV station, remember? So, you say you closed the deal?" Maybe there was still time to get out of this. He could just say Joanne was difficult to work with or something. But did he want to do that?

"That's right. You didn't have any problems working with her, did you?"

Nice of her to ask *now.*

"Of course not." What exactly had Joanne told the producers? "It just would have been nice if you'd consulted me."

Shanda exhaled a little too loudly, and he realized she'd been holding her breath. Had she expected a fight?

"Truthfully, I was worried she was an old girlfriend and you wouldn't want to work with her. She really was the best candidate who was willing to work for the least money. I didn't want to have to pass because you broke up badly or something."

"Some people are capable of keeping their clothes on at work, Shanda."

She cleared her throat. *"I don't let my personal relationships cause problems at the office."*

"Are we done here? I'd like to get five minutes of sleep before I have to get up at five AM."

He ended the call and put the phone back on the bedside table, his mind racing. Surely Joanne wasn't going to blab anything to the tabloids. He knew far more embarrassing things about her than she knew about him.

Working with her wouldn't be a problem, even if it did remind him of that one time he actually caught feelings for someone.

No problem. He wouldn't be doing something stupid like *that* ever again.

8

GOOD MORNING, SURVIVING CANDIDATES. I see you're all enjoying the continental breakfast."

Bryan walked past the couches, eyeing each contestant. Bob Brumley had been praying over his food for the last five minutes. If he didn't hurry up, he was going to have to eat on the run. Phil Foster's plate was piled with bacon, which he ate with so much enthusiasm even people who wore bacon-patterned underpants would have to laugh at him. Bob Fuller wrinkled his nose at Foster and sipped a green smoothie, probably chockfull of kale.

"I hope you got plenty of rest, because you're going to have a busy day." The feeds from last night had been disappointing—nobody had sex, snorted cocaine, called a psychic hotline, or did anything else that would make for great television.

"I'm eager to solve this country's problems." Ronald Chump turned his squinty gaze to the nearest camera. "As you know, once I'm elected, I plan to solve our country's illegal immigration problem by building a giant moat between the US and Mexico."

"With a drawbridge we can lower whenever we want to outsource jobs or import something we used to make in this country?" Ronda Harper asked.

"I'm thinking of adding nuclear weapons stationed every five miles to keep us safe." Chump adjusted his gold cufflinks.

It was another great moment for the crickets, as the other eight candidates fell silent. Bryan was impressed—it took a lot to make nine presidential candidates shut up.

His teleprompter blinked *RECALCULATING RECOMMENDATIONS* at him. Time to tap dance. "Uh, I'm not an expert, but I think that might be in violation of a few international treaties."

"So what?" Chump shrugged. "What country is going to attack us if we've got our entire border studded with nukes?"

Buckshaw was the first candidate to recover from his moment of speechlessness, which was a relief to Bryan because he had no idea how to respond.

"Do you hear this? Mr. Chump's inane plan to protect our borders is exactly why you should vote for *me*. I won't get us in World War Three by the end of my first day in office—Mr. Chump here will."

"Don't you know what a nuclear war would do to the trees?" Fuller flung his plastic smoothie cup into the nearest trash can. "I don't think you need votes, Mr. Chump, I think you need psychiatric help."

"The trees? What about us?" Harper asked.

JUST GET ON WITH THE CHALLENGE the prompter flashed.

"Well, this has been an interesting discussion, and the top five will get plenty of time to explain their plans for this country later in the season, but right now we need to move on to our next competition," he said. "I'm glad Mr. Chump mentioned the moat, however, because it actually ties into your next assignment. You will all go out and work at regular, low-paying jobs.

"Now, I know some of you are thinking you've already done that. Yes, we've all seen the campaign photos many of you have taken. Standing behind the counter of a diner, wearing aprons and handing out coffee, serving the less fortunate in a soup kitchen line, breaking ground on new development projects in your private sector days.

"But this time you won't have any aides or assistants to help. The owners or managers of the workplaces you go to won't be big contributors who want to make you look good in exchange for voting their way on something. You won't get to take off the apron and leave after a few photos. You will be treated like a regular employee. You will not be allowed to buy or bribe your way out of anything—attempting to do so, or to use your wealth and power to influence your new boss in any way, will result in immediate termination from this competition."

He turned to the camera that had his tight shot so he would appear to look directly at the audience. "Because the candidates will all be going to different places, and we want to air all the segments again in prime-time, it will be another week before the audience votes again. However, you can watch all the challenges live via the Candidate Cams, and highlights will be shown every night in prime-time. Again, you can catch instant replays at any time on our website."

The camera operator waved him to the other camera, the one that had his wide shot, and he faced the candidates again. "Do any of you have questions or concerns?"

"This is ridiculous." Willard crumpled up his napkin and tossed it on the coffee table. "Everyone in the country knows who we are. People are going to recognize us. It won't be a real experience at all."

"It might be more real than you think." Bryan arranged his face in what he hoped was an indulgent smile. "You're right, everyone will recognize you—and at least some of those people hate every one of you. But you're going to have to work with those regular people who hate you. You'll have to face them as customers or coworkers, and you won't have your private security people to remove the hecklers. You'll just have to deal with them yourself."

"What does all this have to do with his moat?" Haverty scowled at Chump.

"Well, since Mr. Chump plans to make that a job for, I'm guessing, thousands of Americans when he's elected, America has decided it's only fair that he get to dig it himself."

Chump's jaw dropped. "That's ridiculous. This show only lasts a few weeks. You can't possibly expect me to dig a moat that size in such a short amount of time."

"You're right." Bryan's face hurt from fake-smiling. He'd never gotten used to it. "Since you can't realistically be expected to build a moat across the entire

American/Mexican border in one day, we're going to let you dig the first half a mile yourself. Don't worry, it only has to be thirty feet deep and thirty feet across. Due to security and legal concerns, I don't think the Department of Defense will let you handle any nukes, so you won't have to worry about that, either. I'm sure it'll be a piece of cake, Mr. Chump."

"Well, I, I, I... I'm running for president so I can make America awesome again" —he grinned as he repeated his tired campaign slogan— "not dig ditches."

Bryan shrugged. "That's the challenge. If you want to stay in the race, you'll do it."

"Wait a minute, you mean our assignment is to help build his asinine idea for national security?" Finnegan glared at Bryan.

"Of course not. You'll all be given regular jobs, but each of you will have a different one, voted for by the American people via social media polls. We asked voters to select jobs based on the candidates' prior experience, voting record, or campaign promises. Mr. Chump gets to dig the moat because, and I quote, 'It was his idea and he has no experience doing anything but counting his money,' according to the poster whose suggestion received the most likes, shares, and retweets. You, Ms. Finnegan, have campaigned on a platform of business expertise from your years of running Hewitt Computers, so you will get to work in a retail store, selling Hewitt computers."

"Oh, well, I'm sure I can manage that." Her fake smile matched his.

"What about me?" Phil Foster asked.

"Since you campaigned so hard for the pork industry in your state, we're sending you to work on a hog farm... with the hogs."

"Well, that sounds like... fun." Foster made a concerted effort to un-wrinkle his nose. "As you all know, I'm a big supporter of the hog farmers in my state. I'll enjoy working alongside them... and the swine."

"So do I get to work with cattle in my home state of Texas?" Buckshaw did a slightly better job of masking his disgust. Or maybe he was genuinely happy because he thought he'd get paid in Big Macs.

"In an indirect way, yes." Bryan aimed to do the exact opposite of Foster, trying to hide how much he was enjoying this one. "Remember, I said these jobs are tailored to your experience, your campaign promises, and your voting record. Now I'd like to call your attention to this video. That is you, standing on the floor of the Texas state senate, making the speech that's credited with getting the minimum wage bill shot down there last March, yes?"

That was the control room's cue to roll the video on the giant screen behind Bryan. He turned as it came to life.

"Ask yourself this," Buckshaw said to the bored-looking members of the Texas state senate. "Does the person who screws up my order at the drive-through window every single day *really* deserve fifteen dollars an hour to forget that I wanted extra bacon on my double bacon cheeseburger? To give me the stale fries from the bottom of the bin even though I asked for fresh ones?"

The video froze and Bryan turned back to Buckshaw, who stood with his arms folded over his beer belly. "We're sending you to work in a burger restaurant, Congressman, so in a way you will be supporting the beef industry in Texas. I'm sure you'll get along well with your new coworkers. Now, let's move on. Senator Brumley, we have the perfect assignment for you, too."

Brumley turned and awkwardly tried to figure out what to do with the copy of *I Vote God's Shares* he'd been waving at Ronda Harper seconds before. Ultimately, he stuffed it under one arm and tried to stand up straighter to hide it.

"I can't wait to hear what it is."

"Well, we know you're an avid supporter of abstinence-only sex education," Bryan read off the prompter. On the monitor below, Brumley shook hands with a supporter whose protest sign screamed CLOSE YOUR LEGS AND OPEN A BOOK.

"Will I be teaching, then?"

"Not quite. You'll be working at a state-run facility in Alabama that provides reduced-cost daycare to low-income parents, almost half of whom are younger than twenty-one. You might recall voting to cut their funding yesterday. But don't worry, they'll be happy to have you as a volunteer."

"I'm in favor of comprehensive sex education," Haverty said.

"For yourself, or other people, too?" Finnegan asked.

"Don't worry, we haven't forgotten about either of you." Bryan turned to Haverty first. "Since you voted against the bill that would have forced medical records to be streamlined and stored online, your job will be to work in an insurance company call center. You, Mr. Morganstern, will be working at one of your banks, and you, Congresswoman Harper, will be working at a coffeehouse."

Harper feigned a smile. Everyone and their dog had seen the video of her grumbling that the barista getting her coffee wasn't working fast enough. "Doesn't she know I'm a congresswoman and I have important things to do, that I can't just stand around waiting while she stuffs her face with bagels?" went viral. Donations started pouring in to help the barista go to college after she explained she was eating a bagel at the window because a coworker called in sick and she had to work a twelve-hour shift without a lunch break.

"What will I do?" Fuller asked.

Bryan tapped his tablet. "You'll be working at a natural foods co-op. Now that you all have your assignments, you have an hour to get your luggage together. Then you'll be taken to your new work sites, where you will stay until you're told otherwise. Your staff, personnel, et cetera, will remain here."

Bryan left the grumbling contestants and headed to his limo, which would take him to the airport. He had a busy schedule as well, visiting as many of the candidates as he could each day. Meanwhile, the other reporters would fill in where he couldn't be. Eventually, he'd meet up with all of them.

Including Joanne.

9

BRYAN'S FIRST ASSIGNMENT TOOK him to the Mexican-American border, where Ronald Chump was prepared to build his moat.

It was hard to tell who looked more confused and unclear how to proceed—Chump, or the bulldozer crew who had been put in place to protect the expensive equipment he was going to operate.

At least, that was how *Shanda* explained it. "Chump will be doing all the work himself. The crew is just here to make sure we don't break a three-hundred-thousand-dollar piece of equipment we're paying five thousand dollars a day to rent. The insurance company won't cover us unless a licensed crew is on hand."

Bryan pulled back the curtain from the tiny window of his makeup trailer. "Is he actually going to drive that thing? Don't you need a special license or something?"

"Not in this state. Don't worry, everyone's signed waivers, and Dan over there is a certified instructor for this type of, um, equipment, I guess?" Shanda pointed a red-white-and-blue nail at a tall man whose arms were folded over his chest. He stared at Chump with a look that suggested he'd rather vote for Joe the Plumber's dog.

"I assume we've cleared the area so he can't run over any people when he gets on that thing?"

"Not a whole lot of people around here, but yes. He might hurt a few tumbleweeds, but that's it." Shanda scrolled through something on her phone. "We're going to stay for the first hour, then we go visit Sara Finnegan at Buyers' Best Electronics. Now get out there and get started."

"And where will I be when Chump starts driving that thing?" Bryan stood up and went to the door.

"Relax, our insurance company wouldn't let us put you in harm's way, either. After you finish interviewing Chump, you'll step out of the shot and come back behind the line." She yanked open the trailer door and pointed at the string of orange tape, tied around wooden stakes to block off the trailers their production department had set up. "We have cameras back here getting wide shots, mounted on the bulldozer itself, one on Chump's hard hat, also ones on the crew—"

"I get it. Good to know the *insurance company* cares about keeping me alive." Bryan climbed down the steps, made his way to the orange tape, and stepped over it. Shanda stayed behind as he approached the bulldozer.

Texas, or at least this part of it, was just as boring and barren as Oklahoma had been, with at least as many tumbleweeds. Nothing else around for miles— except the network's trailers and equipment, the bulldozer, Dan, and one confused-looking bazillionaire.

Bryan reached them with a fake smile in place. "Well, Mr. Chump, are we ready to get started?"

"Well... I guess so." Chump tugged up the visor of his baseball cap, which featured a picture of a fist and the catchy slogan, *"Pumped for Chump!"*

"I'm ready whenever ya'll are." Dan hooked his thumbs through his belt loops and stared at Chump. The implication was clear—just waiting on you, buddy.

"Do you feel like you're well-equipped for this task?" Bryan asked Chump.

"I'm sure it's just like the business I run." The trillionaire waved at the bull-dozer. "I'll figure it out in no time."

"So when you're president and you encounter situations you have no prior experience with, are you just going to wing it?" Bryan asked.

"Obviously, I'll surround myself with advisers who are experts in their fields."

"Well, that's what Dan is, and he's willing to give you a lesson." Bryan gestured at the crew leader. "Now, if you want the chance to become president, you're going to have to start digging. You only have until five PM to dig your portion of this moat, you know."

Chump reached his right hand toward his left arm, like he was about to adjust his cuff links—something he did in every campaign photo Bryan had ever seen of him—then stopped, apparently realizing he was wearing a polo. At least his campaign manager had talked him out of the suit today. He turned and looked at the bulldozer.

"Why, that machine is huuuuge." Chump held up his hands in front of his face. "Just like my hands. Have you ever noticed how puny that Phil Foster's hands are? Mine are twice as big. You know what they say about men with large hands, right?"

"That they should get to work if they want to dig half a mile today?" Dan rolled his eyes.

"All right, then. But since I'm a beginner, maybe it should only be a quarter of a mile. After all, this is really a job for... for, ah, someone more...."

"Poor?" Dan said through gritted teeth.

"Someone who, well, who has worked in construction for longer than a few hours," Chump finished.

"Don't worry, I'll teach ya." Dan waved his arm at the cab door. "After you."

"Good luck to you both." Bryan walked backward, keeping his eyes on Chump. A strong wind blew their way as the mogul climbed into the cab, his nose wrinkled with disdain. It sent dozens of tumbleweeds scattering, but neither Chump's over-moussed, orangey hair nor his over-starched trousers moved in the gust. Dan's jacket whipped in the wind as he climbed in after the trillionaire.

Bryan quickly ducked under the orange tape and Shanda thrust a tablet into his hand. "This is going to be great. Check it out. **#billionairebitesthedust** is already trending."

"Let's hope he lives up to the hashtag."

"You should have asked him more questions." Shanda took a sip of her eight-dollar latte. "You know what else is trending? **#seafoamissoft** and **#don'tcheerleadchump.** "

"I wasn't cheerleading." An assistant handed him a bottle of water and he twisted it open. A drop landed on his shoe, clearing a single spot of dust off the shiny black leather. "And you know what's going to happen when I start playing hardball. Hashtags will go from **seafomissoft** to **seafoamsucks.** They'll accuse me of being too mean to the candidates, say I'm not a real journalist even—"

"Well, you can't be mean to them, but you can't be too nice, either. You just have to—oh, wait, this is getting good." Shanda pointed at the tablet.

"Now don't tell me what to do. The commander-in-chief doesn't need a boss," Chump said to Dan. "I can figure this out."

"Of course. I'm just here to ensure your safety." Dan smiled tightly.

Chump moved his well-manicured hands over the various buttons and levers on the control panel, finally reaching for something that looked vaguely like the gearshift on a car.

Dan cleared his throat loudly. "You need to turn it on first."

Chump's mouth pulled into a frown, but his Botoxed forehead didn't move.

Dan pointed at a dangling key fob, his face twitching like he was trying not to laugh. "It's, ah, in the ignition."

"Of course. It's been a while since I did this, you know." Chump turned the key, and the sound of a motor hummed to life.

"Since you did this? I thought you'd never operated a bulldozer before?"

"I mean, turned an ignition key. My limo driver does that."

Dan sucked in a breath. "When was the last time you drove a car? Or a ve-hick-ul of any kind?"

Bryan cringed at Dan's pronunciation of vehicle, something he hadn't heard since the last time he saw a car commercial in Oklahoma.

"I don't really remember." Chump yanked on what looked like a joystick and the large machine lurched forward. "College, I think. I had this Ferrari, really impressed all the girls. That's how I met my first wife—"

"You might want to go a little slower at first." Dan gripped the dashboard, his knuckles white.

"Didn't you hear that smarmy host of theirs? I've only got until five PM to dig up thirty feet for a mile."

"See?" Bryan rolled his eyes at Shanda.

She waved a hand. "That's the opinion of a trillionaire who called one of his staffers a lazy quitter for taking a bathroom break, after the guy had been handing out buttons for ten hours straight without relief. Just because he thinks you're smarmy doesn't mean the audience agrees."

Back on screen, Dan tried to get Chump's attention. "Right, but it's going to take longer if you—"

"Oh, just shut up and tell me where to start digging."

"I believe those stakes with the red tags mark off the area. The moat goes inside them." Dan's face tried to fight the smirk. It lost.

But Chump didn't pay attention to him. He jerked the stick to the right, and the bulldozer turned in the general direction of the nearest stake.

"You might wanna slow down," Dan said.

"I told you, I have a deadline. In my line of work, you meet deadlines. I don't make excuses, like that blowhard Buckshaw. Took two weeks off from his job as governor because he had a *little* heart attack."

"If you don't slow down, you're going to overshoot your—"

Thwack. The nearest stake went down.

"It was in the way anyway." Chump slammed on the brake. "Now, how do I, ah, dig up the dirt?"

Dan pointed at a screen on the dashboard. "That helps you line up the blade. Now, what you want to do—"

"But which one's the blade?"

"That one." Dan pointed at another gearshift-looking thing. "But you have to be careful, because—"

"Don't worry, I know what I'm doing." Chump grabbed the stick and the camera feed blurred.

"What's happening?" Shanda screeched into her headset.

"Whoa, easy there, you almost tipped us over." Dan yanked the gearshift back. "You need to be more careful. This ground is extremely hard. If you go in at the wrong angle, you could get the blade stuck."

"You know what I do, Don? I solve problems." The camera briefly blurred again, then stabilized, as the cab of the bulldozer turned at a right angle.

"What the hell is he doing?" Shanda squinted at the nearest monitor.

"What the hell are *we* doing? We've got a politician driving a bulldozer when we should be asking about his many grandiose campaign promises. You want me to ask the hard questions, but not too hard, and be really nice about it, but instead we're wasting time on this." Bryan pointed at the bulldozer as it wheeled around, the blade scooping into the ground.

"I told you, that part is coming. The candidates have to do this stuff first, to prove to the viewers they're worthy of consideration. No one wants to choose which privileged rich person they want to vote for this time." She raised her voice over the horrible screeching sound the blade made as it tried valiantly to scrape through the earth. The dozer careened forward. "But if you don't ask the candidates *some* serious questions now, the audience will think this whole thing is fake, meant to make the contestants look good. On the other hand, if you're too critical, you might be seen as opposing one of them."

"At this point, I think I oppose all of them equally, but acting like their therapist isn't getting us anywhere, and it makes me look like a yes-man. You think I can go get a job at a real news network after this, like all the stringers you hired to interview the other candidates?" The second he said it, he looked around to see if anyone had overheard. To everyone else, it would sound like he was complaining about a job most people in the business would kill to have.

But no one had heard—not even Shanda.

The noise from the bulldozer continued to grow, mixing with the sound of Dan screaming. Chump had managed to get the machine more or less centered between the rows of stakes, and pushed the blade into the unforgiving ground. It was hard to tell, since neither Bryan nor Chump knew much about digging up dirt, but he was pretty sure Chump was trying to dig the whole moat at one time.

Dirt sprayed in all directions. The rotating thing that covered the wheels—Bryan had no idea what it was called, he'd have to find out so he could explain it to the viewers—churned at the ground, struggling to move forward.

"Put your foot on the brake, you can't go that fast with the blade extended," Dan yelled. "You're stuck on something, probably a big rock. You need to back up and try again."

"Can we isolate that audio and turn it up?" Shanda shouted into her headset.

Bryan turned back to the tablet. The argument in the cab was difficult to hear over the noise, but he made out snatches of it.

"Going to burn out the—"

"—a go-getter, always have been—"

"—too hard, at this pace—"

"—built my empire with just the measly ten million in my trust fund—"

"—need to slow down before—"

The rest was drowned out by the sound of the bulldozer's motor, whining louder as it spit chunks of earth everywhere.

Bryan ducked as one flew over the orange tape. "Will the insurance company cover us if mud takes out a camera?"

"Everybody get back." Shanda turned and waved her arms at the crew behind them. "You too, Seafoam, I am not going to be the producer who gets the country's most beloved host killed."

A solution to Bryan's problems popped into his head. "No. You want me to ask serious questions? I'm going to do it right now, and you can't stop me."

Before he lost his nerve, he jumped over the orange tape and ran toward the bulldozer, dodging dirt bullets. Maybe he'd look like a real reporter again if he did something dangerous to get a story. Back at the station in Oklahoma, his coworkers constantly tried to get video of themselves chasing tornadoes to put on their audition reels, no matter how many times the station manager told them not to get in harm's way. One of the reporters even tried to make a mock weather video in front of the green screen, with a fan to fake a strong gust of wind, until someone pointed out how painfully fake the whole thing looked.

If Bryan could just get a candid shot of himself, questioning Ronald Chump while dirt flew at him, maybe he could escape this reality show nightmare and get the job he'd always wanted—reporting for a real news network.

He was halfway to the bulldozer when security tackled him. If he hadn't been so intent on the big yellow machine and its imbecile driver, he might have seen the blur coming at him sooner, but because he was so laser-focused, he didn't notice the three-hundred-pound former bouncer for Hollywood's most exclusive nightclub barreling toward him until it was too late. The guard hit him from the side, and he went flying.

Which would look great to producers from a national news network.

Except they would never see this video, because Shanda would make sure it was deleted. She would never let the world see security tackling "the most beloved reality show host in America" to keep him from being a real journalist.

The bouncer landed on top of Bryan. Three hundred pounds felt like three thousand, crushing the air out of his lungs. The guy was in great shape, and bounced up almost immediately.

Bryan, not so much. While the guard gripped his shoulder with a beefy hand, he struggled to breathe normally. Spots swam in front of his eyes. His back hurt. His knees hurt where they'd kissed the ground. His shoulders hurt where the security goon's fingers grabbed him.

Somehow, the hands succeeded in pulling Bryan to his feet and hauling him back toward the orange tape. He tried to struggle, but it was no use. This guy could bench-press a Mack truck, and Bryan was lucky if he made it to the gym twice a week. The show made him wear a tux all the time, so Tiffany and all those other female fans who tweeted him sex proposals would never know he didn't have a six-pack.

They were almost to the row of tape when the whining of the bulldozer's motor suddenly grew louder, then cut off completely.

The goon stopped dragging him. Shanda halted her screaming at the crew, now twenty feet back from where they had been.

"At least give me a tablet now that you stopped me from getting the story," he yelled at her.

Shanda sighed and flicked a hand at the security guard.

"Let him go. The danger's passed now, anyway. But you need makeup before you go back out there, you look like crap," she added for Bryan's benefit.

He rolled his eyes. "The money moment has passed. What the hell is going on in that cab?"

She scurried under the tape and showed him a tablet, as two assistants rushed up with makeup brushes. One of them wiped dirt off his face while the other reapplied foundation. A third assistant ripped off Bryan's soiled suit jacket and tugged another one onto his arms. He couldn't see Shanda's tablet, but he heard the audio.

"What happened? Why isn't this thing going anymore?" Chump sounded dumbfounded.

"I told you, the ground is extremely hard and difficult to dig through, and you can't just step on the gas while ramming the blade into a big rock. The motor finally overheated. I hope it shut down before you did any permanent damage."

"So how will I dig my moat?" Chump looked at his Rolex. "I only have seven more hours."

"Well, we can call a mechanic and wait to find out how bad the damage is to the bulldozer, but I doubt the repairs can be completed in that length of time."

"So let's get another bulldozer."

Dan spread his hands, unable to stop the grin from spreading across his face this time. "That decision is above my pay grade."

Shanda shook her head. "The deal is he can't buy his way out of this. He got one bulldozer, we're not getting him another. Go tell him that."

Bryan made his way to the big yellow-speckled brown lump—that was pretty much how it looked now, covered in dust—at a more sedate pace this time, his bouncer injuries begging him to slow down. When he reached the cab, climbed up, and opened the door, Chump was still sputtering.

"You!" He whipped his head around to squint beady eyes at Bryan. "You need to get me another of these things immediately."

He rapped the dashboard in case Bryan couldn't figure out what he meant by these things.

"I'm afraid that's not possible." Bryan put on his nice-guy show-host smile again. He had to at least start out friendly. "The rules of this assignment say you get all the equipment and training help you need, and you did. They do not say we have to replace an item you broke."

"All right, I'll pay for it." Chump looked at Bryan like he was an idiot.

"As you'll recall, the rules also say you can't use your money or influence to succeed at this challenge," Bryan said. "You'll have to do the best you can with the equipment you have."

"But this thing's not working!"

"It's not working because you didn't listen to my instructions and pushed it too hard," Dan said.

"Well, how else can we dig the moat?"

Dan looked like a kid on Christmas morning. "There is one other way. Come on."

Bryan hopped down and let them both climb out of the broken bulldozer. Dan reached behind the seat and pulled out a large shovel, which he handed to Chump.

"Go ahead," he said. "Start digging."

"Now ask him the tough questions," Shanda said in Bryan's ear.

Yeah, now when he would look like a wannabe reporter instead of a serious journalist who faced danger and dodged dirt bombs to ask Ronald Chump what the hell he was doing. Great idea.

But he had to at least try. Consulting the social media feeds on the tablet, he followed Chump around the bulldozer. The trillionaire stabbed the shovel down into the dirt, then shoved it a few inches away.

Dan rolled his eyes.

"Mr. Chump, why didn't you follow your instructor's directions?"

Chump grunted. "I don't follow directions. Haven't since I started my own business—"

"With just the ten million from your tiny trust fund, I know. But some of our viewers—and voters—think this proves you would be an unfit leader for our country. Cindy M. in Las Vegas has the most-liked question on Facebook. 'Mr. Chump, someone who can't listen can't lead. Why should we even consider voting for you now? Will you take such cavalier chances when our country's security and prosperity are at risk?'"

Chump stuck the shovel in the ground and leaned on it. "Cindy M. needs to understand that in business, as in politics, a leader has to forge ahead, regardless of risks—something I explained in detail in my book, *The Art of the Steal*. This incident today just proves that I have the guts and perseverance to do whatever it takes to move our country forward."

Bryan took a deep breath. "Real reporter" time. "Does it? Or did it just prove you'll do what it takes to get our country stuck in the mud?"

"My voters know the answer is that I'll do whatever it takes to keep illegal aliens out of our country, even if it means digging a moat with my bare hands." With that, Chump straightened up, lifted the shovel, and flung the dirt aside—right into Bryan's face.

10

ARE YOU OUT OF your *mind?*" Shanda slammed the trailer door shut behind her and swiped dust off her face. More of it clung to her pale pink blouse.

"Am I out of *my* mind? You had me tackled by security! How would it look if that video got out?" He knew the answer was Shanda wouldn't let it, but wanted to make her worry about it.

"I had you restrained because the insurance company won't cover your death benefits if you get within twenty feet of a bulldozer being operated by an unlicensed, untrained individual...." She trailed off, apparently realizing how that sounded. "I'm sorry, what I meant was, I didn't want anything to happen to you."

"Especially with cameras around." Bryan sat in his chair, yanked off the suit jacket, and wiped off the combination of makeup and dirt on his face.

"No, really, it isn't like that." She sat on a folding chair next to him. "That dirt was flying fast and farther than we expected, because obviously we didn't know he was going to try a trick like that. And there were rocks in some of it. One of them took out a monitor. *Of course* I didn't want you to get hurt or killed. Chump and Dan were fairly safe in the cab, but you were running around without even a hard hat on. Did you remember you were supposed to wear one when you interviewed Chump?"

"Oh, uh... I guess I forgot." Great. Now he was going to look even more like a wannabe reporter.

"Anyway, I had the director cut away from you before I sent security to tackle you. Are you, um, okay?"

"Nothing injured but my pride." He got up and grabbed his coat. "What are people saying on Twitter?"

"Oh, ah, you know the usual... Chump's a moron, I'm not voting for him, blah, blah. Although some of his rabid supporters are agreeing with his assessment that he does whatever it takes to get the job done. Can you believe how stupid some people are?"

"I used to host a singing show where people consistently voted for the contestants who couldn't sing worth a damn but had great sob stories. Yes, I can believe it." Something was wrong with Shanda's response. She was telling the truth about Chump, sure, but she didn't want him to know what viewers thought of him....

"Well, we need to get going. What's next on the itinerary?" He opened the door and walked out of the trailer toward the limo that was parked about a quarter of a mile from the "construction" site. Hopefully the limo company had a good insurance policy, too.

Shanda got up and hurried after him. "Los Angeles, where Sara Finnegan is working in a retail store, selling Hewitt computers. You'll be joining Joanne there for the final interview with Finnegan, then on to Texas, where Valencia is wrapping up with Buckshaw. I'm sending you the video from both their interviews now so you can review it on the plane."

"Thanks." He reached the limo and got in, Shanda right behind him. After buckling his seat belt—wouldn't want to get in trouble with the insurance company for that—he pulled out his tablet and rolled the first video she'd sent. On the screen, Sara Finnegan babbled about the amount of money Hewitt had spent developing its latest processor while a bored-looking teenager rolled her eyes and slowly backed away.

"She obviously knows nothing about retail sales." Shanda's eyes were on her phone, fingers frantically flying over the screen.

"Yeah, that's really awful. I bet she doesn't sell a single computer." Leaving the video tab open, Bryan opened another and went straight to Hootsuite, where he typed in **#bryanseafoam #americanpresident.**

"The vids of Buckshaw are even better. He and Chump are getting the most attention on social media right now."

"I'll check that out." As Bryan scrolled through the posts, it quickly became apparent what Shanda didn't want him to see.

Where is that wuss Seafoam when this shit is going down? **#bryanseafoam #seafoamsucks**

What kind of political reporter scurries behind a safety line while a presidential candidate runs amok on a bulldozer? **#americanpresident #americanwimp**

At least they have a real reporter on Sara Finnegan. Seafoam is just a poser who barely interviewed his subject. Dan did a better job asking Chump questions than he did! **#americanpresident**

Love the shovel! I bet Chump isn't used to holding such a large tool in his tiny hands! **#americanpresident**

Why didn't Seafoam ask Chump any real questions? Was he too busy hiding his pretty face from mud? **#americanpresident**

Dan interrogated Chump while he burned up a $300,000 piece of equipment. Seafoam showed up later and lobbed a couple softball questions. Can I vote for Dan to host the show? **#americanpresident #seafoamsucks**

Seafoam was so mean to Chump. Can't he see the guy is a real American hero trying to save us all from illegal immigrants taking our jobs and communists

trying to overthrow our government? He should have helped Chump dig,
but I guess he didn't want to get his hands dirty. **#americanpresident**
#Americanhero #pumpedforChump #screwseafoam

Bryan cringed. Damned if he did, damned if he didn't. How would he ever
get out of this reality show mess in a way that would let him move to a real
news network?

11

SARA FINNEGAN WAS ALMOST unrecognizable in her Office Cheapo uniform. Her frozen brown bob and the large cross necklace she always wore to remind people she was a Republican were still in place, but everything else about her looked wrong. Instead of her usual suit starched as stiff as her hair, Finnegan wore a bright yellow Office Cheapo polo and khakis. She looked about as uncomfortable as Kim Kardashian without a selfie stick.

Joanne, on the other hand, looked just like Bryan remembered—only better. When they worked in Oklahoma, she'd bleached her own roots and bought blazers at Goodwill to wear on-air. She usually couldn't find matching pants, so she wore the same pair of black slacks with everything. Now she had a hundred-dollar haircut and a perfectly-matched designer suit.

Bryan realized he was staring and was immediately grateful he was in one of the production trucks and not on camera. He turned his gaze to the multiple monitors banked along the truck's walls. On the nearest one, Finnegan greeted a customer like she was glad-handing a wealthy donor.

"Has she been doing that all day?" he asked Joanne.

"Yes. She hasn't noticed how much it annoys everyone." She handed him a corded mic for the interview. "It's good to see you again, even if they did pick you to host this show instead of me."

He blinked. "You wanted to host *American President?*"

She gave him the *are-you-really-that-stupid* look he used to see at least three times a day. "Of course I did. Don't you think the job should have gone to someone with experience as a political correspondent? But of course I'm sure they expected you'd get better ratings because of Sing Your Heart Out's popularity."

"Um...." It had never occurred to him that NNN reporters—the same people whose jobs he wanted—had tried to get this position. Now on top of all the other reasons Joanne had to be pissed at him, she thought he'd gotten a job she deserved. Great. "I, ah, really don't know why they picked me, I was just glad they did. I mean, um, I do have a lot of experience at this sort of thing. I don't think I'm bad at this job."

He just needed to stop talking, he was making it worse.

"Of course not. I'm sure they made the right choice." She turned to her tablet and scrolled through a social media feed. "I suppose you want to take the lead on this interview with Finnegan?"

"No, you can do it. I'll just ask a couple questions at the end." Maybe that would make her hate him a little less.

"Time to get in there," Shanda said in his ear, and he could tell by Joanne's wince she heard it, too.

She opened the truck doors and they climbed out, security guards materializing to shadow them to the door. There didn't seem to be any rabid fans hanging around in the back parking lot anyway, probably because the entire lot was cordoned off for *American President's* crew.

Guards flanking them, they walked through the back door and into a large storage area with boxed furniture stacked to the ceiling on all sides. The crew had crammed as many monitors, cameras, mics, and other gear into the narrow aisle between shelves as possible. How much was the show paying Office Cheapo to take over the store this way?

Shanda shrieked instructions the second she saw them, while makeup artists swarmed around Bryan and Joanne. "Do you see what they're doing?"

"No." He stared at the ceiling because the makeup artist had pointed his head in that direction with a very firm hand.

Shanda turned up the volume on the monitor nearest his head. Finnegan was explaining the fifty-two-week highs and lows of Hewitt's stock to her customer.

"I'm guessing she's never worked in retail a day in her life," Joanne mumbled.

"No shit," Shanda said. "Are you done with their makeup? I need them out there now, so I can get Bryan to Texas to meet with Valencia and Buckshaw."

The hand released his chin as a final puff of powder speckled his face.

Security ushered Bryan and Joanne through the store, which was mostly deserted except for the area around Finnegan. Everyone watched as she pitched a Hewitt 5000 model to a middle-aged man in a *Vote for Harper* t-shirt.

"Oohh, this is a good one," Shanda said in his ear. *"You guys stand off to the side and watch for a few minutes. I want to let the customer beat her up for a while before you go in for the kill."*

That almost made Bryan feel sorry for Finnegan—and the rest of the contestants—but then he remembered they'd all volunteered for this madhouse of a show.

"I told you, I won't buy a Hewitt," the man in the Harper shirt said. "What other computers can you show me?"

"Well, I'm sure this store has other brands, but I'd really like to recommend the Hewitt—"

"Listen, I know who you are, and I know all about that company. More than you, actually. Did you know I used to be one of your employees when you were the CEO?"

"Oh, well, thank you for your hard work." Finnegan's fake smile never wavered. How had she learned to talk around that thing?

"I remember when we introduced the 2000 line. We were told to install the cheap hard drives even though our tests showed almost ten percent of them failed right out of the box," he said. "Then a few weeks later, we heard the terms and conditions of the warranty had been changed to exclude coverage of the hard drives."

"I don't know what time period you're talking about, but I didn't supervise day-to-day operations of every manufacturing facility, obviously—"

"No, but I bet you supervised whoever was in charge of cutting costs and raising the bottom line. Probably the same person who sent my job overseas. How much of a bonus did that person get?"

"I had to cut jobs to keep the business afloat." Finnegan smoothed her already-perfect hair. "If I didn't outsource some of our manufacturing, the company would have gone bankrupt, and far more people would have lost their jobs."

"But it did go bankrupt—right after you left." The guy shook his head. "You got out with your retirement and probably a nice bonus. The next CEO filed for bankruptcy, reorganized the company, and sold it to a foreign company that moved even more of its jobs overseas."

Finnegan shrugged and relaxed her practiced smile into an equally practiced look of concern. "I'm sorry to hear that, but I can't comment on what my successor did after I left."

The customer leaned over and glanced past Finnegan, at a bored-looking sales associate whose name tag said Callie. "Can you show me the other models your store offers? I'm not buying a Hewitt."

Callie quickly pocketed her cell phone and plastered on a fake smile to rival Finnegan's. "Of course. Follow me."

"Go in now," Shanda said.

Joanne moved into Finnegan's shot, standing to the left of the former CEO. Bryan positioned himself on the right.

"Looks like things aren't going too well for you today," Joanne said.

Finnegan straightened her shoulders, lifted her chin, and launched into what sounded like a campaign speech about overcoming adversity. She was thirty seconds into it when another customer approached.

"We'll get out of your way," Bryan said as he and Joanne backed into an aisle full of printers.

"How are you today?" Finnegan enthusiastically pumped the hand of a middle-aged woman in a tie-dyed tube dress. Her other arm was wrapped tightly around a laptop.

"I came to return this defective computer." Tie-dye yanked back her hand

and placed the device on the nearest shelf, knocking boxes of anti-virus software to the floor. The Hewitt logo sparkled on the laptop's cover. "But the lady up front told me I can't."

Callie scurried back over as the Harper t-shirt guy headed out the door empty-handed. "That's because it was purchased more than a year ago, which is outside of our fourteen-day return policy on electronics."

"I remember you, you're the one who sold me this defective piece of crap." Tie-dye jabbed a finger in Callie's direction. "I told you I was buying this thing for one reason—to write my memoir about growing up in a hippie commune with psychic dreams about the location of dead bodies the police will never find because they won't listen to me."

"That sounds fascinating." Callie fingered the laptop. "What seems to be the problem?"

"The hard drive failed and I lost my entire two-hundred-fifty-thousand-word prologue." She turned her gaze to Finnegan. "I called the manufacturer and they said there's nothing they can do."

"Didn't you have your work backed up anywhere?" Finnegan asked. "A thumb drive, the cloud...."

Tie-dye recoiled as if the politician had just suggested printing all 250,000 words and immediately setting them on fire. "Oh no, I don't trust the cloud."

Callie started to roll her eyes, but then she must have noticed the camera to Bryan's right, and pushed her face into a neutral expression instead. "As I recall, I told you how safe the cloud is when you purchased your computer, and recommended a subscription, since I knew how important your book must be to you."

Tie-dye shook her head. "No security. Anyone could steal my novel from the cloud and get rich off my work."

Who would want to steal that story? Bryan suppressed a smile.

"I told you, the cloud doesn't work that way. It's very secure, and with the premium plan, you can even control your own encryption key," Callie said through gritted teeth. "Had you bought the subscription, your novel would be safe in the cloud, regardless of what happened to your hard drive."

Tie-dye turned back to Finnegan. "I've been doing some reading, and a lot of other people with Hewitt computers have had bad hard drives, too."

Finnegan shrugged. "I haven't been CEO of Hewitt in several years, so I really can't comment."

Of course she couldn't.

Bryan blinked to keep his eyes from rolling.

"You drove that company into the ground and forced them to cut corners and buy cheap hard drives." Tie-dye slapped the laptop for emphasis. "Now what are you going to do to get my book back?"

Finnegan smiled. "You know what, I still know someone who runs the data recovery division. Why don't I—"

Bryan coughed loudly. "Can't use your money or influence to get out of this one, Ms. Finnegan. You will have to handle this situation as if you were a regular Office Cheapo employee."

"We offer a data recovery service," Callie said. "It costs eight hundred dollars and takes two weeks, because we have to send off your hard drive—"

"To some foreign facility where some stranger can steal my novel?" Tie-dye whirled back to Finnegan. "Why don't you fix it?"

"I—don't fix... computers." Finnegan licked her lips. "I was the CEO. The CEO's job is to steer the company in the right direction—"

"You were the CEO of a computer company and you don't know how to recover my data?" Tie-dye's voice sounded like an old clunker trying to turn over—and failing.

"As I said, the CEO's job—"

"Is to make millions and do nothing. Now you listen to me. I am not going to pay eight hundred dollars for a recovery service where my data gets stolen." Spittle flew from Tie-dye's mouth, sprinkling Finnegan's yellow polo. "You are going to get me and my defective computer on a plane to wherever this facility is, you're going to put me up in a hotel while I'm there, you're going to pay for all my meals, and you're going to allow me to watch while the technician recovers my data, so I can ensure my masterpiece isn't stolen."

"Wouldn't it be cheaper to buy her a bottle of whatever medication could treat her paranoia?" Shanda mumbled in Bryan's ear.

For once, he agreed with her.

Finnegan blinked. "I can't do that."

"There's no way our store manager has the authority to do that, either," Callie said.

"Then I demand you give me...." Tie-Dye trailed off for a second, looking around the aisles, then slapped her palm on the keyboard of the nearest laptop. "This laptop for free, so I can rewrite my two-hundred-fifty-thousand-word prologue to my magnum opus. You'll also need to pay my bills for the next month so I can stay home from work and write."

"That's ludicrous." Finnegan's smile was replaced by a frown that didn't quite reach her frozen forehead. "Neither this store nor Hewitt Computers owes you anything. I may not be a repair technician, but I know any hard drive can fail at any time, and you should always back up any data you wish to see again. Now you should have taken... um, Carrie's advice and purchased a cloud backup service when you purchased your Hewitt computer. Since you didn't, you need to rethink this entitled attitude and buy your own replacement unit. I recommend you get that backup service this time."

"I will do no such thing—and I will *never* vote for you." Tie-dye lifted her hand off the laptop's keyboard, closed the device, and yanked it off the display. An attached wire popped off and an alarm sounded.

Bryan blinked. Was she stealing a laptop in front of the Secret Service?

"I'm sorry ma'am, you'll have to pay for that at the register." Callie's face shone with perspiration.

"I will do no such thing. I'm exchanging my defective Hewitt for this new one, and if you don't like it, you can take it up with their former CEO here." Tie-dye dashed for the door, braless boobs bouncing in different directions under the top of her tube dress.

"Security!" Callie rushed to the register.

"Now throw Finnegan some hard questions, but in a nice way," Shanda said.

Bryan and Joanne popped back into the shot with Finnegan.

"I'm afraid your time here is almost up," Joanne said. "And you haven't sold a single Hewitt computer. Also, you antagonized a customer who then stole a laptop."

"That wasn't my fault." Finnegan sniffed. "That woman was a lazy, entitled mooch who probably milks the system every chance she gets. Those people always vote Democrat, anyway. I'm not worried."

"Are you suggesting all Democrats steal computers?" Bryan asked.

"Of course not." Finnegan twisted her face back into its fake smile again. "I just think the majority of Americans understand that unpleasant scene wasn't my fault."

"How about what that other customer said earlier—that Hewitt knowingly installed bad hard drives?" Joanne asked.

"I have no knowledge of that." Finnegan shrugged. "Hard drives have been failing as long as they've existed. That's why Hewitt offers its own cloud backup service, for a reasonable fee."

Bryan took a deep breath. Now was his chance to prove he was a real reporter. "Ms. Finnegan, regardless of the hard drive failure issue, the fact remains that you haven't sold a single computer, and you escalated a volatile situation instead of de-escalating it. Do you really think that's the kind of leader this country needs?"

Finnegan's frown returned to the lower half of her face. "I didn't escalate anything, that woman did. When I'm president, I will not be giving away free handouts to everyone who demands it, because I believe in fiscal responsibility. I'm also tough on crime, and if I'm elected I'll make sure shoplifters like her are prosecuted to the fullest extent of the law."

Joanne shoved her tablet in front of Finnegan. "One of our followers just tweeted a picture of a Hewitt company memo from when you were CEO. It appears to be a letter directing the manufacturing division to 'continue using the DL200 drives and delete the obviously erroneous early test data on them.' Is that your signature at the bottom?"

"Anyone could have Photoshopped my signature onto anything." Finnegan's face turned redder than her party's mascot.

Joanne narrowed her eyes at the candidate. "Are you—*denying* writing this memo?"

"I can't recall every memo I ever wrote when I worked at Hewitt, and I can't comment on a tweeted picture I can barely read. I promise I'll have my people look into it." Finnegan straightened her shoulders and turned to the nearest camera. "I can assure you, though, if I did write a memo like that, it was because I truly believed the data was erroneous and should be disregarded. I would never knowingly direct an employee to use poor-quality parts. When I was at the helm of Hewitt, our mission was to deliver a high-quality product. That's all I'm going to say on the subject."

"That's great," Shanda shrieked in Bryan's IFB as he and Joanne worked their way back to the production van. *"Joanne, that was wonderful. Twitter is blowing up about how you cornered her. Great job!"*

She didn't screech anything about Bryan.

12

BRYAN HAD NEVER SEEN so many people lined up outside a fast food place—even the day they had that free-nuggets-with-fries-purchase deal two years ago, resulting in riots and people across the country being treated for fast-food injuries. One guy, interviewed the next morning on all the talk shows, required retinal surgery after he was stabbed in the eye with a particularly hard, overcooked french fry—or so he claimed. His girlfriend said it might have been a plastic spork, but it was hard to tell in the melee.

But the line of people who wanted to hear Governor Milton Buckshaw ask, "Do you want fries with that?" stretched from outside the burger joint, down the block, and around the corner.

"This will be a good opportunity for you to ask some hardball questions. Well, not too hardball, we still want the audience to like you, but just a little hardballier than usual." Shanda shoved him through the back door, security team trailing them.

"I don't think *hardballier* is actually a word, Shanda." He felt like he was intruding on the restaurant's storeroom. Bags of buns dangled off shelves, edges of plastic fanning his face as he walked through and nearly tripped on a case of bottled water.

"There's a little more room once you get out from between the piles of food." Shanda nudged him with her elbow to make him move faster.

"Good." He didn't plan to stay back here any longer than necessary. It made him claustrophobic.

She tapped a monitor set up on what was probably the store manager's desk—it was strewn with paperwork, kids' meal toys, and walkie-talkies. He had watched footage of Buckshaw in action since his plane landed, but he took a last look before leaving the back room. The portly governor squinted at the cash register, apparently searching for the right button. Beside him, a twenty-something with a nose ring and a permanent scowl rolled his eyes at the politician's incompetence.

"Valencia isn't a political correspondent like Joanne. You'll have to ask the serious questions," Shanda said. "And remember, you're not the candidates' friend, okay? You're here to grill Buckshaw like one of those cheap cheeseburgers—but politely and in a non-offensive way, of course."

"I'll keep that in mind."

Leaving Shanda behind, he walked out of the tiny office and into the fast food kitchen. After squeezing past drink fountains, ovens, and grills, he made his way up to the customer service area.

Valencia Mills stood in a corner, taking selfies on her phone. She had long, dark hair, a face that had sold a lot of makeup, and a rear end that was voted *Best Ass on Instagram* three years in a row. Her phone had a custom case with the picture she'd won *Best Selfie* for on the back. He approached Valencia and stuck out his hand. "Hi, I'm Bryan Seafoam. It's nice to meet you."

"Fifty bucks if you want a selfie with me. A hundred if you take a pic with my ass." She did not look up from her phone. He didn't know how she did it, but in the space of about three seconds, she'd made him feel like he was sixteen and being turned down for a date to the prom. Again.

Wait—why should *he* feel bad? This was *his* show—she had no right to treat him like one of her adoring followers.

"Um, I don't want a picture. I'm Bryan Seafoam—you know, the actual *host* of this show?" He waved a hand in front of her phone.

She finally turned her ice-blue eyes on him and waved the hand that wasn't holding the phone toward the cash register, where Buckshaw still pecked at the register. "Well, it's your turn. I've been babysitting this bore all day."

"Thanks for your help. Pleasure working with you." He hoped she'd notice the sarcasm dripping from his voice, but she'd gone back to her phone and did not seem aware of his existence.

He turned around and headed to the counter, fixing a fake smile on his face. "Governor Buckshaw, how are we doing here?"

Buckshaw returned the faux smile. It showed signs of wear around the edges and didn't come close to reaching his eyes.

"I'm happy to support the cattle farmers of my great state by providing these delicious meals."

"That's good to hear. How are you getting along with your coworkers?"

"I'm always happy to meet and engage with my constituents."

"Could you engage with the next customer? We're getting a line." The nose-ringed supervisor rolled his eyes at Buckshaw. His name tag said *Matt* and his facial expression said *shoot me now.*

"Of course." Buckshaw spun around to face the four lines of customers, all trailing out the door. Each line led to a register. Outside the window, the other three lines ended halfway through the parking lot, while the one to be waited on by Governor Buckshaw stretched farther than Bryan could see.

"Hello, how can I help you today?" the politician asked his next guest.

A short blond woman stepped forward and fixed her gaze on the presidential candidate. "I'd like a job, Governor. How about one of the jobs you promised to create if you were elected?"

Buckshaw smiled through gritted teeth. "I'm sorry to hear you're out of work. I did, in fact, sign a job-creation bill not long ago that improved the unemployment rate—"

"Do I look stupid? And yes, that is a rhetorical question." She waved her phone at him. "I have the unemployment numbers here. They've been stagnant for the two years you've been in office."

The governor smiled. "They were steadily increasing for five years before that. Since they're no longer in a steep upward trend, they have in fact improved. Hopefully they'll go down someday."

"Would you like to order something off the menu?" Matt's voice rose on the last three words.

The customer's eyes flicked over to Bryan. "And you, how come you never call this guy on his bullshit? He created ten jobs by building a statue of himself, and made it harder to collect unemployment, so it would appear the numbers were no longer increasing. How come you've never asked him about that?"

He tried to look at his tablet without being too obvious. *RECALCULATING*, Artie flashed.

Buckshaw cleared his throat.

"We have a lot of customers to serve today," Matt said. "If you don't order something, I'm afraid we'll have to ask you to leave."

"Fine. I'd like half a cheeseburger."

"*Half* a cheeseburger?" Buckshaw squinted at the buttons on the cash register.

"We don't sell half burgers." Matt folded his arms across his chest.

"I can't afford a whole one. I'm unemployed, thanks to the Governor here."

"Then order a small fry, it's half the price of the cheeseburger," Matt said.

"Fine, I'll have a small fry." She pulled open her purse, a worn LV knockoff with lipstick stains on the handles, and dug her arm inside, eventually pulling out a handful of change, which she painstakingly counted out to Buckshaw. Most of it was in pennies.

"*You should ask a probing and relevant question,*" Shanda growled into Bryan's ear.

He cleared his throat. "Governor, I think you should address this customer's question. Is it true you made it harder for people to collect unemployment so your numbers would appear to be improving, or at least not getting worse?"

Buckshaw's fat fingers fumbled the coins into the drawer, and he had to dig several out of the wrong slot. "I overhauled our state's jobless claims system to eliminate waste and improve efficiency. It should actually be easier for a person to claim unemployment."

The customer snorted. "Easier? The bill you passed not only requires recipients to pass a drug test, it also requires us to spend a week in a job-training seminar."

Buckshaw shrugged. "You don't think you'll have better luck finding a job if you improve your skills?"

An employee behind Bryan shoved a tray with a bag onto the counter. "One small fry!"

With a sigh of relief, Buckshaw handed it to the woman.

"Improve my skills?" She looked at him as if he'd just said Kim Kardashian should win the Nobel Prize for physics. "I spent a week hearing where I could take classes to learn English as a second language, how I could take a low-cost program in massage therapy, how to sign up for an adult literacy program, and how to take night classes so I could get my GED."

Buckshaw shrugged. "Getting your GED would probably make more jobs available to you."

"Yes, I'm sure it'll go great with my two bachelor's degrees, Governor. Unfortunately, the only jobs you've brought to this state don't require any education, only a desire to work for minimum wage."

"Which we all know isn't very much." Matt was suddenly no longer concerned with moving the customer along. He propped an elbow on what looked like an ice cream machine. "Around the same time you signed that unemployment-efficiency bill, you also vetoed one that would have increased the minimum wage, after giving a speech to convince the state senate not to pursue it."

Buckshaw glanced at Matt, then put on his grip-and-grin smile and turned back to the blonde woman. "Thank you for your business. Now please, I'll have to help the next customer."

"Thanks for nothing." The customer rolled her eyes and stalked away.

The next person behind her was a redhead with three kids and a t-shirt that said *Supermom*. She was so busy trying to dig some sort of gooey pink mess out of her youngest daughter's hair she didn't appear to even notice Buckshaw behind the register. "I'll have three kids' meals, please. And extra napkins."

"Three kids' meals, right away." Buckshaw frowned at the register, poked a button, frowned deeper, stabbed another button, then grimaced.

"Why isn't it taking the order?" he asked Matt.

The supervisor rolled his eyes. "It's waiting for you to enter a quantity."

"Right." Buckshaw poked a few more buttons, then appeared satisfied. "That'll be—"

"And I want the healthy options." The redhead turned and shouted at her older children. "Stop playing with the ketchup pump. If they charge me for that again it's coming out of your allowance!"

She turned back to the counter, finally seeing Buckshaw. "I mean, I want the orange slices instead of the fries, and extra lettuce on the burgers."

"Mo-om! I hate oranges. I want the *fries!*" The middle child, a chubby, sandy-haired boy, wandered over with ketchup smeared on his face, shirt, and the tiny paper cup he clutched in one hand.

"Billy, we've talked about this. I said if we were going for fast food, you had to get the orange slices instead of the fries. You can't eat fries every day."

"But I got ketchup for my *fries!*" Billy screeched.

"Okay, one kids' meal with fries, two with orange slices," the mother said to Buckshaw. Then she turned back to the kids. "Now, you're going to share those fries with your sisters, okay?"

"But she'll eat them all!" He pointed at his big sister, who had just joined him with more ketchup. She was old enough to be more dexterous, and carried two paper cups of liquefied tomatoes in each hand, plus two more tucked in the crook of each arm. Her juggling act looked to Bryan like a ketchup disaster waiting to happen.

"Billy, you are sharing the french fries and that's it." The mom swiped her credit card and Buckshaw handed her the receipt. "Thank you ma'am, I wondered if you've been voting for—"

"I won't be voting for you," she snapped.

Buckshaw's eyes widened. "What? Well, I hope I can change your mind—"

"Governor, you've done nothing but promote unhealthy habits for children in this state. My kids all have BMIs that are too high for their age, and they won't eat anything but junk thanks to you."

Buckshaw forced a smile. "I actually implemented a healthy lunch program for our schools."

"Yes, and our childhood obesity rates have gone up ever since. Now that my daughter can't get chips at school" —she pointed at the oldest— "she stops at the convenience store on the way home every day and eats two bags by the time she makes it to our street. She trades her school lunch for whatever candy some other kid has brought from home. She eats more fattening food now than she did when the school had a pizza day and chips were a side item."

"I'm sure the obesity rates will come down eventually," Buckshaw said as Matt slid the tray with the three kids' meals across the counter.

"Like unemployment rates will come down?" Matt sneered. "Like employers will raise all our pay if they get enough tax breaks? You approved a law that lets big companies like this one save a fortune through tax breaks a year ago, but I'm still working for minimum wage here."

"So am I," said a middle-aged man who stepped up to the counter as the redhead moved to the side and gathered her food and kids. He wore a t-shirt that said *Byte Me* and an expression that said he wanted to stuff a french fry up Buckshaw's nose.

"We should address that," Bryan said before Shanda could yell at him again. "I looked at the numbers on the way here, and it doesn't appear that wages for low-income workers have—"

Billy let out a blood-curdling scream and pointed at his older sister. "She took all my french fries!"

"Nuh-uh, I didn't," the older girl said around a mouthful of food. It was hard to tell, but the mashed-up white stuff in her mouth was probably a fistful of fries.

"No, you did!" Billy pointed at the tiny paper bag in her hand. "Those were all the fries!"

"The kids' meal only has a handful," Matt explained patiently.

"Did I just tell you to share with your brother?" the mom asked.

"I didn't eat them." The daughter swallowed. "There was only one in the bag. He must have shorted us."

"All I got were these stupid things." Billy pulled a plastic baggie of orange slices out of his bag. He flung the baggie and the paper cup of ketchup across the counter at Buckshaw. "I want my french fries, *give me my french fries.*"

The mother eyed Buckshaw. "You look like you've been stealing a lot of fries."

"Yeah, my mommy says you cheated the people of Texas, I bet you cheated us out of our fries." The older daughter followed suit and flung one paper cup after another at Buckshaw.

Bryan immediately dove for cover, then realized a second later that he looked like a wimp. Peeking around the corner of the ice cream machine, he saw ketchup flying at the governor.

A Secret Service officer popped out from behind the soda machine and threw himself between Buckshaw and the kids, as if flying ketchup posed some serious harm. "Ma'am, you'll have to control your children, or I'll arrest you."

"Well, why don't you replace the order of fries you stole from us?" the mother demanded of Buckshaw, but she grabbed the last of the ketchup cups from her daughter.

Nice parenting. Bryan stepped out from behind the soda machine.

"What's wrong with you? Get over there and ask him if he stole the kids' fries," Shanda said in his ear.

With a sigh, Bryan made his way to the counter, relieved to see the kids were finally out of ammo. "Governor, how do you respond to these allegations that you stole french fries from chil—"

Too late, he realized the bigger problem wasn't being doused with ketchup, but slipping on ketchup. One second he was taking a step forward, the next his foot slid out from under him, and the next he was flat on his back, ketchup soaking through his dry-clean only suit jacket.

"Are you okay?" Matt asked, kneeling beside him. Show photographers swarmed around, making sure to catch every second of his embarrassment.

"I'm fine." He sat up and tried not to wince as all the bruises from his live shot with Chump reminded him they were still present and accounted for. "Nothing's going to stop me from asking Governor Buckshaw the hard questions."

"That'll be fifty cents," Buckshaw said to the redhead as Matt snatched her order of fries from a large bin in the back.

"Fifty cents! You stole my kids' fries and you want to charge me for them?"

"There's no charge, ma'am." Matt slapped a button on the register and handed her the bag.

"But I didn't steal her fries. Her kid ate them." Buckshaw pointed at the little girl.

"Have a nice day, ma'am," Matt practically yelled through a fake smile that rivaled even the politician's.

"But why are you—"

"Because the customer is always *right,*" Matt hissed as the redhead walked away. "You may not need this job, but *I* do. Because when you make minimum wage, you have no savings. I can barely pay my bills as it is. If I lose this job, I won't be able to pay my rent or buy ramen noodles anymore."

Bryan finally pulled himself to his feet, even though he had to lean on the counter to do it. "Why don't you answer his question from earlier about shooting down the minimum wage law, Governor?"

"Yeah, stop dodging his questions," the guy in the *Byte Me* shirt said, pulling out his wallet. "I want to hear your answer, too. And give me a chocolate milkshake, too, while you're at it."

Buckshaw rang up the milkshake and Byte Me swiped his credit card. "Raising the minimum wage wouldn't have helped either of you in the long-term. Instead, I chose to use that money to help businesses expand, so they would need to hire more workers and lower the unemployment rate."

"They hired more workers all right." Byte Me rolled his eyes. "My company hired only part-time workers, so I can't work more than twenty hours a week and I'm not eligible for benefits. I have two part-time jobs, no insurance, and a bill from the government for not being able to afford any."

"That's a federal mandate." Buckshaw grabbed a napkin and wiped ketch-up off his face.

"So you're saying you don't care about minimum wage workers?" Matt turned around and fiddled with the milkshake machine.

"Of course I care." Buckshaw straightened his humongous apron. "I also invested in a state program to encourage kids like you to pursue higher educa-tion, so you can get better-paying jobs."

"Yeah, we didn't have that when I was in school, but my teachers and par-ents still harped on me to go to college, to improve my prospects for the fu-ture." Matt's customer service smile finally escaped from his face. "I worked in a place like this all through high school to save money for college. Then I worked in another while I was in college. While all the rich kids in my class went on spring break to places I've never seen, I worked extra hours in a job like this, so that one day I could have something other than a job like this. I still didn't have enough money, so I sold my blood, rooted through Dumpsters for stuff to sell online, and took out a bunch of student loans."

Buckshaw frowned. "So what are you still doing here?"

"When I graduated, I found there were no jobs for anyone in my field, except a few that required two years of experience for an entry-level position. I'm not the only one, either, in case you're thinking that I just picked a bad major or had a lousy GPA or misspelled university on my résumé or something. Most of the people I graduated with found themselves in the same boat. A lot of them are working in places like this, or standing on street corners with Cash For Gold signs, or stocking shelves at a big box store. The only ones who found gainful employment in their fields were those rich kids whose bigshot executive parents gifted them with jobs when they graduated.

"This isn't my only job, either. I still have those student loans to pay back, despite not having the income to pay them, so after I get off work here, I go deliver pizzas. And on my days off from here and the pizza place, I hand out samples of smoothies in the mall."

Buckshaw's eyes widened, and he looked from Matt, to the crowd, then back again. "See? There you have it. Unemployment is going down. This young man has not one, not two, but three jobs. If he can get all those positions, no one should be applying for unemployment. Obviously those numbers are inflated by those who don't want to work!"

The crowd fell silent. All the people talking on phones shut up or hung up. The parents screaming at their kids stopped in mid-bellow. Even the children quit whining about their orange slices.

"Say something!" Shanda screamed in Bryan's ear.

"Uh, uh..." He stammered, trying to think of something to say that wasn't an outright insult. A question, he needed a question. "Uh, Governor, are you actually saying that the situation Matt here just described is a good thing?"

"Well, it means I lowered unemployment, just like I said I would." Buckshaw tugged the apron down to cover his gut and stood up straighter. "Imagine, all those thousands of people on unemployment who could be working for a living, just like Matt, instead of sucking up the taxpayers' money. I'm going to call an emergency meeting of the state senate to figure out how we can get people off Texas's bankroll, since jobs are so easy to come by that some people have three of them. Maybe applicants should be required to apply at places like this, where business is obviously booming."

Byte Me finally broke the silence that followed. "I don't know who I'm going to vote for, but it won't be you, Governor Buckshaw. I worked my ass off to pay for college too, and I'm working two low-paying jobs to fork over money for my student loans, and I find your job-creation plan despicable. If one of your competitors decides to stop selling the lie of a college education leading to a better life, that's probably who will get my vote. If not, it'll be anybody but your entitled, out-of-touch ass. Now get me my goddamn milkshake!"

"You heard the man, and like I told you earlier, the customer is always right." Matt waved at the machine behind him. "I have to put somebody else on register who can clear out this line faster than you. Get that milkshake *now.*"

Buckshaw went to the machine, managing to avoid slipping on the ketchup.

I should say something. Bryan wracked his brain. He couldn't openly criticize or support any candidate, but he was supposed to ask serious questions. What could he quiz Buckshaw about?

As the portly governor put a cup under the spout and studied the buttons, something finally came to him. "You can't call an emergency meeting of the state senate right now if you want to stay in the race, but I do have a question for you. Governor, did you work in college?"

"Ah, er, yes, I volunteered with the Young Leaders Society, because even then, I knew I wanted to—"

"I don't mean volunteer work to further your future career, I mean a paying job in a place like this that you *had* to do to pay for school," Bryan said.

Buckshaw cleared his throat. "Well, no, I was fortunate that my parents could pay for my education, but that didn't stop me from wanting to help the less fortunate. That's why I started my program to encourage low-income kids to attend college, too."

"Which obviously works so well," Byte Me said.

"Look, it's not my fault if there are no jobs for some recent graduates who don't want to apply themselves." Buckshaw glanced over his shoulder. "I've talked to many business leaders in this state, and they all tell me when they hire Millennials right out of college, all they get are kids glued to their phones, who cry or get angry when anyone asks them to do anything, wail that their feelings are hurt, and demand a union strike if the Wi-Fi goes down for five minutes."

"How could they possibly know that when they won't hire us in the first place?" Byte Me demanded. "I'd work my ass off if an employer would just give me the chance. I was told I needed five years of experience for an entry-level position, but how can I get experience in my field if no one will hire me to do anything except stock the dairy case at a big box store? I even tried getting an unpaid internship, but every company says they only give those to students for legal reasons."

"Well, you've just got to work hard at that big box store and an opportunity will come along." Buckshaw turned back to the machine and jabbed a button.

"I bet when those tax breaks for corporations really kick in, you'll find your wages go up a little too—"

He was cut off by a spray of milkshake to the face. "What? What's wrong? What's going on?"

Bryan stood his ground, even though liquid chocolate ice cream was flying his way, too. Matt's back was to him, but it shook like he was laughing. How did he know what had happened? Wait, wasn't he just toying with the machine? He suddenly had a whole new appreciation for Matt.

He looked over at Byte Me, who was bent over the counter laughing. Actually, so were all the customers.

Matt turned around and walked over to Buckshaw, ducking out of the line of fire, and reached behind the machine. It whirred to a stop, leaving the governor standing in a pool of melted ice cream. "You've caused a mess. You're going to have to mop it up."

"Oh, uh, of course, but what did I do wrong?" Buckshaw asked.

"Everything," shouted a woman in line.

Matt grabbed a mop and bucket and dragged them over to the governor. "Here you go. I hope you learned how to use one of these in college."

Valencia looked up from her phone and blinked at the two of them. "What's going on? My like *traffic* just went way down."

"That's probably because people are liking... hang on let me find it...." Bryan tapped his tablet. "This. That's a picture of the governor here covered in milkshake. Now, Governor Buckshaw, why don't you tell us—while you mop, of course—how you plan to help graduates who are deeply in debt and only able to secure low-paying jobs like this one?"

"By keeping them off unemployment, that's how," Buckshaw huffed. "Once they get on that, they become dependent and never get off."

13

BRYAN MANAGED TO GET a few hours of sleep on the plane to Alabama, then spent the morning doing interviews to publicize the show. Around eleven, he and Shanda finally got in the limo and headed to the daycare where Bob Brumley was scheduled to work.

"Do you think it was fair to dump this assignment on Jeremy?" he asked as they drove past shuttered businesses and houses with peeling paint.

"What are you talking about? All our correspondents beat out hundreds of other people for these jobs. We didn't twist anyone's arm."

"I know, but we're making Jeremy deal with that homophobic moron Brumley. Years ago the guy said if we let gay people serve in the military, they'd bedazzle their rifles and twirl them around like batons instead of shooting people."

Shanda rolled her eyes. "Jeremy Hayden is a gay man who hosts a dating show for gay people. I'm sure he deals with bigoted idiots on a daily basis. Besides, he asked for the Brumley assignment. I think he's enjoying it. Here, look at this video from earlier, it's already got five million hits."

Bryan took the tablet and pressed play. Brumley stood in front of the daycare center, arms at his sides, trying to smile while squinting into the morning sunlight. He actually looked like a dog baring its teeth and growling.

Jeremy walked into the shot, greeted Brumley and stuck out his hand. Brumley managed not to wrinkle his nose too much when he shook it.

"So are you excited about working at the daycare today?" Jeremy asked, friendly as always.

"Yes, I'm happy to do whatever I can to prove to the viewers that I'm the right person to lead this beautiful country." Brumley slowly inched away from Jeremy. "Like I explain in chapter five of my book—"

"What are you doing, Congressman?"

"What?"

Jeremy pointed. "You're backing away from me. Why?"

"Oh, uh, no reason, I'm just, ah, antsy to get in there and get to work."

Jeremy nodded, his face deadpan. "So it's not because I'm gay?"

"No!" Brumley took another tiny step backward. "Of course not."

"Good, because you don't have to worry." Jeremy took a small step closer to Brumley, still leaving a good foot of personal space.

"Worry? About what?" Brumley folded his arms over his chest.

"I don't know, but I've met a lot of people who seem to think being gay is contagious or something." Jeremy shrugged. "I can assure you, it's not. I mean, I've been around heterosexuals my whole life, and it's never turned me straight."

The Congressman nodded. "That's nice."

"Okay, should we go inside now?" Jeremy opened the door, which was covered in decals of tiny hands.

"Are you coming too?" Brumley asked as he walked into the daycare center.

"Of course I am. I'm going to be your shadow all day."

"Oh, look, it just went up to five-and-a-half million hits." Shanda took the tablet back. "You should try to be more like Jeremy. And Joanne. You know, have a real debate with the candidates. All the correspondents are currently outranking you right now, even Valencia, and she barely said two words to Buckshaw. I'm not sure she knew who he was."

"Outranking me?"

"Their hashtags are trending higher than yours. Joanne got a bump after her segment with Sara Finnegan, then Jeremy trended after that video you just watched aired. Of course, Valencia always trends, so it doesn't matter that she didn't do anything, but you could trend if you'd do a better job of grilling the candidates. Without openly criticizing them, of course."

"Of course." No problem at all. The first week of *Sing Your Heart Out,* he'd casually asked a contestant if she found it difficult to sing with so much collagen in her lips, and Shanda screamed at him to stop being mean to the contestants. Ever since, he'd been handing out tissues and asking people how they felt, and he felt a little more like a robot every day.

"Don't worry," Shanda said as they pulled up behind the building. "I'm getting some great stuff for our surprise segment, the one you're going to help me with. We won't use it until after we've eliminated another contestant, though."

When he walked into the daycare, he found Bob Brumley sitting on the floor, playing blocks with a group of small children. Kneeling on the carpet made his pant legs ride up, and flashed his argyle socks to the world. As he leaned over to grab a green block, his tie dragged in what appeared to be Cheeto dust on the worn gray carpet.

"Who in the hell wears a tie to volunteer at a daycare?" Jeremy asked when Bryan joined him. They stood next to a cartoon-covered wall, out of earshot of the congressman.

Bryan shook his head. "Someone running for president, I guess. How's he doing?"

Jeremy shrugged. "The kids haven't thrown ketchup at him yet. Although they haven't had lunch, either...."

"I think I'll interview him before that happens." Bryan walked over to Brumley and the gaggle of children and joined them on the floor, hoping he didn't look as ridiculous as the presidential hopeful. At least he was wearing khakis and a polo, not a three-piece suit from the best tailor in Nowhereville, Alabama.

"Congressman, how are we doing here?"

"Just great." Brumley flashed them a toothy grin. "I'm enjoying this assignment immensely."

"Probably because the kids aren't old enough to ask him any real questions—but you are," Shanda said pointedly in Bryan's ear.

"What do you kids think of, um, Congressman Brumley?" Bryan asked, because several of the children were staring at him like he had three heads. Did they recognize him from TV?

A little girl with auburn pigtails looked up from the toy truck she was running over the end of Brumley's tie. "That's not what my mommy calls him."

"Oh? What does your mommy call him?" The second he said it, Bryan realized he'd just made a huge mistake. Embarrassing the candidates was one thing—they'd signed up for this freak show—but the kid and her mother, on the other hand....

"Whenever he's on the TV, she always calls him Cocksucker Brumley," the little girl said. "Then she changes the channel."

"Ohmigawd that's going viral!" Shanda screeched in Bryan's ear so loudly he only heard ringing for a few seconds after. He blinked and tried to surreptitiously pull his IFB out just a tad, hoping it looked to the viewing audience like he was scratching behind his ear. Not that anyone was probably paying attention to him.

The little girl tugged on his sleeve. The ringing in his ear diminished just in time for her to ask, "What's a cocksucker?"

"Uh...." He had never before been so aware of the presence of TV cameras. What the hell was he supposed to say? There was probably an appropriate way to handle questions like that, but he didn't have kids, and his parents' solution had been to lie to him. At the age of eight, he asked them what a blowjob was and they said they'd never heard of it, and it probably wasn't a real thing. One of his friends explained it to him, and he never asked his parents a question about sex again, since he knew he wouldn't get a straight answer.

Besides, he got a great education on the subject of blowjobs a few years later, when details of the president's Oval Office activities led the news every night. Hell, that was what got him interested in journalism.

"Oh, you poor child of God," Brumley said, saving Bryan from his inability to speak. "I'm sorry your mother has taught you such deplorable language. I guess she didn't stay in school long enough to learn anything better. Well, let's pray for forgiveness."

One of the daycare workers ran over, nearly tripping on the ragged hem of her stained sweatpants. There probably wasn't any point in wearing new clothes to work with forty kids every day.

"I'm sorry, uh, Congressman, but this is a state-run facility. You can't, ah, pray with the children."

"But the kids can swear like sailors? Ridiculous." Brumley patted the little girl on the head and lowered his voice an octave. "Just another example of how our freedom of religion is being taken away every day in this country, a travesty *I* intend to correct when I'm elected, don't worry."

"*Now's your chance—remind him of the definition of religious freedom,*" Shanda said.

Bryan cleared his throat. "Uh, Congressman, you're free to practice any religion you like—"

"There's only one true religion, and if we all used our religious freedom to practice it, these poor children wouldn't be in this situation." Brumley waved his hands at the perfectly-happy-looking kids.

Bryan consulted the summary Shanda had sent to his tablet. "Freedom of religion means *you* can practice *your* idea of the *one* true religion, but not that the government has to teach your idea of the 'one true religion' to children in a government-operated school or daycare facility like this one."

Brumley shook his head. "Religious persecution, that's what this is."

Jeremy joined them and took a seat next to the congressman, who scooted closer to Bryan. "Respectfully, sir, I don't think you know what religious persecution is."

Brumley pointed at a TV mounted on the opposite wall. "Look kids, there's Barney!" When the children turned around, he said in a lower voice that was still easily picked up by his lapel mic, "I know these kids are all here because of their parents' immoral behavior."

"You mean sex?" Bryan blurted, then looked to see if the kids had heard him. None of them were looking at him, but who knew what they heard? He was going to be voted worst reality show host in America before this day was over.

"You told me yourself more than half of these children were parented by teenagers, probably unwed." Brumley shook his head. "They're in this facility because their parents make less than twenty-five thousand dollars a year. What kind of life are these poor kids going to have? One little boy told me he eats all his meals here. The little girl with the potty-mouthed mother is barefoot because her shoes don't fit anymore and her mother hasn't bought her new ones. This is a tragedy of our Godless nation."

"So, don't you think you should change Alabama's policy on abstinence-only education?" Jeremy asked, while Bryan tried to formulate a good response.

What had happened to him? He had always had a snappy question ready the second a subject stopped talking when he was a reporter in Oklahoma. Too many years of handing out tissues and being a shoulder to cry on must have wrecked his journalistic skills.

Brumley jerked even farther away from Jeremy, shoving Bryan against the wall. "Of course not! In addition to abstinence-only education, we need God back in our schools, and a return to the moral standards our founding fathers held dear."

"But you just expressed concern about these children from low-income families." Jeremy waved around the room, with its tattered cartoon-character curtains, scratched-up walls, and crayon-marked plastic furniture. "Studies have shown teen pregnancy rates are far lower in states with comprehensive sex ed."

"Teenagers shouldn't be having sex! Or any unwed couples, for that matter," Brumley snapped.

"But the fact is that they do." Bryan consulted his tablet, which blinked with new messages from Shanda and the automaton, Artie. "And the studies Jeremy references are correct. States with comprehensive sex ed do have lower rates of teen births, and fewer underprivileged kids like these."

Brumley shook his head. "When I'm president, I'll abolish those immoral programs in all fifty states, or die trying."

"**#i'dliketoseethat** is going to trend now," Shanda said.

"So you'd like to see an increase in abortions then?" Jeremy asked.

Bryan tried to conceal his surprise, before again realizing no one was paying attention to him right now.

"Of course not," Brumley said so loudly a couple kids turned around and stared. He waved and rolled a rubber ball in their direction. In a lower voice, he said, "You know I'm pro-life."

"I know you're strongly opposed to abortion." Jeremy picked up one of the blocks and turned it over in his hands. "But you've also signed several bills reducing funding for clinics that provide low-cost birth control, you've campaigned on a platform of reducing welfare and other government benefit spending, including free school lunches for kids from low-income families, and you've repeatedly shot down efforts to introduce comprehensive sex ed in schools. So if you don't want any abortions, then have you changed your mind about reversing the legality of gay marriage?"

"I—what? No, I firmly believe marriage should be between a man and a woman, and when I'm elected, I'll see to it that our laws reflect—"

"If you want to limit access to birth control, ban abortion, and stop all comprehensive sex ed programs, and you want to spend less money on social welfare programs like this very facility, then the only solution is for everyone who can't afford a child to try a homosexual relationship, at least until their finances improve." Jeremy looked so smug Bryan realized he'd been planning this since he asked for the assignment.

"*Blasphemy.*" Brumley jumped to his feet, and Bryan followed, much more slowly because of all his bruises. And also because no one was watching him, anyway.

Brumley jabbed a finger at Jeremy. "You're just trying to push your gay agenda on all of us."

"I'm not, but so what if I was?" Jeremy shrugged. "I'm a private citizen. You, on the other hand, are a public servant, the governor of this state, and running for the highest office in the land, and you want your religious and personal opinions to dictate the laws of this country."

Bryan consulted his tablet. "Congressman, the top trending question right now is from Paul in New York. Paul wants to know what your plan is to fund the increase in social welfare programs that will be needed after you end all comprehensive sex ed programs, ban abortion, and cut off access to reduced-cost birth control for low-income individuals?"

"Well, I don't plan to lead a *gay parade.*" Brumley straightened his tie. "And I'm not rewarding immoral behavior by forcing the taxpayers to support kids like these."

"So you'd rather see *kids like these* go hungry? Didn't you just say some of them eat all their meals here?" Jeremy waved at the group of children staring at the television.

"Of course not. I want to lead our nation back to God, so we don't have these problems."

"By *problems*, do you mean" —Bryan lowered his voice and pointed at the group— "these children?"

"I mean the immoral behavior that *led* to these children is a problem." Brumley buttoned his jacket. "Now, if you'll excuse me, I need to go tell my students about Adam and Eve, and why they shouldn't have sex before marriage."

The harried-looking aide ran after him as he rejoined the kids in front of the TV.

14

BY THE TIME BRYAN arrived at Twentybucks Coffee, social media was ablaze with compliments for Jeremy, harsh criticism for Brumley, and—mostly—total indifference to Bryan.

Jeremy Hayden explained everything that's been wrong with Brumley's hypocritical and contradictory platform from the beginning. No wonder that guy is in last place. I wish all his relatives would stop voting for him and put him out of our misery already. **#byebyebrumley**

Someone should make Brumley support all those kids himself. Maybe he could put them up in one of his three beach houses. **#byebyebrumley #americanpresident**

First Joanne, now Jeremy. Seafoam always needs a real reporter to prop him up. **#seafoamsucks**

#seafoamrocks was still trending, but it lagged far behind Jeremy, Valencia, and Joanne's hashtags. Would that Barnaby dope from *Strip Club Idol* be beating him by the end of the day?

No, absolutely not. By the time they got to Shanda's surprise segment in a few days, he was going to be the most popular host again. All he had to do was take a hard line with Ronda Harper, which shouldn't be difficult considering how badly her day was going.

Slipping into the back entrance of the coffeehouse, trailed by security, he glanced at the live feed on his phone. Harper stood at the drive-through window, juggling coffee cups, sloshing lattes onto the counter, and jerking her headset away from her ear every few seconds, probably to relieve the pain of listening to another screaming customer.

"Barnaby doesn't know how to do anything but make sexual innuendos," Shanda said in Bryan's ear as he moved down a tiny hallway and into the "employees only" area. "You can easily trend higher if you come back with intelligent questions for Harper. I'll try to help you out."

Help him out? He had trained as a journalist, she hadn't. He didn't need help. He needed to forget about being the nice guy who didn't ask if it was hard to sing with ten pounds of collagen in your lips. Before he nodded sympathetically to sob stories, he had been a real reporter once. That guy hadn't gone anywhere, he'd just been locked up in a cage, and it was time to let him out.

"But remember, you can't appear to be too mean or out to get the candidates," Shanda added while he shook hands with Barnaby.

Rock, hard place. So much for being a real reporter again.

"I'm so glad you're here. This assignment blows—and not in a good way." Barnaby looked at himself in the nearest monitor, undoing another button on his shirt and flexing his pecs, which he'd obviously spent hours working on at the gym.

They were in the back of the coffeehouse, camera equipment wedged between bag after bag of coffee grounds, every one with a different flavor listed on the label. Stone-ground Kenyan Odyssey. Amazon River Dark Roast. South American Star-Light Roast. And he used to think the names on Joanne's twenty tubes of lipsticks were ridiculous.

"Listen, I'm going to slip out and meet with a few fans while you interview the dragon lady."

"What? You're not sticking around for the interview?" Even Valencia stood in the corner and played with her phone the whole time, but she didn't leave.

Barnaby wrinkled his nose. "Harper's tough, man. Good luck."

"What do you mean, tough? I know she's a politician, but so are the rest of them."

Barnaby stared down at his alligator boots. "To be honest, I don't really know how to talk to women who aren't dancing around a pole or burning up the dance floor at a club. Like, she has all her clothes on, and there's no alcohol in this bar—"

"That's because it's a coffeehouse."

"—and she wants to talk about stuff I don't understand, like the economy and fiducious, fiduci-um...."

"Fiduciary concerns?"

"Yes! I need a fucking dictionary to talk to this chick, man."

Bryan bit his lip. *Surely* she must hold Barnaby in the same high regard. "That's all right, I'll interview her myself."

Bryan squeezed past a stack of Moonlight Madness Mongolian Extra Dark Roast and walked to the drive-through window, where Ronda Harper stood, wearing a blue pantsuit, a black Twentybucks Coffee apron, a headset, and a strained smile.

"You messed up my order," said a young woman in a Mazda Miata. Her blonde hair blew in the wind, some of it sticking to her face. She brushed it away with one hand and shoved her coffee cup back at Harper with the other.

Harper frowned and took back the cup. "Iced soy no-foam decaf café mocha, wasn't it?"

"Behind you," said a woman with a name tag that said *Brenda* and a facial expression that said *I wish I could fire her.* She shoved two cups of some sort of fruity red beverage toward the window, and three bags of pastries into a separate pile.

Miata Girl glared. "I said a peach green tea lemonade, no sweetener."

"Sorry about that." Harper handed the cup to Brenda with an apologetic smile. "As you know, I never was one to stay home and bake cakes and make tea." She turned her gaze to Bryan. "That's why it's so unfair that they gave me, *a female candidate,* this job, serving food and beverages. It's just another attempt for the old, white, male crony establishment to try to force women into subservient roles, and if you want to fight them, you should vote for me—"

"Here's your drink." Brenda leaned around Harper and handed over the iced tea-and-fruit-flavor cocktail.

"For the record, we didn't choose anyone's assignment, America did," Bryan reminded her. "And I just left Bob Brumley caring for small children in a daycare. Would you prefer that task?"

"She prefers the assignment where she gets paid six figures to give an ass-kissing speech to the old cronies she claims to be fighting against." Brenda shoved the pastries and red drinks toward Harper and gestured for her to hand them out the window to the next carload of coffee fiends.

"Yeah, you claim to support the poor and middle-class, but you live in a mansion and took half a million dollars from that guy Morganstern's bank last year to speak at some financial summit they threw themselves," said the customer, a man in a security guard's uniform. "Then you voted to cut taxes for the one percent, and didn't lower them at all for the other ninety-nine. Isn't that true?"

Harper pasted on her best campaign smile. "Well, I think it's wonderful that we're finally having a debate about crony capitalism. And remember, the important thing is that we beat the Republicans this year."

"Force her to answer that question," Shanda said in Bryan's ear.

"Congresswoman Harper, that's not an answer to this voter's question." Bryan pointed at the security guard. "What's your name, sir?"

"Bob Martin. I'm one of the ninety-nine percent."

Obviously. He was driving a clunker that looked older than Bryan's grandmother and holding out a handful of change plus a crumpled one for his $3 plain coffee.

Bryan turned to Harper. "I'm sorry, but if you're going to grandstand and tell people to vote for you, you're also required to answer their questions—no dodging. Now, did you or did you not take money from Cheatham Bank for some sort of speech, then vote to lower taxes on the largest financial institutions in this country, of which Cheatham is definitely one?"

"Try not to sound too adversarial when you do that," Shanda whined.

Harper cleared her throat. "I take many speaking engagements each year. I enjoy speaking with business leaders to learn more about how we can improve the economy for everyone—"

"Did you make a speech for the bigwigs at Cheatham Bank?" Brenda asked. A car behind Bob honked.

Brenda winced. "We really need to keep the line moving."

"Anyone coming here today has to know the lines are going to be insane. Congresswoman Harper is going to answer your and Bob's question, and if anyone doesn't like it, they can go to one of the twenty other coffee shops on this block." Bryan grabbed a cup and filled it with Panama Canal Mid-Roast Coffee. He took a long sip. "Cheatham Bank?"

Harper glanced at Bob, then at Brenda, then back to Bryan. Finally she took a deep breath, lifted her chin, and put on a stump-speech face. "I delivered a talk about corporate responsibility, a subject that concerns me greatly, of course, to Cheatham executives, yes."

"And when you voted to lower taxes on financial institutions like Cheatham?" Bob pulled out his phone and leaned out the window, apparently trying to get video of himself with Harper. Maybe he wanted to vote for her after all.

"That was to help the ninety-nine percent," Harper said. "It was to stimulate the economy, creating more jobs and leading to raises. I also voted to raise the minimum wage, although some of my fellow members of Congress, sadly, did not," she added, looking at Brenda.

"We already make five bucks an hour more than minimum wage here." Brenda leaned on the counter. "Can I be in the picture, too?"

Horns blared behind Bob.

Bryan leaned out the window. "Can't you people see we're in the middle of a presidential debate here? Go buy your coffee somewhere else!"

"Hey, whoa, I need this job!" Brenda grabbed Bryan's arm and yanked him backward. He tried to turn around, but his polo shirt caught on the edge of one of the many metal machines he couldn't identify, throwing him off balance, and he tripped. The next thing he knew, he was slamming into the coffee machine. He tried to catch himself by grabbing the giant coffeemaker, but burned his hand on the metal, so he grabbed the nearest non-metal thing in sight, a piece of plastic.

Unfortunately, that piece of plastic apparently controlled the flow of liquid out of the machine, and grabbing it unleashed a flood of hot coffee onto his other hand, which was gripping the lower part of the coffeemaker.

He jerked his hand away, but the searing pain momentarily blotted out everything else, including his usual on-air language filter.

"Son of a *bitch.*" Shit, did he just say that out loud?

"Bleep that!" Shanda screamed.

"Privileged white males like yourself don't realize how offensive and sexist comments like those are," Harper said. "You never hear anyone yell *son of a bastard,* do you?"

Brenda grabbed his elbow and yanked him over to the sink, practically dislocating his shoulder. "Hang on, we have a first aid kit for burns."

"I also gave a speech to the Restaurant Owners Association about how important it is to protect workers' safety." Harper shoved the coffee cups aside and waved for Bob to come closer with the camera. He ducked back into the car, turned off the engine, opened the door, and got out. Then he leaned on the counter while Harper launched into a speech about protecting the workers of establishments like Twentybucks Coffee.

Bryan's hand was on fire. Brenda ran cold water over it and applied a bandage. "You should go have that looked at by a medic."

But all Bryan could think about was how this incident would trend on Twitter. People would scream about how he was too hard on Harper, how he was somehow being sexist by yelling a commonplace phrase while in incredible pain, what a wuss he was for whining after being burned by a coffee machine that was, in his estimation, hotter than the surface of the sun, how he wasn't a real reporter....

"You don't look so good. You should really sit down and wait for the ambulance," Brenda said.

"Ambulance? You called an *ambulance?* No, I don't need one, I'm fine." He waved her away with his slightly-less burned hand. Besides, how would it get through the traffic?

"There's been one parked outside all day. You think we want to get sued?" Shanda asked.

"Don't worry, despite your crude comments about women, I'm working hard to protect your rights, too," Harper continued in her best campaign voice.

"This is bullshit, but I want to be on TV." Bob leaned in the window and waved at the camera capturing Bryan's embarrassment. "Have you guys ever considered starting a reality show for underpaid security guards at soup companies?"

"I voted against a bill to cap personal injury lawsuits against big corporations like this establishment." Harper waved around the coffee house, where people had stopped sipping lattes to stare at Bryan. "I realize you're a privileged white male, so this injury doesn't affect you. After all, you can afford the best health care. But what if Brenda here had been seriously injured by your fumbling with the coffee machine? I want to protect workers like her in the event that their employers allow them to be injured due to a careless mistake, so I voted against the lawsuit cap."

"Helping the American Bar Association make more money. You gave them a speech too, didn't you?" Bob asked.

"I think the important thing to focus on is protecting the blue-collar workers of America and defeating the Republicans this year, how about that?" Harper yelled, leaning around Bob to shout out the window.

Horns blared—whether in agreement with her speech or because people were desperate for caffeine, Bryan wasn't sure.

15

I HAVE TO HAND it to Harper, her numbers didn't take as big a hit as everyone else's after their segments," Shanda said as they rode to the airport. "I mean, every candidate's numbers have fallen after their challenge. And hers did, too, but not as steeply as Brumley's or Chump's. And they're going back up faster, too."

Bryan rubbed at the bandage on his hand. "So she'll still be in the race after tomorrow night's vote?"

"Probably. But we haven't seen all the candidates yet, either." She set down the tablet and drummed her red-white-and-blue fingernails on the console. "We need to talk about *your* numbers, though, Bryan. I think after today you should probably abandon taking a hard line with the candidates, at least for a little while."

"But I wasn't trying to be sexist! Everyone uses that expression."

"I know, and if it had been any other candidate, no one would care. Except maybe Brumley's 'crumbling morals' friends." She hooked her fingers into air quotes with one hand and picked up her phone with the other. "I know Harper just took advantage of your little outburst to tell the country they should vote for her because she's a woman and not voting for her is sexist. That's not your fault, but because she was able to turn the situation her way, the viewers are turning on you—in droves. Look at these."

With a sigh, he took the phone and read the latest social media buzz about what had apparently been labeled **#sexistseafoam.**

#sexistseafoam *should apologize to Ronda Harper for demeaning her like that.*

#sexistseafoam *doesn't want a woman to win the White House. He probably thinks she should be cleaning the Oval Office instead of working in it!*

Stop saying **#seafoamsucks** *is* **#sexistseafoam** *because he was hard on Harper. He's mean to all the candidates. Didn't he used to be a nice guy when he was on* **#SingYourHeartOut**?

"You've got to be kidding me." He shoved the device back to her. "This is ridiculous. You wanted me to ask tough questions, but still be a nice guy, and people are criticizing me for both being too hard on the contestants and not acting like a real journalist. Plus now they're all listening to Harper's nonsense because I had a momentary slip of the tongue and used some profanity when I was burned with scalding hot coffee."

"I know, and I'm sorry. Harper is just grandstanding and this thing will blow over. But I do think I was wrong, pressuring you to play hardball with the candidates. For now at least, why don't you just go back to being the supportive host? I mean, we already have a real reporter. Joanne can take a hard line with the contestants."

He stared at her. "A *real* reporter? I used to be a *real* reporter, too. I worked in the same TV station as Joanne—"

"Then you went on to host game shows, then reality shows, while Joanne went on to work for NNN." She fished a compact out of her purse and patted her hair. "Look, you trying to be an investigative journalist while hosting this show just isn't working, okay? It works for Joanne, because people have been seeing her do the same thing for years."

"So that's it? All I ever do for the rest of my career is wipe noses and ask people how they feel?" He turned to look out the window of the limo, which suddenly felt like a tomb. The dilapidated houses and rusted clunkers on cinder blocks rushing by reminded him of the area where he'd lived in Oklahoma. Everything looked gray and old and run-down.

"I don't know, Bryan. A career is a long time." The compact slammed shut with a click and the sound of fingers flying over a screen filled the car. "But for the remainder of the show, I think it's best if you let the candidates make their own controversies, okay? What is it they teach you in journalism school? The reporter is not the story?"

16

THE GREEN THUMB CO-OP in downtown Seattle was overflowing with customers, and Bryan was pretty sure it wasn't because they all desperately wanted to save fifty cents on carrot juice.

"Of all the contestants, I'd say he's enjoying his assignment the most." Joanne pointed at Bob Fuller, who was engaged in an animated conversation about the health benefits of organic grapefruit.

"No one's given him a hard time?" Bryan stood next to Joanne in the clearance corner, between a ten-pound bag of vegan dog food with a starburst sign that screamed *WAS $49.99, NOW 48.99*! and a stack of whole wheat cereal marked down to the low, low price of $7.99 a box.

She shrugged. "A few cranks told him marijuana was a gateway drug. He asked if they were worried their kids would end up here."

He watched a couple picking through different varieties of kale. "Who has money for drugs when they're paying fifteen dollars a pound for leaves that don't get you high?"

She snickered. "I forgot how funny you could be."

For the first time since the show started, he remembered what it was like when he and Joanne worked in that piddling Oklahoma TV station in a town where there were more cows than televisions. How he used to go to work every day anticipating that he would learn something new, even if it was that the city council wanted to change every street sign to have all capital letters. How he used to love it when Joanne laughed at his jokes, even though she always went home with—

Shanda's shrill voice cut off his reminiscing, which was probably just as well. *"If you guys are done catching up on the good ol' days, I suggest you wrap up the interview with Fuller. This guy is boring our viewers and tanking our ratings. Ask him a couple questions, and get out so you can go visit Phil Foster and his porcine friends."*

"You're coming to the pig farm?" he asked Joanne as they walked toward Bob Fuller.

"Didn't Shanda tell you? Valencia was supposed to go there, but she says she's allergic to pork or something, and her skin breaks out in hives if she gets anywhere near mud...."

"Surely there's an Instagram filter to fix that?"

She snickered. "You really are funny, Bryan. It's a pity our viewers haven't gotten to see that side of you since the first night, when you put the candidates in their place."

"Well, that side of me is on lockdown for the moment." He stopped a few feet away from where Fuller inspected a grapefruit. "You take the lead on this one. I'll hang around and hand him a Kleenex, if necessary."

She frowned, but stepped forward and joined the candidate at the fruit stand anyway. "Mr. Fuller, how are you doing there?"

"Just great." Fuller scratched at the hairnet that covered his long brown ponytail. "I feel so at home here in this store. When I become president, I'm going to mandate a federally-operated organic food co-op in every city."

Her eyebrows shot up. She used to spend hours plucking them herself, but now she could probably afford to have them waxed.

"Ah, you're suggesting the government should go into the grocery business?"

Fuller picked up two tiny paper cups of freshly-squeeze grapefruit juice and handed them to Bryan and Joanne. "That's right. Think of all the jobs we'll create! And we'll provide healthy food at a reasonable cost to all our citizens."

Bryan nearly choked on a sip of the sour juice. "You're going to... that's um, an interesting plan. Tell us more about it."

Joanne's eyebrows remained elevated. "Yes, please tell us how we're going to pay for that, within that budget you just voted to approve."

Fuller waved a hand. Bryan caught a whiff of pot. "That's for the coming year. It'll take me that long to get the proper legislation through Congress and all. So my national co-ops won't be operating until the year after."

"And how will you pay for them then?" Joanne asked.

"Well, first I have to explain how the plan works, see." Fuller leaned back and propped an elbow on a pile of grapefruit. "It'll pay for itself in no time. People eat healthier food, they get sick less often, and we simply spend less on health care. Also, we raise the age to collect Social Security to eighty, eighty-five or so, since healthier people can work longer."

"Let me get this straight, Mr. Fuller—you want to reduce spending on health care, and raise the Social Security age to eighty to pay for free food for the masses?"

"*#socialismsucks is trending on Twitter,*" Shanda squealed in Byran's ear.

"Well, we're not cutting anything people really need." Fuller shrugged. "If people are in pain, they can just smoke some pot. That'll also be available in our co-ops, at a subsidized low rate. As for raising the Social Security age, everyone's going to be living longer, and our current system is just not sustainable."

"*Well, he's lost the AARP vote,*" Shanda mumbled. "*Although, I doubt he had it in the first place.*"

Joanne consulted her tablet. "Mr. Fuller, what would you say to critics on social media who are calling this plan 'socialism' or, and I'm quoting here, 'Worse than socialism, even, this is like communism plus socialism plus a nanny state telling us to eat our vegetables.' End quote."

Fuller flashed his not-quite-white teeth in something resembling a smile. "To that I would say, 'Did I mention marijuana will be legal?'" She glanced at Bryan as if expecting him to jump in. What could he say that didn't sound too critical?

"Ah, Mr. Fuller, that's an interesting idea, but what if you can't get it through Congress?"

"Then it'll be Congress's fault we can't move this great country forward, not mine."

Joanne cleared her throat. "I don't think I've ever heard a presidential candidate blame Congress before even being elected."

Fuller shrugged. "I am a progressive candidate."

She looked at the tablet again. "You're also an independently wealthy candidate, who has lived on a hundred-acre estate here in Washington for the past ten years."

"I'm okay with sharing my wealth." The Green Party candidate poured himself a cup of grapefruit juice. "I'm also in favor of increasing taxes on big corporations, like those evil pharmaceutical giants that sell pills to make people sicker."

"I see." She tilted her head like she was thinking. Bryan had seen that look before—she got it just before she went in for the kill.

"How do you plan to collect taxes off the big drug companies if you get everyone eating health food and smoking marijuana? Won't that lower their profits?"

"Sure it will. That's why we also reduce spending on health care," Fuller said.

"Of course. So how will you force people to eat only healthy food? Your co-ops won't stop people who can afford to eat elsewhere from clogging their arteries with cheeseburgers and fries, will it?"

"No, we'll just tax people who put an unnecessary strain on the health care budget. We'll start right away, and soon we'll have enough money to fund the co-ops."

"You're going to tax people for getting sick?" Bryan asked.

"Not all the time. Just for preventable illnesses, like when people have a heart attack after eating cheeseburgers every day for years." Fuller grabbed the nearest grapefruit and raised it in the air. "This is the solution to all our problems. Healthy food reduces health care costs and—"

"So now you're shifting the tax burden from the wealthy corporations to the poorest individuals, right?" Joanne asked.

The contestant jerked back as if she's punched him. "Of course not! I said we'd tax Big Pharma and individuals—of any income level—who abuse our health care system."

"But studies show that the poorest people are also the sickest, and are more likely to develop preventable illnesses like heart disease and diabetes." She waved her hand at a wall of dried goods, topped by a sign that screamed Stock up on nuts! "Even with government subsidizing, organic food isn't cheap. This is going to cost a fortune, and historically, every time Congress passes legislation to make large corporations pay more money, the wealthy CEOs of those companies lobby Congress for exclusions to get their businesses out of paying. Isn't there a good chance you're just going to increase the tax burden on the poor?"

That was exactly the kind of investigative reporting Bryan had pictured himself doing when he chose broadcast journalism as a major in college. Too bad he wasn't the one doing it.

"I think she has a point," said an older woman in a pink sweater. She leaned over her shopping cart to glare at Fuller. "And I will never vote for someone who wants to take away my Social Security."

Fuller offered her a grapefruit. "Eat more of these, and you might feel like working longer."

"I think all the pot has clouded your thinking. But you're right, I am feeling pretty spry right now." The woman hauled back her arm and flung the grapefruit at Fuller, who ducked out of the way just in time—

For the grapefruit to go flying at Bryan.

Not one to be outdone by a pothead—it didn't seem to have affected the guy's coordination, he had to admit—Bryan also jumped out of the way, nearly knocking over a display of $7.99/lb grape tomatoes.

Without asking if he was all right, the nearest photographer shoved Bryan out of the way, trying to get a shot of the flying grapefruit. It hit a large silver coffee maker and bounced off, heading right toward—

SPLAT! All the TV monitors littered around the store for Bryan, Joanne, and the crew to watch went dark as the grapefruit smashed into the camera lens, covering it in pink goo.

The monitors didn't stay picture-less for long. Shanda screeched at the director to pop up one of the dozen or so static cameras scattered around the store, and Bryan found himself looking at a wide shot of Joanne asking the woman how she felt about Fuller's suggestion. Meanwhile, he stood off to the side, looking like the useless lump he was, at the moment.

"Ask Fuller a question while Joanne interviews the customer," Shanda shouted.

"So, uh, Mr. Fuller, what do you think about—"

But Fuller wasn't done with the lady in the pink sweater. He stomped past Bryan and stormed up to her. "You know, I've had enough of your generation. You've been trying to stop progress since the sixties. You want your Social Security, but you don't want to support jobs for the people who will continue to pay into it. You just want to live off us, tell us we can't smoke pot, and help Big Pharma get richer. You and everyone else down at the AARP are wrecking this country, and I will not cater to you or beg for your vote. If it was up to me, I'd use your next Social Security check to roll a joint."

"That'll be a great GIF," Shanda mumbled.

"You may not like my generation, but we spend a lot of time watching TV, and *we* vote." With that, the lady in pink grabbed Fuller's pitcher of grapefruit juice and poured it over his head.

"Mr. Fuller, have you ever actually *paid* into Social Security?" Joanne asked as he stood there dripping pink juice onto the faux wood floor. "As I understand from your bio, you've never actually had a job. After college, you moved onto your family's estate and have lived off various investments—including one in the largest pharmaceutical company in the country—ever since."

Bryan slowly slunk away as the candidate spluttered about how the establishment was trying to ruin him. Joanne had things under control, and the cameras had cut away from him a long time ago.

"That's good Bryan, make a quick exit," Shanda said in his ear. *"I need you to go interview some contenders for that surprise segment we have coming up after the vote."*

17

BRYAN HAD NOT BEEN in favor of the Pop-Up Presidential Candidate segment, but as usual, Shanda didn't care what he thought. "This is a reality show. We have to throw a monkey wrench in things every now and then. The surprise new contestant move is to reality shows what plot twists are to fully scripted dramas."

Fully scripted, because of course Shanda and her ilk constantly ran around doing everything they could to manipulate the contestants into a more dramatic/funny/shocking scene.

Although initially he hated the idea of letting absolutely anyone in America audition to be the next president, after spending almost a week with the fully vetted career politician candidates, he didn't think the average person could possibly do any worse. An hour after the Bob Fuller interview, he met Shanda at a non-descript office building in a strip mall.

"We've selected these people from our Skype pre-auditions." She bounded down the hallway of the rented building and he struggled to keep up. "We called it the Talk Back America segment, and we asked people what they'd do if they were president."

"I remember. I recorded the promo asking people to participate." He followed at a slower pace. How could she have so much energy after such an exhausting several days?

"We've told the finalists we asked here today they were being considered to win a trip to see the finale in person." Shanda stopped just short of two heavy double doors. "You're going to ask them to explain what they'd do as president again, then throw them some random questions about handling global problems—I've sent those to your tablet. I'll take notes and our algorithm will rank them on a variety of pre-selected attributes. When I've made my decision, you'll let them know why they're really here, and ask if they'd like to run for president."

"Are you sure this is legal? I don't remember any mention of this in the By the People, For the People Act."

She threw her head back and laughed, and her American flag earrings tinkled. "I had a team of lawyers go over this. The By the People, For the People Act did away with the Electoral College, and many other trappings of our previous election system. In order to make everyone happy, so the bill could pass, they had to throw in a provision that ordinary people be allowed to audition as well as long-time politicians and the financially obese."

He rubbed his eyes. They felt like they were full of sand. When was the last time he'd slept? "Why would anyone in Congress want that?"

She rolled her eyes and gave him that *you-should-know-the-answer-are-you-sure-you-trained-as-a-reporter* look. "So they could claim to be representing the interests of real people. Anyway, it's not like some average shmuck we pick off the street is actually going to win, and everyone in Congress knew that when they voted. This is an aspirin to soothe the headache of the pissed-off voting public, nothing more. But we have to give the impression it's serious and whoever we pick has a real chance. Now go in there and sell this thing, okay? We need people to forget about the coffee house debacle."

He nodded and shoved the doors open.

The first contestant had *redneck* written all over him, from the Bud Light trucker cap to the Confederate flag tattoo to the monster truck rally t-shirt with the sleeves ripped off to the camo pants.

"Nice to meet you, Bubba. Please, tell us again what you'd do differently if you were president of the United States," Bryan read off the teleprompter.

Bubba leaned forward in the metal folding chair, which was placed six feet from the table where Bryan and Shanda sat. "First thing ah'd do, I got three words for ya—nuc-u-lar launch codes."

Bryan clenched his fists under the table. What he wouldn't give to punch the moron who suggested this provision in the Act. "Okay. What would you do with those nuclear launch codes?"

Bubba reached behind him, and for a second Bryan thought he was going to scratch his ass while auditioning to be president, but instead he pulled a toothpick from a back pocket—at least Bryan hoped it was stored in a back pocket, he couldn't really tell from here—popped it in his mouth, chewed at it for a few seconds, then rolled it to the side with his tongue.

"One word—China. Never liked them taking all our jobs. Then North Korea—never liked them either. 'Specially their president. Cheeto-eatin' couch potata pussy, wants to cry and hide behind his hackers' skirts cuz we made a few movies he don't like. I ain't gon' stand fer that when I'm president. That sissy keeps testin' nukes, out there round China or some other place he thinks we don't care about. If we don't nuke 'em first, they'll turn this country into an ashtray."

Bryan pressed his lips together to suppress a laugh. Stealing a glance at Shanda, he saw the corners of her lips twitching like his ex-girlfriend trying to twerk in a club.

Suddenly, it was all clear to him. These weren't the *real* real-people contestants. These were the "no-chancer" comic relief contestants, brought on so the people at home could laugh at their stupidity and feel superior. It was sort of like when the assistant producers of *Sing Your Heart Out* sent through people who couldn't sing on key to save their lives—they were there for the sole purpose of making asses of themselves.

At least, he hoped that was why they'd dragged all these regular people here. It was getting hard to tell, considering how certifiable some of the real contestants were.

"Thanks for your time, Bubba. You'll be advised of our decision later. Next!" Shanda yelled.

18

THE IOWA PIG FARM was every bit as awful as Bryan anticipated. Maybe it was just the recent rainfall, but everywhere he looked, all he saw was mud. Mud on the ground, mud on the fences, mud splattering the lower half of the white limo he, Shanda, and Joanne had arrived in.

An aide provided them all with thigh-high rubber boots, and he and Joanne squelched along through the muck toward the barn where Senator Foster was working.

"Remember the last time we saw this much mud?" Joanne waved at the brown sea surrounding them. "When it rained every day for almost two weeks, and no one in Oklahoma had ever seen that much flooding?"

"And every day, they made us stand outside in the rain and point at the sky and tell people it was raining and the roads were slippery when wet, because apparently all our viewers had TVs but not windows." He shook his head. "That's one of the things I don't miss about news—having to stand around and repeat the obvious a hundred times an hour."

"Is that why you got out and went into hosting?"

He shrugged. "There were a lot of reasons. I guess I never planned to host a reality competition. I took that first game show because the money was so much better, honestly. Plus I could kind of be myself, you know, have a personality and not just recite facts and keep my opinions to myself."

She gave him a sideways glance. "But you don't do that anymore."

"How can I? This is a presidential election. As the host, my job is to remain neutral."

"I've read the contract. You can't endorse or oppose any candidate. That doesn't mean you have to kiss anyone's ass." She stopped at a low fence, threw one leg over, then, after a couple tries, pulled the boot of the other out of the mud, eventually landing both feet on the other side. Then she reached behind her and twisted a dial on her mic pack, turning it off. "I know Shanda's been telling you to be the nice-guy host, because she thinks that's better for ratings."

"You think she's wrong?" He followed her over the fence—not nearly as gracefully, but he managed not to fall in the muck—and turned off his mic, as well. If their conversation was brief, Shanda probably wouldn't notice the lack of chatter.

Joanne scrunched up her face and smoothed her already-perfect ponytail. "She's not looking at the big picture. This is a reality show to elect the next president. People are going to watch whether they like the host or not. Personally, I think they'd find it refreshing if at least one person on the show wasn't full of bullshit. That's why I aim to give every candidate I talk to a hard time. I'm not playing favorites. I'm making them all show their true colors."

"I know, and you're trending a lot higher than me." He started toward the barn. "But I can't just start acting like a... like the reporter I really am right in the middle of the show."

"Why not? What are they going to do, fire you? You're the host of the first-ever *American President*. They can't fire you for acting like a journalist instead of an ass-kisser. If they do, the public backlash will be insane, and possibly overshadow the election, which no one wants."

"I hadn't thought of it that way." He turned his mic back on. They were almost at the barn.

Joanne did have a point though—what was Shanda going to do if he went for the jugular on Foster?

As they entered the barn, an attendant handed them paper masks like the one that obscured his own face. Even with it on, Bryan could still smell the heavy odor in the building, despite the row of industrial fans churning near the ceiling.

"It's like when someone leaves a burning pile of dog crap on your porch, times one-hunnerd, right?" Another guy in a mask walked up to them and offered his hand, which was caked with something brown. Bryan hoped it was mud and reluctantly shook.

"Are you the owner of this farm?" he asked.

The man nodded. In addition to the mask, he wore a hairnet like the employees at Buckshaw's fast food joint, faded denim coveralls that were more brown than blue at this point, and thigh-high rubber boots like the ones Shanda's assistant had provided.

"I'm Jimmy Wilson, and this 'ere farm's been in my family for generations." His expression clouded. "We're one of the few family farms left. The big corporations have been trying to buy us out for years."

"Whatever you do, don't ask him any questions about the pigs' feelings," Shanda mumbled in Bryan's ear. *"It took me three days to convince him we weren't working undercover for PETA."*

"It's a lovely farm." Bryan looked around at the cramped stalls of pigs. "Where is Senator Foster?"

Even with the mask on, it was obvious Jimmy's face had turned up in a smile that reached the crinkles around his eyes. "Down at the end. He's mucking out the manure pits under the pig stalls."

Joanne also smiled under her mask. "So to be clear, you've assigned your resident politician to shovel manure, Mr. Wilson?"

"That's right, and I'll put it less politely than you. He's a politician, he should know how to shovel shit."

"Well, let's get to it." Bryan headed to the end of the barn, Joanne and Jimmy following. The sooner he got this interview over with, the sooner he could breathe clean air again.

Senator Foster was wearing about five masks, and sweating like... well, like a pig. He'd opted to leave his usual suit behind at the hotel, instead donning jeans and a Foster campaign t-shirt, which was now streaked with mud—hopefully, it was mud.

He looked up as they approached, sweat matting his gray hair to his forehead. His smile was completely fake, and just barely peeked around the corners of his mask, while his eyes screamed get-me-out-of-here.

"So good to see you, Bryan. Joanne, I enjoyed our chat yesterday afternoon during my training session."

Bryan had seen the interview, in which Foster babbled his campaign talking points and related them all back to working on a "wonderful family farm like the many we have here in Iowa" in ten seconds or less.

"How's it going today, Senator?"

Foster stuck his shovel in the mud—no, it wasn't mud—and leaned on it. "You know, I've developing a renewed appreciation for the hard work our farmers do here in Iowa to produce the wonderful food we all eat."

He straightened up, leaned the shovel against a wall, approached them, and slapped Jimmy on the back. "That's why I'm doubly proud to have stood my ground during the Congressional budget challenge, defending the farm subsidy package when all my colleagues wanted to kill it—because I support Jimmy and all the farmers like him here in Iowa, and the rest of the country, who make our—"

"Lemme stop you right there, Senator." Jimmy stepped back, brushing aside Foster's hand. "I saw that, and so did the rest of America. Oh yeah, you were 'standing up for farmers' when you were on TV in front of millions of people trying to win their votes for president of the United States. But last year, in a closed Congressional session, you voted to increase farm subsidies for big factory farms, and reduce those for small farms like ours."

Joanne nodded. "That is true, Congressman."

Foster cleared his throat. "Well, last year's budget was very different. Sometimes compromises have to be made, and money has to be allocated where it will do the most good—"

"With big business?"

"Now, the most recent subsidy package in this year's Congressional budget included money for independent farms like yours. I try to make improvements to help small businesses every chance I get—and I didn't see anyone else in that room standing up for *any* farmers."

"I think Governor Buckshaw opposed dropping the subsidy," Bryan said.

Foster waved a hand.

Bryan tried not to cringe as it came inches away from his face.

"Buckshaw doesn't understand what it's like for the farmers in his state. *I* do. I've worked my whole life to help businesses, big and small, produce our food with the least government intervention and the most assistance—"

"That's why you give the big national farms huge tax breaks? You voted to keep that in the budget too." Jimmy held up his phone. "I've watched all the video of that debate, every minute. You insisted on providing tax breaks to the largest businesses in the country, including the farm giants that have been trying to run us out of business for twenty years. With those savings, they can afford to sell at much lower prices than we can."

Foster nodded. "I hear your concerns, Mr. Wilson, and I have a plan to address them once I'm president. I plan to introduce to Congress a Small Business Support Bill—"

"With all due respect, Congressman, why wait till you're president?" Joanne said. "You could have introduced a bill at any time during your last twenty years in Congress."

"Exactly." Jimmy folded his arms across his chest.

Foster went to adjust his tie, realized it wasn't there, then awkwardly hung his arms at his sides. "My bill will get much more publicity and positive press once I'm president. Besides, these things take time, and I've been working on legislation to improve the lives of small business owners for years, because I understand and care about all my constituents."

"No, you don't," Jimmy's voice boomed in the large, high-ceilinged room. "Here you are, mucking out manure, and you claim to understand my job. No, you don't. You're here for a few days. You'll smile and pretend not to notice the smell and act like you're having a good time so you can get into the Oval Office. If you don't, you'll go back to your comfy seat in Congress, or a cushy job in the private sector. I've done this job every day of my life, and I will have to do it every day after you leave, because this is who I am. I didn't go to college, intern for a Congressman for a couple years, then get myself elected with my family's wealth and influence, like you did. You may be from my state, but you are not me, you do not understand me and my business, and you never will. Now I think we're done here." He snatched the shovel and waved at the open door behind him. "You're fired, Congressman Foster. Get out of my barn."

Foster wiped his brow with an elbow—clearly his hands were too dirty for the job.

Bryan desperately wanted to wash his.

"Wait a minute. I want to continue this dialogue."

Jimmy rolled his eyes. "I don't. Not only are you an idiot who doesn't care about real people, you're the worst employee I've ever had. You've barely cleared three stalls in the two hours you've been here. After twenty years in Congress, you should be better at shoveling shit."

"I'll work faster, then." Foster grabbed for the shovel. Jimmy waited until the politician's fingers grazed the handle, then jerked it away and stepped to the side.

Foster pitched forward, landing on his hands and knees in the mud... or whatever it was. Even with coveralls, gloves, hairnet, and a mask, he cringed as the brown goo splattered all over him.

"Oh, sh...." He trailed off, and Bryan wished he'd done the same in the coffeehouse.

"That's what it is, all right." Jimmy chuckled and shook his head. "I wish every Congressperson had to live with the laws they created, I really do. See, up there in Washington, you shovel the shit onto the rest of the country, but you never have to step in it yourselves."

"I'm really trying here." Foster grabbed the nearest pillar and hauled himself to his feet. A pink nose poked out between the bars and made a snorting noise in his direction. "I'm sorry you feel that way, Mr. Wilson, but my assignment is to—"

"Your assignment is to do your job, but once you've been fired, you're done," Bryan said. "Those are the rules. Getting along with people is a required skill for the commander-in-chief. Wouldn't want to start any wars by angering some dignitary at your inauguration ceremony, right?"

"Well... well... what happens to me now?"

Joanne shrugged. "You go back to the house and wait for the vote tomorrow night, like the rest of the candidates. Being fired doesn't immediately disqualify you, although it might affect how the voters feel."

Sweat beaded on Foster's forehead again. "Wait, please, let's talk about this," he pleaded to Wilson. "I may not understand you, but I want to. Please, tell me what you want me to know about your business."

"I already did," Jimmy said. "I told you I want you to stop giving all the breaks to the big corporations and allow small businesses like mine to make a living. I wrote you a letter every year you've been in Congress, sometimes two or three a year. Sorry you weren't willing to listen then. You're still fired. Now get out before I shovel you out."

"I'm sorry that we'll have to agree to disagree, but I still very much value your perspective on this, and will take it under advisement." Foster offered Jimmy his hand, waited a few seconds, then gave up and left.

Wilson turned to them. "Did you have any more questions for me?"

Bryan looked around the stalls, wishing he'd thought of a hard question to ask Foster. Unfortunately, Wilson had done all the work himself, and now Bryan just looked like a useless lump. While he was desperately trying to come up with something, Joanne proved she was still one step ahead of him.

"Do you have any bulls on this farm?" she asked Wilson. "If so, I'd like to ask you to give Foster just one more assignment before he leaves."

Wilson guffawed. "Unfortunately, all we have here are pigs, but I like how you think. You're welcome to send the rest of those politicians here to shovel shit any day, though."

19

AS SOON AS THEY left the farm, Bryan went straight to his hotel for a long, hot shower. Jimmy was right though—he could still smell the stink of the barn even after scrubbing his skin pink and blowing his nose five times.

Or maybe that was just the stink of the election. It was hard to tell anymore.

His phone rang while he finished getting dressed. No surprise, it was Shanda.

"What's taking you so long to take a damn shower?" she asked as soon as he answered.

"Unlike you, I had to go stand in that barn and soak up the smell of pig manure," he snapped. "It took me a while to get clean."

"Well, you were a little tough on Foster, but you're still trending okay." The sound of Shanda's fingernails drumming on the limo's seat rest wafted through the phone. "They really loved Joanne's question about the bulls though. She's trending higher than any of the candidates or correspondents, and definitely higher than you."

"Great." He gripped the phone with one hand and grabbed his bag with the other.

"Well, hurry up, we need to get going. You still have to interview Haverty and Morganstern before tomorrow night." The drumming stopped. "Jeremy is with Haverty now, and Joanne is on her way to pre-interview Morganstern."

"I'm on my way." He disconnected and headed for the door, Shanda's words still ringing in his ears. *Joanne is trending higher than any of the candidates or correspondents, and definitely higher than you.*

I'm not jealous, he told himself. I'm not jealous, and I'm not having feelings for Joanne again, either. I'm happy she's doing well, even if it's what I really wanted to do, and I'm stuck being a hand-holder on this show.

Anyway, he was going to show her up at the Haverty interview.

He just hadn't figured out how yet.

20

JEREMY'S INTERVIEW WITH HAVERTY proved bland. The senator yammered about not wanting to hamper doctors' efforts to treat their patients. He harped about how hard he worked to make health care "reasonably priced for everyone." Despite efforts to goad him, he stayed on topic.

Well, that wasn't going to happen today.

Bryan had a plan.

He found Haverty in a dull, nondescript cubicle farm. The carpets were gray, the walls were gray, the employees' prospects for career success were obviously gray judging by their expressions. The squares surrounding Haverty's had been cleared to make room for the cameras and crew, and so he could put his callers on speakerphone.

The phone rang and Haverty, wearing his usual suit and tie, pushed a button to answer. "Hello, you've reached Independent Allies, a government contractor hired to assist individuals with their health care questions and concerns. My name is Senator Fred Haverty, and as you may know I've been assigned to work here as part of my bid for president of the United States. As such, your phone call will be recorded and may be used on a national television broadcast later. You will need to sign a waiver to allow that to happen. If you prefer to be transferred to another operator, I can do so now. Continuing this call constitutes agreement to being recorded. Do you agree?"

Bryan blinked. What a mouthful of legalese. Glad I don't have to read that every time the phone rings.

An angry female voice blasted through the speaker. "Oh, I definitely want to be on TV. I want to tell *everyone* about the lousy health care plan I bought through this so-called exchange. Especially since you, Senator Haverty, voted for all the legislation that's driving me to bankruptcy."

"I'm, uh, sorry to hear that." Haverty cleared his throat. "What kind of problem are you having?"

"My name is Maggie Smith, and I make less than twenty thousand dollars a year, and I signed up for the 'affordable' plan, after you voted to expand coverage so more people would qualify for cheaper plans last year."

"It sounds like that would be helpful to you...."

"It does sound like that, doesn't it?" Impatience and frustration dripped from Maggie's voice. "But after I entered my information, it told me the cheapest plan available would cost me three hundred dollars a month, with a twenty-five-hundred-dollar deductible before any of my health expenses would be covered."

"I'm sorry to hear that. I've been hearing concerns about this all day, and I've looked into it," Haverty said. "As it turns out, before the expansion that *I* did indeed vote for, that same plan would have cost you almost four hundred dollars a month."

"But I can't afford three hundred dollars either," Maggie snapped. "I can't go to a doctor for anything other than preventive care, because it won't be covered. If I saved that three hundred a month, I might be able to see a physician and pay for some of my medications, but I definitely can't now. But when I failed to sign up for this policy, your government sent me a bill fining me for not having coverage."

"I'm sorry to hear that," Haverty repeated. "But in order to expand coverage so more people could have lower-cost options, premiums had to be raised for everyone."

"So you're saying fewer people have affordable health care coverage now, thanks to your brilliant plan?"

"Well, it's not exactly my plan, I didn't write it—"

"But you did vote for it?"

"Well—yes. I firmly believe all Americans deserve affordable health care."

"But you just said you made it less affordable for more people."

"That's not what I said." Haverty used the end of his navy tie to dab the sweat on his forehead. "I said premiums had to be raised *slightly* so that more people could have lower cost coverage. Previously, tens of thousands of people paid four hundred dollars a month. Now all of those people, including you, only have to pay three hundred dollars a month, and that deductible went from three thousand dollars to two thousand five hundred dollars."

"But my health care still isn't affordable under either of those plans. You know what? I worked out the math, and it's cheaper for me to pay the fine and go without doctor visits and medication than it is for me to pay the three hundred dollars a month, and still go without doctor visits and medication, since those are my only options."

"I'm sorry to hear that." Was that the only phrase in his vocabulary? "When I'm elected president, I plan to introduce a bill to overhaul the health care exchange and eliminate some of these problems—"

"That you voted for in the first place?" Something crashed in the background, and Bryan wondered if Maggie had thrown something at the wall. He could understand the impulse after witnessing the conversation.

"I will never vote for you for president," Maggie continued. "If you want to help me, why don't you try living on twenty thousand dollars a year and paying three hundred dollars a month for health insurance you can't use until you get sick enough to rack up a twenty-five-hundred-dollar bill?"

"I will take these excellent suggestions to heart and use them in crafting my first bill as president—"

"Screw you and screw your acts as president. You need to see how real people have to survive in this shitty economy that you also failed to fix before anyone gives you the keys to the White House." That was followed by a dial tone.

"That was unfortunate." Haverty turned to Bryan. "I really do want to help these people, and I'm glad I have the opportunity to work here. It really will inform my attempts to improve our government's health care coverage options for everyone. I know our current system isn't perfect, but that's just because the Republicans wouldn't vote for good coverage. Once I'm president, I'll lobby all of Congress to—"

Bryan cut him off. "Let's be honest, once you're president the Republicans will still be Republicans. Aren't there other ways to improve coverage?"

"Yes, and I'm considering all of those. Lowering deductibles but raising pharmacy co-pays is one option. I know it will also anger a lot of people, but it would allow low-income individuals like Maggie to have better coverage than they do now. At least she could go to the doctor and get *some* help with prescriptions."

"And what about her challenge?" Bryan asked. "If you're not voted off the show tomorrow, would you be willing to live on... I've done the math here on my tablet... three hundred eighty-four dollars a week, minus taxes? Minus seventy-five dollars a week for health insurance? I'm sure we could arrange that as part of whatever your next challenge is—if the American people vote for it on Facebook and Twitter, of course."

"What?" Shanda shrieked. *"Whoa, wait, we'd have to plan that out and—you don't have the authority to ask him that!"*

"I just did," Bryan said as Haverty stammered and spluttered. "I mean, I just asked you a question, Senator, how do you respond? You have to admit Maggie had a point. You and the other contestants really have no idea what it's like to live like the average person in this country does. Would you be willing to do that for a period of time, to prove you can handle the job?"

Haverty nodded. "Of course I would. I meant what I said to Maggie—I really do want to help her and all Americans find affordable health care. Maybe when I'm president and my competition has gone back to Congress, they'll have a better appreciation for what people like her go through—if they have to take the same challenge."

"It's up to America." Bryan turned to his close-up camera. "What do you think viewers? Would you like to see all the contestants live like a real person for a change in the next challenge? We'll post an official poll on our page in just a few minutes, and you can vote using the **#getrealcandidates.**"

"What did you just do?" Shanda screamed. *"We haven't even vetted this idea. Now I have to post a poll, when we don't even know how much this challenge will cost."*

Bryan thanked Haverty for his time and excused himself from the set. The crew stayed behind to record the senator's next call. As soon as he was away from the cameras, he pulled out his phone and checked his social media traffic. **#seafoamshootshescores** was the highest trending hashtag in the last five minutes.

21

BRYAN FROWNED AT THE Kevlar vest. "I really don't understand why I have to wear this thing. I mean, I know sometimes people try to shoot presidential candidates, but this is a *bank,* for crying out loud. Don't they have metal detectors at the door? And what about all those guys in dark suits and sunglasses from the Secret Service who are following all these people around?"

Shanda rolled her eyes. "Take off the shirt, Seafoam. Metal detectors can fail or be deactivated, and the Secret Service already stopped three armed idiots at the perimeter. I know there are crazies who hate all the candidates, but Morganstern's bank repoed a lot of people's homes. There seems to be an inordinately large number of people who want him dead."

"So... the Secret Service isn't confident they can stop every nutcase with a gun at the perimeter?" He reluctantly pulled off his suit jacket and unbuttoned his starched white shirt.

She shrugged. "I don't know. They've been busy. Besides, guns aren't the only threat. Metal detectors are useless against bombs. Someone could lob a grenade through the door, slide a gun under the detector...."

"Would this vest protect me from a grenade or a bomb?" He set the starched shirt aside and slipped his arms into the vest, which weighed a ton and reminded him of those lead aprons the dentist made him wear every time he got his teeth X-rayed. He fumbled with the Velcro straps, finding it hard to maneuver with such a bulky item covering his torso.

"I don't know, but you wearing one made the insurance adjuster happy. Here, let me do that." Shanda secured the straps, then helped him pull the shirt on over it. "Oh, that's not going to button. I'll have them send you a bigger one. Don't worry, you don't look *that* fat."

He gritted his teeth. "I see **#livelikearealAmerican** is still trending."

"You're lucky I got you the vest after that stunt." Her fingers flew over her phone. "Fortunately for our budget, too many people don't believe it would be a real challenge, because these people all still have money and influence, even if they can't use it *during* the competition. Did you even think about how hard that would be to schedule, how expensive it would be, how we don't have time to add that to the schedule?"

"I guess not." He grabbed a promotional flier and fanned himself. He didn't know if the Kevlar would stop a bomb, but it did a great job of suffocating him with his own body heat. "But it was a question I could ask without hurting the poor candidates' feelings, or taking sides, or being too nice."

"Maybe, but it just wasn't a good idea," Shanda grumbled.

Twenty minutes later, with the help of two aides, he was bundled into the vest, the shirt, and the suit jacket, and felt vaguely like a beached whale. Due to the "advanced security concerns," two Secret Service officers escorted him into the bank and behind the bulletproof glass window where Morganstern worked. He moved stiffly while he counted change, probably because he was also wearing a bulletproof vest.

"Mr. Morganstern, good to see you. So they've got you working the teller window, huh?" He sat down next to the former CEO of Cheatham Bank.

Morganstern nodded, puffed out his chest, and cocked his jaw forward, a sure sign he was about to launch into a speech of some kind. "Yes, they had me scheduled to work in loans, but I wanted to do every job in this bank, so I could get a feel for what regular people's lives are like. I want to get to know my constituents—"

"Again, Mr. Morganstern, you don't have any constituents—"

"And that's why I should be president. Unlike some of my competition, I've never turned my back on the people who elected me. I've never voted for legislation that places an unfair financial burden on those who need healthcare the most, or those who need help to grow our food. I will start with a clean slate, and I will truly serve the people of this country."

Bryan smiled and nodded. Say what you wanted about Morganstern, he was smart—or he hired smart people to run his campaign. Knowing the last two contestants the show had visited were raked over the coals for their previous votes, he had taken full advantage of their failures to promote himself. It was actually a brilliant plan.

Until Bryan showed up.

"Mr. Morganstern, that's interesting. The Secret Service just told me they put you back here behind the bulletproof glass for further protection against anyone who might want to cause you harm, because so many angry people came in to complain about their loan foreclosures. They also said the bank president has been walking those people over here one by one so you can hear their concerns."

The banker's smile slipped almost imperceptibly, but he fixed it fast. "Like I said, I want to learn about all the jobs in this bank. Yes, I have spoken with some people who were upset that their failure to pay their loans resulted in repossession, but I've also cashed checks and made deposits here at the window."

Bryan blinked. "People still go into a bank to deposit money? I haven't done that since I was fourteen and had a paper route."

"It was one old lady. He's obviously going for the AARP vote," Shanda said in his ear. *"Don't worry, though, the bank president is heading over with a real problem customer."*

Morganstern shrugged. "We still have good old-fashioned customer service at this institution, even though we also offer online banking for those who can't make it here in person."

The bank president was a tall, dark-haired woman wearing a blue pantsuit and a nametag that read, *Cindy Lawrence, President.* Did she always wear a nametag, or did she have one specially made for her appearance on the show? Probably the latter.

Accompanying Cindy was a middle-aged woman with bloodshot eyes, unkempt hair, and a long brown coat that looked like it hadn't been washed in weeks. Her pale pink tote bag was covered with stains and splotches and so overfilled it appeared to be straining at the seams. Bryan recognized the look from the street people he sometimes handed twenties. How long had she been homeless?

"How may I help you today?" Morganstern appeared oblivious to the woman's appearance.

"This is Evie." Cindy's smile looked tight on her face. "She'd like to talk about her home loan."

"Evie Marie Bauman." The homeless woman stepped closer to the bullet-proof glass and bent down to peer through the six-inch hole at Morganstern. "You don't know me, I'm sure, but I used to have a home loan at this bank."

"I know I appreciate all the customers who patronize this establishment," Morganstern said.

Typical.

"I know a few things about you." Evie pulled a deposit slip and a chained pen from the offerings on the counter, turned the slip over, and wrote on the back. Bryan tried to see what she scribbled, but she blocked it from view with her other hand. "I know three years ago you and some other 'zecutives at this bank lobbied the Fed to raise interest rates, so you could make more money off loans. I know two years ago you lobbied Congress to bail you out when your whole banking group almost went under."

Morganstern cleared his throat. "We asked for a bailout because almost a hundred thousand employees would have lost their jobs if we failed. And now we're profitable again, and hiring more people."

"See, I get that." Evie scribbled furiously on the slip, then grabbed another and continued. Bryan tried again to glimpse what she wrote, but she pulled the papers closer to her and shielded them with one arm. "And I don't blame you. But what I don't understand is why, with all your money and in-fluence and power and all, you had to stop at just your company. You didn't lobby to keep the mid-size corporation I worked for from going under two years ago. In fact, you begged Congress to legislate tax breaks for the biggest businesses, leaving small and mid-size companies out in the cold. Guess who was more likely to survive and remain profitable? Not the company I worked for. They had no one to lobby for them, to bail them out, and they folded. I lost my retirement savings when the fund that your bank managed suffered. I couldn't get another job when businesses like my previous employer were laying people off."

"I'm sorry to hear that." Morganstern folded his hands in front of him, another pose that signaled a talking point was coming. "When I'm elected president, I have a ten-point plan to improve our economy and help displaced workers like you—"

"Displaced?" It came out as a half-laugh, half-cry. "Displaced? I wasn't just *displaced* from my job after you lobbied Congress to give big businesses like yours the advantage, and I wasn't just displaced from my savings when this bank mismanaged a few hedge funds, Mr. Morganstern. I was displaced from my home when I couldn't pay the mortgage and your bank foreclosed."

"I'm very sorry, but we do have a right to foreclose on property when the loan account is in arrears."

"I tried to work with your bank." Evie licked her lips, poked her tongue into the cracks in the corners. Something tickled the back of Bryan's brain, something he'd seen on that medical drama that used to come on right after *Sing Your Heart Out* that was always playing in his dressing room after the show. What was it?

"I called up here and talked to three different people." Evie grabbed a third deposit slip and a fourth, scribbled furiously, grabbed a fifth. "I explained I was looking for another job, that I just needed some time, that I'd pay what I could out of my unemployment, and catch up when I was employed again."

Morganstern's face looked like he wasn't sure whether to smile or frown, the curve of his lips bouncing back and forth between up and down. Sweat beaded his upper lip.

Bryan didn't blame him. The stupid vest was hot as hell. He wanted to grab a deposit slip to fan himself, but couldn't because he was on TV.

"I'm really sorry," the banker said. "Unfortunately, if we accepted less than the minimum monthly payment from you, we'd have to do it for everyone, and then no amount of bailout would keep us in business and our employees working."

"Yeah, I get it. You gotta do what you gotta do." More deposit slips flew across the counter. She scribbled furiously. "But I'm not here to talk about that. I'm here to ask you to give me a new loan, so I can get back on my feet. I want to start a new business."

Morganstern pressed his lips together. His forehead wrinkled in a slight wince. "I'm sorry, but we can't give you a loan if you haven't paid back the last one."

"But I have a great new idea for a business I want to start. I just need the money to do it." She shoved the slips, all of them, across the counter and stuffed them through the hole. Some of them crumpled. "See? That's my business plan."

Morganstern gently picked up each one, un-crumpled it, and laid it out on the table in front of him. After the first it was clear to Bryan that they would all be the same. Doodles, scribbles in unintelligible handwriting, pure gibberish. Her business plan consisted of stick figures and scribbles.

Bryan felt even filthier than he had after the pig barn. This was what the show had come to? The woman was clearly deranged, probably mentally ill, and they were using her misery to gain ratings.

Morganstern decided not to fight the expression of dismay off his face. "I'm very sorry, ma'am, but you'll have to fill out a loan application. You'll be asked for proof of income, a permanent address...."

"But this plan can work, can't you see?" She used the chained pen to point.

"I'm sure it's a wonderful plan, but we can't give loans without some assurance we'll get our money back. Otherwise, no amount of government bailouts could help us." He pushed the papers back toward her. "I'm very sorry. I really am going to fix the economy when elected, with my ten-point plan to—"

"But how can you help everyone when you can't help one person? You're just as bad as all the rest of those politicians. I know, I've been watching. I walk into the electronics store every night so I can watch you people on TV. You say you're the candidate who cares because you've never been in Congress, but you're worse, because you spent years *leaning* on Congress to pass laws that hurt people." Evie shook her head. "You'll never help anyone but yourself if you get elected."

With that she grabbed the deposit slips, yanking them through the slot. Morganstern reached out to shove the remaining slips through, and that was when she made her move.

In one swift movement, she brought the pen down on the back of his hand.

"Ow!" he yelled.

"Security!" Cindy screamed.

Morganstern tried to pull his hand back, but the pen was stuck too deep in his flesh, and the skin tore further. Evie slapped her hand down on his wrist, yanked out the pen, stabbed it down again, then again.

The Secret Service agents tackled her, and she went down as hard as Bryan had in the desert with Chump.

But he didn't have a vise-like grip on a pen that was stuck an inch deep in someone's flesh at the time.

"GAHHH!" Morganstern screamed. Blood poured from his hand and soaked through the deposit slips.

"Get a medic out there now," Shanda screamed.

Still feeling filthy, Bryan saw his chance and grabbed it. "Mr. Morganstern, how do you feel about what she just said? Isn't it true that while you've never served in Congress, you've spent a fortune in time and money lobbying them to do your bidding?"

"I... ahhh.... I can't... I'm bleeding."

"Yes or no, Mr. Morganstern. Do you still want to be president?"

"I... yes, I do... I just need someone to stop the bleeding." He grabbed one of the deposit slips and pressed it over his hand. It immediately turned to mush as the blood soaked through. One of the dark-suited Secret Service agents grabbed the bleeding hand and applied pressure, while the other two hauled Evie out the door.

"Did you or did you not lobby Congress to give tax breaks to big businesses, knowing some smaller businesses might suffer as a result?"

"I... ah... lobbied Congress to do what was best to keep the biggest businesses running and employing... the most people... it was better for everyone...."

A medic rushed in and shoved Bryan aside.

"Thank God," mumbled Morganstern, apparently unimpressed by the Secret Service agent's first aid technique.

"I'd like to suggest another poll for the American people," Bryan turned to his close-up camera. "Who would like to see Mr. Morganstern live as a homeless person for a few days?"

"Wait, I don't even know if that's legal," Shanda said, but she didn't sound as distressed as she had at the last event. His suggestions for Haverty were still trending, impractical or not.

"I really am trying to fix... the economy... for people who deserve it." Morganstern straightened his tie with his good hand. "But that woman was clearly off her rocker. Why should we believe she lost her job because of legislation that helped a few big businesses incrementally? For all we know, she lost her job because she went off on her boss like that."

Bryan consulted his phone. "We'll look into that, but in the meantime, I see **#morgansternhomeless** is trending. I'm sure you'll be fine panhandling on a corner, Mr. Morganstern. You used to beg Congress for money all the time—same thing, right?"

22

THE LAST YEAR BRYAN hosted *Sing Your Heart Out,* someone created a spoof Facebook page called "Cry Your Heart Out" to make fun of all the people who cranked out the saltwater to get votes. There were dozens of different categories, including "Dead relative/friend/lover who inspires me," "Not going to let my illness/disability stop me," "This has been my dream since I was in the womb," and "Music is how I express my feelings to the world."

The parody became almost as popular as the show's official fan page. Shanda made no effort to shut it down because it ultimately encouraged people to watch. Bryan secretly thought the anonymous satirist was right on the money, especially as he handed out Kleenexes and pretended to care.

But with *American President,* he'd expected to avoid the therapy session. After all, these were presidential candidates—hardened politicians, not hormonal teenagers with pipe dreams. Surely no one would expect to win the most powerful office in the country by opening up the fake-tear floodgates.

But on Tuesday night, the first candidate he interviewed got misty—or pretended to—one minute into the conversation, and all Bryan asked was, "Senator Foster, tell me how your experience at the pig farm made you feel."

Foster was a surprisingly poor actor for a politician. He scrunched up his face, squeezed his eyes shut—trying to pop out the tears, Bryan assumed—and held up one hand while covering his dry eyes with the other.

"I just... this is so hard for me, because there are so many wonderful opportunities I want to make available to these... these people who grow our food."

"Take your time." Bryan wished he could look at his watch without the whole country knowing, then realized there was a clock on his tablet. Only fifty-seven more minutes of this crap.

Foster lowered his hand from his face, blinked about thirty times in five seconds, and managed to squeeze out a single tear. "I was so moved by Jimmy and all the people like him working on that farm, Bryan. We have to do a better job of helping our farmers, the people who produce the very food we eat. I vow to do just that when I'm elected president." He wiped the tear away and his voice hardened into its usual bluster. "I promise I'll block Congress's efforts to hand out all the tax breaks to big corporations. I'll introduce a bill with subsidies just for family-run farms like Jimmy's. I want you to know, Jimmy, that I heard you, and I've got your back."

The next candidate to be interviewed about his challenge was Ronald Chump. As much as he hated the guy, Bryan had to give him credit for making no effort whatsoever to pretend he was a human being. Instead, he blathered on about his increased determination to build his moat and "keep our jobs here in America."

"Why a moat?" Bryan asked.

"Because a moat has a drawbridge that we can lower for legitimate trade reasons. I'm also the pro-business candidate." Chump flashed his expensively white smile.

"Oh, trade reasons. Like when your company, Chump Enterprises, produces ninety percent of its textiles in Mexico and imports them back here? That creates a lot of business—and jobs—in Mexico, right?"

"Whoa, let's not be so combative," Shanda said in his ear.

Chump harumphed. "I'm trying to keep American jobs here. If the Mexicans want to work for Americans, they can do it in Mexico, and stay off our welfare system."

*"Oh, **#racistronald** is about to trend again."* Shanda had already forgotten about Bryan.

"You're suggesting illegal immigrants come here just to go on welfare?"

"Of course." Chump shook his head. "Like it isn't bad enough all the lazy Americans are bleeding us dry."

"So, *are* you in favor of American corporations outsourcing jobs to Mexico, like your own company has done for the last ten years?" Bryan forced himself to say it through a smile, so he could tell Shanda he wasn't combative at *all*.

"I'm in favor of stopping illegal immigration. Too many people are sneaking across our borders—"

"Hang on, Mr. Chump, you can tell us your feelings about the border in a minute, but first I want you to answer my question. Are you in favor of legislation that would make it easier for companies to outsource jobs to other countries?"

"Not at all. In fact, I have a plan to bring all those outsourced jobs back here."

"What's he talking about?" Keys pounded in the background behind Shanda's voice.

"Including the ones your own company outsourced over the past decade?" Bryan asked.

"That's right." Chump smoothed his five-inch orange toupee—or was it a hair transplant?—and turned to face the studio audience. "My company was forced to outsource jobs due to restrictive policies here in the US. I can solve that by making it easier for companies to employ people here."

"And, ah, how will you do that?" Bryan skimmed his tablet. Like Shanda, he'd never heard Chump mention *this* plan before.

"By getting rid of the minimum wage, for starters. If businesses can pay employees as little as they want, like in other countries, we could keep more jobs here," Chump said. "Then we'll get rid of all these labor laws that restrict American corporations. No more forty-hour workweek and overtime pay for hourly employees. No more requiring companies to provide luxury conditions to workers. This country wasn't built by pansies crying for shorter work days and paid time off and compensation for being hurt on the job."

"The fuck did he just say?" Shanda shrieked in Bryan's ear.

"Uh, Mr. Chump, let me make sure I have this straight." There were so many things wrong with the guy's plan he didn't even know where to start. "Basically you're suggesting we bring sweatshops to America?"

Chump shrugged. "Americans are okay with buying things made in other countries' sweatshops. Why not buy things made in American sweatshops?"

23

NEXT IN THE HOT seat was Bob Fuller, who resumed the practice of crying while pandering. He cried about the lady in the health food co-op. He cried because Ronald Chump hated immigrants. He cried over the pigs at Foster's pig farm. He cried because marijuana wasn't legal. The worst part was, Bryan didn't even think the guy was faking—it seemed more like the kind of crying his college roommate used to do when coming down from a particularly good toke. After several minutes of acting sympathetic and trying to ask questions—all of which were answered with sobs—Bryan thanked Fuller for his time and moved on to Bob Brumley.

Brumley didn't cry either, but he scrunched up his forehead and manufactured a pained expression to rival any actor in a heartburn medication commercial. "My heart goes out to those poor children at that daycare center. After thinking about it, I realize the only solution is to require all schools to teach abstinence-only education."

Bryan cleared his throat. "But statistics show states with comprehensive sex ed have much lower rates of teen pregnancy."

"I wasn't finished yet," Brumley said. "In addition to requiring abstinence-only education, schools would be required to pass out chastity belts and instruct students on how to use them."

Bryan frantically googled chastity belts on his tablet as the studio audience booed. "Uh, it seems that chastity belts are designed for women, Congressman Brumley. So your suggestion is to make female high school students wear chastity belts?"

Brumley shrugged. "It prevents the male students from having sex, too, you know. Besides, if girls have to wear chastity belts, they won't be wearing those scandalous low-cut jeans and other distracting clothes. Then the male students can concentrate on learning instead of sex."

"Well, he just lost the female vote," Shanda said.

Haverty explained how he now supported a single-payer health care system, although he'd previously opposed it, after he had originally supported it. He then explained his plan to pay for yet another health care overhaul by taxing junk food.

Bryan consulted the notes on related legislation Artie and Shanda had produced on his tablet. "But Senator, didn't you also vote against a soda tax last year saying, and I quote, 'Why don't we just give tax breaks for gym memberships instead?'"

"It was a good plan." Haverty flashed a smile at the audience. "I work out in my home gym every day, of course, but I want to help the many Americans who can't afford their own personal treadmill. My tax break—for the average person, not big corporations, I might add—was shot down, but I plan to reintroduce it once I'm president. Unlike many of my opponents, I don't believe we should punish the middle class for their food choices, but rather reward them for taking their health seriously."

"But isn't it true your last reelection campaign accepted a million-dollar donation from the largest soda producer in the country?" Bryan asked.

Haverty cleared his throat and looked directly into the nearest cameras. "I have many donors. Some of them are large corporations, but I don't work for them—I work for you, the people."

Sara Finnegan said she'd learned a great deal about the many hardworking Americans who would depend on her once she was elected. "I now know that as president, I will have to devote my time to strengthening our economy and bringing jobs back home."

"So do you agree with Mr. Chump's suggestion that we should abolish the minimum wage and other labor laws?" Bryan looked at the tablet. Thirty-three more minutes.

Finnegan rolled her eyes. "Of course not. We need those laws to protect American workers. But we also need tougher import tariffs and higher taxes on corporations that outsource their labor."

"But when you were CEO of Hewitt Computers, you spent a fortune lobbying Congress to do the exact opposite of that, isn't that right, Ms. Finnegan?"

She shrugged. "If Senator Haverty can vote three different ways on health care reform in one term as a senator, I can change my mind as our current job market evolves."

After another commercial break, he interviewed Milton Buckshaw. "Governor, how did your experience in the fast food restaurant make you feel about the minimum wage issue?"

Buckshaw folded his hands over his stomach. "I have newfound appreciation for the hard work fast food employees do every day. It sure isn't easy using that milkshake machine, heh heh...." He looked around, waiting for the audience to laugh. They didn't. He moved on.

"But I also learned that college graduates don't have as many opportunities as they should. For that reason, when I'm elected president, I'll introduce a bill to provide companies of all sizes with tax breaks for hiring people right here in the US. And that's not all—I'm going to overhaul our country's unemployment program. Anyone who wants to collect will be provided a list of local companies that are hiring, and will be required to apply at all of them."

"Even if they have no relevant experience?" Bryan considered the implications. "Wouldn't that result in a lot of paperwork for HR people in these companies? Won't they spend a lot of time ruling out people who are under- or over-qualified for each position? Plus, how much money would it cost the unemployment program to verify all those applications?"

"See? That creates more jobs in HR and the public sector!"

"So you're saying that private sector inefficiency and government waste are the solutions to our unemployment and economic problems?" Eighteen more minutes until he announced it was time to vote.

"Like it or not, that's always been true." Buckshaw looked directly into the camera. "Think about it, folks. When was the last time the economy was really booming? It was back before computers were commonplace. Technology made things more efficient, but eliminated jobs in the process. My plan will solve that problem, while still allowing everyone to enjoy the comforts of the digital age."

Ronda Harper also claimed her experience working in food service had given her a bright new idea to help the country. "I want to implement a school program to teach children how not to make offensive comments when angry and upsetting things happen."

Bryan rubbed the scab on his burned hand. "Are you saying you're joining the family values crowd?"

"Of course not. I just want children to learn that sexist comments about a person's gender, or race or religion or sexual orientation, are not appropriate."

"If the candidates have to address the tough issues, so do you," Shanda said in Bryan's ear. *"Just apologize to her, okay?"*

"My producer wants me to apologize to you," Bryan said, and he heard Shanda scream the same phrase he'd yelled at the coffee shop. "When the coffee burned my hand at Twentybucks, I admit I yelled some profanity. It's a common expression used every day, and I've never heard anyone call it sexist before. Now I'm not going to apologize because I momentarily made a poor choice of words when I was in pain, but I do want to reiterate that it had nothing to do with your gender, or anyone else's. Plus I'm pretty sure the coffee machine I was yelling at doesn't have a gender.

"Also, one of our viewers posted some old video of you to the show's Twitter account last night. Artie, can you pull up that Tweet I asked you to save earlier?"

Harper's face had that expression Bryan often saw on overly-Botoxed celebrities, the one where he could tell their foreheads would be wrinkled if they could move.

He turned the tablet toward the camera. "Now, can we zoom in on this so the audience can see it? Hopefully my friends in the control room can make this full screen for everyone."

"Well, now we have to take the video," Shanda grumbled to the director. *"It's okay, Artie wouldn't play anything too offensive—I don't think."*

The director popped up the frozen video from his tablet, and Bryan hit play. It was an interview Harper had done about fifteen years ago, in which a reporter had asked her, off the record, what she thought of an opponent.

"I think he's a lying son of a bitch," Harper said.

Artie bleeped *bitch.*

"I remember this was a case study when I was in journalism school," Bryan said to Harper. "We talked a lot about whether the reporter should have aired something she promised was off-the-record. But journalistic integrity isn't really the issue here. It turns out you use the same language you're trying to skewer me for using, don't you Congresswoman?"

"That's different. I'm a woman." Harper waved her hand at the tablet. "And that video is fifteen years old. We've all said and done things in our past that we've since had other thoughts on. Hey, Senator Haverty changed his vote three times in one year, didn't he? Now, can we get back to the issues here? I want to help low-income Americans improve their quality of life."

"Would you stop harping on me and my evolving concerns for our health care options?" Haverty yelled from the U-shaped ring of chairs on stage left where the other candidates sat.

Morganstern went last, and he managed to squeeze out a few tears, too. "I was so moved by Ms. Bauman and her story. What happened to her is just devastating, and I'm sure contributed to her mental health issues. That's why I'm not pressing charges." He wiped away a tear, then straightened up and put on his game face. "It's also why I'm now more determined than ever to fix our economy, with my ten-point plan. The first thing I'm going to do—"

"Slow down there, Mr. Morganstern," Bryan interrupted. "I appreciate your desire to implement a ten-point economic recovery plan, but let's go back to Ms. Bauman for a moment. Do you know how she's doing? Do you care?"

Morganstern frowned as if he didn't understand the question. "Well, I realize her situation is unfortunate...."

"Did you ask anyone on your staff to find out if she'd been released from jail? To ask how she was doing or where she was going after she got out?"

"Well... I... ah.... Look, I dropped the charges against a woman who assaulted me with an ink pen for crying out loud. Don't try to make it sound like I don't care."

Bryan nodded. "I'll take that as a no. Well, I did, Mr. Morganstern. Because as far as I can tell, all nine of you are only interested in promoting yourselves. But we here at the show actually care about the regular people you all interacted with in your jobs this week. I personally asked our legal department to provide representation to Ms. Bauman after her arrest. I also arranged for a doctor to check her out, a hotel room for her to stay in for the rest of the week, and a career counselor to help her find a job."

He held up a hand as the audience started to applaud. "No, I'm not the only one who cared about Ms. Bauman. Social media has been flooded with people expressing concern for her—and not just her. Viewers all over the country wanted to help the pig farmer in Iowa and the fast food manager in Texas and the coffee shop manager in Virginia and all the other people we encountered this week. How many of you even asked how those people were doing after you left them? This is an open question for all the candidates, not just you, Mr. Morganstern."

He turned and looked at the ring of candidates, shifting uncomfortably on their chairs and looking everywhere but at the audience and cameras. No one spoke.

He glanced at his tablet. "Well, look at that, it's time to vote."

24

AS YOU KNOW, THIS week we'll be eliminating the bottom three contestants, just as we'll do next week. Then we'll have the top three fight for that top spot." Jeez, the crap Shanda put in the prompter got worse every day. "I'll call the contestants up here one by one, in no particular order, and let them know if they'll be continuing this journey with us.

"First, Mr. Chump, will you please join me right here in the middle of the stage? Thank you. Now, as you know, this has been a long and difficult week for all the contestants—"

"But I emerged victorious." Chump flashed his expensive smile and waved at the crowd. His hair looked higher and his head wider every time Bryan looked at him.

Just a few more minutes until this is over, he reminded himself. "In this envelope, I hold the answer to your fate. Are you ready to find out if you're moving forward in the competition or not, Mr. Chump?"

"Well, obviously America wants me to stay in the competition. Let's open that envelope and make it official." A mixture of cheers and boos rose from the crowd.

Bryan ripped open the envelope. What the hell? Had the voting public lost its mind? "Mr. Chump, according to these results... you will be back tomorrow to continue the competition. Congratulations."

Chump grabbed his hand and shook it so enthusiastically Bryan was afraid he might dislocate his shoulder. He breathed a sigh of relief when the business-man finally let go so he could wave both hands at the crowd—then he remembered the public had actually voted for a guy who wanted to bring sweatshop labor to America.

Bob Brumley was next, and he was the first to leave the competition. No surprise there. Even he didn't look too surprised, and his speech, in which he promised to keep the faith and run again in four years, sounded rehearsed. Bryan gave him thirty seconds to finish quoting Bible verses, then ushered him to the right side of the stage, where the losers would stand until the show was over. The other winners would join Chump on the couches to the left.

Fred Haverty and Ronda Harper were both selected to stay in the competition, and managed to thank the voters quickly. Milton Buckshaw seemed to think he'd been elected president already when told he'd survived another week, and launched into what sounded like an acceptance speech, waxing poetic about all the great work he planned to do for the country. After thirty seconds, Shanda had the sound guys play "shut up" music—some sort of up-tempo synthesized elevator jazz—and Bryan had to shout "Thank you, Governor!" and gesture to the left.

When Buckshaw failed to take the hint, he tried again. "Thank you, Governor, you'll get a chance to tell us more about your plans on tomorrow's episode, I promise—"

"Of course, but right now I want to remind the voting public that I am here to stay, and I will not be silenced by my detractors, I will keep fighting for—"

He kept talking, but his mic cut off as two National Guard officers marched onstage. One grabbed each of the governor's arms, then they hauled him over to the couches, planting him next to Ronald Chump, who was also still waving at the crowd like an idiot. Buckshaw's face furrowed in a confused frown, but he got the idea and stopped speaking.

"Thank you, officers, for your assistance." They could have used the National Guard on *Sing Your Heart Out*. Once a contestant who lost had to be dragged away by her stage parents, after loud music and boos from the crowd failed to silence her impromptu, a capella, and completely off-key swan song. "In fact, let's have a round of applause to thank all the men and women who serve or have served in our military."

After the applause died down, he moved on to the next contestant, Bob Fuller, who, not surprisingly, had been eliminated.

"This is so unfair." He raked a hand through his unkempt hair. "You know who voted against me? Corporate America. The same people who poison our food and sell drugs to make us sicker are all out to stop the only candidate who really has your best interest at heart. I bet they all hired hackers to rig the results."

"I can assure you, the CIA has its best cyberterrorism people working round-the-clock to make sure that doesn't happen," Bryan said. Why did stoners always get more paranoid when they weren't stoned?

"But I won't be stopped," Fuller continued as Shanda cued the "shut up" song. "I'll continue campaigning to legalize marijuana, and I will run again in four years."

At least he took the hint and slunk off to the right without an assist from the National Guard.

That left Sara Finnegan, Joe Foster, and Martin Morganstern as the final three. Bryan gestured for them all to join him center stage, then reminded the audience how important and suspenseful this moment was.

"There are three contestants left, and only two spots available on those couches." He pointed to the left, at the blue microsuede sofas and coffee table, waited a few seconds for dramatic impact, then turned to his close-up camera and held the final envelope in the air. "Inside this envelope lies the name of the last person whose journey ends tonight. Who will it be? We're about to find out... right after this break."

25

AND THE FIRST PERSON I'm sending to the couches, who will appear again on tomorrow night's show is... Sara Finnegan." Bryan paused so the audience could cheer and Finnegan could thank her supporters. Fortunately she was brief and headed to the couches. He still had the surprise segment to reveal at the end.

"And that leaves Mr. Morganstern and Congressman Foster," he read off the prompter. "It's been great getting to know both of you, but unfortunately, only one of you can continue. Are you ready for the results?"

Both men bobbed their heads. Facebook and Twitter were predicting a Foster loss by a small margin. Apparently a lot of angry farmers took issue with the Congressman and flocked to social media to vote, but unofficial "who did you vote for?" polls weren't always accurate.

"And the person leaving us tonight is... Martin Morganstern. Mr. Morganstern, do you have anything you wish to say?"

The banker's face fell only slightly. "I'm truly sorry for Ms. Bauman, and everyone I met at that bank. I know it may not seem like it, but I really do care about all Cheatham's customers, and I want to make this country great again. Maybe I'll get another chance in four years."

Foster thanked his voters for their support and rushed to the couches, while Morganstern started to join the others on the right.

"Wait just a moment, Mr. Morganstern. Will you stay here just a little longer? Thanks. Would you two also join us out here?" Bryan waved to Fuller and Brumley, who walked—trudged, in Fuller's case—back to center stage.

"Before you three go, I have an announcement to make." Bryan stared down his tight-shot camera. "There's a chance *one* of these contestants *might* get back in the competition."

Fuller was the only one who looked surprised. Judging by their poker faces, Morganstern and Brumley had obviously watched reality shows before.

"But all three of them will have to go up against three totally new contestants," he continued, and the audience went silent.

Fuller scratched his head. Brumley pasted a pleasant expression on his face. Morganstern fixed his stony stare on Bryan.

"Tonight we're introducing a new segment," Bryan continued. "You may remember that the By the People, For the People Act specifies *everyone* who meets the criteria to be president has a right to audition for this show and should be given equal consideration. The top ten contestants, nine of whom you see on stage right now, were chosen by social media votes. But they were all well-known, to some degree, with large followings.

"One could argue that the rich and powerful have dominated presidential and congressional elections for years. Perhaps that's why the By the People, For the People Act specified everyone eligible should have access to the voting public through this venue. You may have noticed the *What would you do as president?* links on our social media pages, where you can browse through various videos from people like yourself who have opinions. We selected the most-liked/favorited/shared submissions, and asked those people if they would like to run for president. Among those who said yes, we chose a select few to continue the process. This week we'll introduce three regular people who will compete against the three of you" —he gestured at the losers— "and of the six of you, whoever receives the most votes tomorrow night will go on to compete with the top six." He waved to the left.

The three candidates stared at him in shock.

Fuller was the first to speak. "Mind. Blown."

"Praise the Lord, it's a miracle," Brumley said.

Morganstern nodded, allowing only a tiny smile to crack his facade. "This sounds like an excellent idea."

"Let's see what the top six think." Bryan walked over to the couches and sat between Harper and Chump. Foster was at the other end of the couch, and he still stank of that pig barn. "Ms. Finnegan, what do you think of this new element of the competition?"

She put on her best fake smile. "I'm happy to compete against anyone."

"I'll kick anyone and everyone's ass," Chump said, and parts of the audience cheered.

"I'm thrilled to be here and willing to debate with any person in America," Foster said.

"I hope you chose a diverse group of new candidates," Harper said.

"America chose, not us," Bryan reminded her. *America chose* wasn't one hundred percent true—they had called in the most liked/favorited/tweeted individuals for the in-person interviews, and America would vote on the three they had finally chosen, but he, Shanda, and a representative from the election committee had selected those three. After all, the guy who wanted to nuke North Korea had one of the most popular posts, and there was no way in hell they could risk letting America vote for *that* guy. How could a voting public that thought Ronald Chump and his sweatshop plan were the best thing for America be trusted not to elect a guy who wanted to send them all into a bad dystopian movie future?

Bryan wasn't sure the idea of a government By the People, For the People was such a good idea anymore.

26

WELL, WHAT DO YOU say we meet the new contestants?"

The candidates all responded with fake enthusiasm.

"Here's a look at their Skype auditions." Bryan turned to face the green screen behind him. He and the candidates would observe nothing there, but the viewers at home would see the video play.

"You're clear," Shanda said in his ear after a few seconds, and he turned around to watch on one of the dozens of monitors littered around the set.

New contestant number one was Clarice Greenforest, a teacher from Indiana. The video opened on her seated at her classroom desk, a whiteboard scribbled over with math problems behind her. She looked very much like a normal person, wearing a faded floral top Bryan had seen at least a hundred times in a JCPenney ad that aired during the last season of *Sing Your Heart Out*. Her brown hair was pulled into a messy bun secured with a Number 2 pencil.

"Hello, I'm Clarice Greenforest, and I know I could do a better job running this country than any of the people I've seen on this show. As you might have guessed from my luxurious surroundings, I'm a teacher. I've been teaching for twelve years, and unlike the morons in Congress, I actually know firsthand what the problems are in our schools. I know because I've lived with them, struggled against them, found ways to work around them. If I was president, the first thing I'd do is fix education—and not just by throwing money at it.

"Do we need better funding for our schools? Sure, that would be nice. I'd love to come to school and not have to spend half my paycheck buying all the pens and pencils and binders and paper towels we can't afford. But that's just the tip of a very big iceberg. You know what schools really need? We need to stop spending every second of every day preparing kids for tests. We need to get rid of rigid curriculums. Each teacher should teach in whatever way he or she thinks the students will learn best.

"Oh, but don't think I'm a one-issue candidate." She stood, walked to the camera, and the shot went blurry for a moment as she adjusted the focus. It landed on a wider shot of the room, and she walked back to the desk. *"If you want someone who can fix our economy, you want to elect a teacher. A person who can run a classroom on the extremely limited budget public schools get every year knows more about economics than anyone in Congress, or even a successful businessperson. Hey, anyone can run a multi-million dollar corporation. They've got millions of dollars to do it. I have to run a classroom on a lot less, and I'm not just making money for a board of directors, I'm shaping the minds of our future doctors and lawyers and business leaders."*

She went to the whiteboard and erased some of the equations, rubbing the eraser so hard it rattled the board. When it was finally a blurry but more-or-less clear slate, she wrote a list of bullet points, which included actually understanding economics and knowing how to get things done—unlike Congress.

"I can handle foreign affairs, too. If you can negotiate with a room full of two dozen seven-year-olds, you can handle negotiating with anyone in the United Nations. In short, I am equipped to deal with all our nation's problems. Which one of the candidates on the show can say that?"

Next was Kevin, a phone company representative from Georgia. He had dark hair, a round face, and what looked like a five o'clock shadow shaped like a goatee. *"I know I could do a better job of running this country than any of the morons you've got running around trying to do real jobs. You know why? Because I've been doing real jobs for fifteen years, that's why. I didn't just do them for a couple days and go back to my cushy office and my limo and blowjobs from my interns.*

"Let me tell you, politicians can't agree on shit because they've never had to develop any real debate or negotiation skills. They went to some expensive prep schools, all paid for by their rich parents, then on to some even more expensive Ivy League colleges, then to jobs working for their rich parents' rich friends, then on to Congress. Some of them, like Senator Haverty there, actually went straight into public office without ever working any other kind of job in their lives.

"So, you've got your politicians running the country. And what do you have there? You've got a bunch of rich, spoiled brats who never learned the meaning of the word no negotiating with other rich, spoiled brats from other countries who never learned the meaning of the word no. You want to know why we have so many wars and military conflicts and so much terrorism? That's" —a loud *bleep* drowned out the first part of his next word— *"—ing why.*

"Me? I went to the school of hard knocks. I've had to work in customer service my whole life. Went to college, got a degree in journalism, found out I couldn't make any money in that field. Wound up working in customer service again because it paid slightly better, and believe me, I ain't making a king's ransom here, but I'm still trying to pay off my student loans twelve years later and I need every extra dime I can get.

"So. Here I am, working in customer service. Every day, I deal with people who are rude, abrasive, abusive, entitled jerks. Sometimes they're rich jerks like the people running our country, and sometimes they're poor people who are jerks because being poor sucks. Either way, jerks, and I have to deal with them. Unlike our illustrious leaders, I understand negotiation. I understand how to win an argument with a moron using reason and logic. Because I don't have the option of acting like a spoiled jerk and throwing a tantrum if I don't get what I want. I need this job to pay my bills.

"You want a president who can actually get things done? I could do that, not these—" BLEEP BLEEEEEEEP BLEEEEEEEP.

The third and last contestant was a balding, middle-aged guy with glasses and a goofy expression. *"Hi, my name is Evan, and I'm a stand-up comedian who's between jobs right now, so I figured, why not go for the brass ring?*

"You're probably wondering why I'd make a good president. Well, think about it—I could do the stupid things real politicians do that we comedians make fun of, then make fun of myself.

"But that's not all I can do. Just imagine what I can accomplish in Congress. I'll get everyone laughing so hard, they forget to veto the legislation I want to put through. And you know what kind of bill I want to pass first? One to fix the economy and bring our unemployment rate down to zero.

"That's right, I said zero unemployment. I have the perfect solution—everyone on unemployment is given a government job. That means they can never get fired. And don't worry about qualifications—they don't need any. The government already employs thousands of people who don't do anything or even know how to do anything—if you don't believe me, just go down to your local IRS office, or federal building, or even the unemployment office.

"The last time I was at unemployment, I waited in line to see a guy at a desk. I explained that I had applied online, and received instructions to appear in person. He told me to go to a phone bank on the wall and pick up a phone, and I would be connected with someone somewhere in the state who was just sitting at a desk doing nothing.

"So if the government can employ all those people to do nothing, why can't they employ all the people on unemployment? They could just pay us all the average salary for our state. It's not like we're asking to be paid six figures a year to do nothing, then get paid six figures a year in retirement—we're not asking for the kind of cushy deal our Congress-people had until last week—and you know they're working overtime to overturn that decision the candidates made for them. Anyway, that's how I'm going to fix unemployment when I'm president."

The video ended, and the spotlight shone on center stage again. For a split second, Bryan wondered if the audience was cheering for him or one of the candidates—then he realized it was neither. They were responding to the new contestants' reel.

Bryan turned to the three losers. "So, what do you think of your competition?

"I'd like to discuss the economics of that unemployment plan," Morganstern said. "Mr.—uh, Evan, he didn't give his last name—didn't explain how we're going to pay for all those do-nothing jobs."

"I think he did a good job of pointing out that we have too much government waste as it is," Brumley said. "And Ms. Greenforest is right that our education system needs an overhaul—but what we really need to do is go back to teaching good moral values. As for Kevin, he could learn some morals himself, with that potty mouth of his."

"I'd be curious to know if any of the new candidates is as dedicated to legalizing marijuana as I am," Fuller said.

"Thirty seconds, wrap up," Shanda shrieked in Bryan's ear.

He breathed a sigh of relief while maintaining a pleasant smile. Thirty more seconds and this circus was over. "Well, there you have it America, your run-off candidates. They'll compete on tomorrow night's show, then you'll get to vote, and the winner will square off against the top six candidates. You won't want to miss it. Be sure to tune in."

27

AFTER TWO HOURS OF signing autographs and waving to adoring fans, Bryan finally escaped to his dressing room, where he collapsed in front of the mirror and counted the seconds. One, two, three, four—

The door slammed open and Shanda stomped in. "I'm glad we finally have a chance to talk. Are you crazy? You do not get to suggest polls for the audience or arrange free services for a crazy homeless woman who bludgeoned one of the candidates."

"With a pen. I talked to the Secret Service agents who hauled her off. Even they admitted she wasn't a serious threat." He grabbed the baby wipes and attacked the first few layers of makeup. "And according to the psychiatrist I insisted she see, she was suffering from mild low blood sugar, probably from not eating all day, and a severe vitamin deficiency from living on the streets and only eating the kind of processed crap they hand out at homeless shelters. That probably contributed to her mental confusion."

"I'm glad we could help her out, but you still don't have the authority to—"

"To do what? Improve our ratings? Increase our social media traffic? Because I've looked at the numbers, and after I explained what we did to help her, our traffic went way up. Not the candidates' traffic, but who cares about them?" He turned his tablet around so she could see it, not that it was necessary. She monitored their social media presence constantly. "Not me. I can't stand these people, and I wouldn't vote for any of them. You want to make laughingstocks of them? I'm all for it. But I do care about some of the ordinary people we've trampled on in the process, and Evie Bauman is just one of them."

Shanda sighed and raked a hand through her hair. "Without them, how would we reveal the candidates' true natures to the audience?"

"You're right." He tossed the tablet on the table, grabbed another baby wipe, and went back to excavating the layers of grease on his face. "But that doesn't mean we can't help the people who get a worse deal than these rich, arrogant morons."

"Well, it did increase our traffic, and as much as I hate to admit it, so did all your new suggested polls." She played with one of her earrings, a red, white, and blue disco ball. Who the hell manufactured patriotic disco ball earrings, anyway? Hell, who *bought* them?

"Yeah, I noticed that, too. So here's what I think." He tossed the last wipe in the trash and stared at his face in the mirror. It was pink from the makeup being scrubbed off, with lavender circles under his eyes. "I think some executive at the network leaned on you to put me in my place, and you need to go back and tell that person you did it. So why don't you do that, and next time you can say that my suggested poll was your idea or you approved it ahead of time?"

Shanda cleared her throat. "You can't just do whatever you want."

"No?" He looked at her in the mirror, standing behind him in her long gold trench coat. "The candidates do, and people want to elect them president. I'm not trying to promote my own interests here. I'm hosting the most popular reality show in history. All I want to do is show people the truth. Shouldn't that be my job as host of *American President?*"

Shanda nodded. "I'll tell the network everything's under control. As long as you don't officially endorse a candidate, or single out any one person for ridicule, I can probably say it was in the interest of ratings—so long as the audience continues to support you."

"I can assure you, I plan to ridicule every one of these jerks. And don't worry. I'll make sure I don't make any more offensive remarks about coffee machines."

Shanda rolled her eyes, then turned and headed for the door.

After she left, he leaned back and closed his eyes. He needed to go home. He couldn't just fall asleep here. Another big day tomorrow, interviewing the dumbest, most stuck-up people America had to—

"Good for you." Joanne's voice startled him out of his half-sleep.

He jolted upright, grabbing the makeup table to keep from falling out of his chair. "I—Joanne, hey, I didn't see you there."

"I figured. It's kind of hard to see with your eyes closed. When you were talking to Shanda I might have been behind the door."

"Oh?" He raised an eyebrow. Back when he and Joanne worked in Oklahoma, he used to tease her that she'd gone into journalism because it was the most appropriate field for someone as snoopy as she was.

"Whatever. That's not why I'm here." She shoved a stack of tabloids onto the floor, revealing part of a red sofa, and sat down. "Let's just say I happened to hear your conversation, and I'm glad you took my advice. You can't let Shanda boss you around, and you're doing a much better job bringing the American people the truth about these candidates now that you're not listening to her."

"Thanks. I guess you were right—she can't fire me for doing my job, and essentially my job is to show the candidates to the world."

She nodded. "Listen, there's something I've been meaning to talk to you about... privately."

Suddenly wide awake, he fumbled for his mic pack, pulled it off the back of his pants, and double-checked that it was turned off. "Okay, we're good."

She waved her hand in a give-it-to-me gesture, and he placed the mic pack in it, after unclipping the lavalier from his tie. Joanne opened the door, stuck her head out, looked both ways, then set the mic on the floor outside and closed the door. "You can never be too careful with those things."

Bryan nodded. Theoretically, if he had the mic turned off, no one should be able to hear him, but it wouldn't be the first time a TV personality leaned against something and accidentally flipped the on switch. When he worked in Oklahoma, their weather guy's mic managed to get turned on in the bathroom, and the entire audience of 327 people got to hear him pee and flush the toilet before someone in the control room noticed.

"So what's this about?" Had she secretly had a crush on him since he left Oklahoma? Or did she want to blackmail him with that embarrassing story from just before he left? Was he spending too much time with politicians?

She sat back down on the couch and leaned forward again. "Are you sure there aren't any more mics in here?"

He looked around the messy dressing room, suddenly feeling a little paranoid. There could be a mic or even a camera hidden anywhere.

"I'm hungry. What do you say we go get a late dinner while we discuss tomorrow's episode?" he said loudly.

She smiled. "Sounds good. I'm starving."

They went to a nearby restaurant that was open until two in the morning for the odd hours of the Hollywood elite. The maître d' seated them immediately at a dark corner table.

Joanne leaned forward and spoke in a low voice. "Do you still want to be a real investigative reporter? Even if it gets you in *real* trouble with Shanda—and the show?"

He frowned. "You know something about one of the candidates?"

She shook her head, a springy curl of hair bouncing beside her face. "Not one of them—*all of them.*"

He leaned across the table. "All of them? What could you possibly know about *all* of them?"

"I...." She glanced around the otherwise-empty restaurant. The only movement was the flickering of the low lighting as it bounced off a humongous sparkling chandelier in the center of the room.

"What? We're all alone here, and I left my mic back at the studio."

"Right." The cushioned seat built into the wall was U-shaped, and she scooted through the curve until she was next to him, instead of across the table. Her hair still smelled like that brand of super-ultra-mega-hold hairspray she used to buy by the case whenever it went on sale. Every time he smelled that hairspray on someone else, it reminded him of all the times he used to fantasize about being with her—

"You know I have contacts in a lot of industries from my job at NNN."

Her words jolted him back to reality. Of course she wasn't here to tell him she'd always wanted him, too, she was here to talk about work.

"Uh, right, yes, contacts in different industries. You must cover a lot of different topics at NNN, not just politics."

"That's right." She paused as the waiter brought their drinks in tiny, fragile-looking glasses. "I think we're ready to order now. Aren't we?"

"Huh? Oh, uh, yeah, I'll have my usual." Good thing the waiter knew him, because he hadn't glanced at the menu.

Joanne ordered a salad with extra croutons, and the waiter left with the menus. Her eyes practically bored holes into his back until he disappeared through the swinging doors that led to the kitchen.

"Okay, so I have this contact who's a hacker. And he has some friends who are even higher up in the hacking industry."

"That's an industry?"

"It is. Professional hackers sometimes claim to offer a legitimate service— cybersecurity, social media marketing, et cetera. But in reality they do things like break into servers, find info about people you don't like, and so on."

Bryan suddenly realized where she was going with this. "You don't mean one of these hackers is going after the votes? We really do have the best people around—including some former hackers who either had to turn their talent and attention to helping the government or go to jail—protecting the voting process. In fact, I've been told the NSA is using the people who usually spy on regular Americans to make sure the voting process stays secure."

She shook her head. "That's just it, Bryan. My friend has a friend who has a friend who has a friend, okay? And this guy doesn't even have a cover business. He only does a few select jobs he really wants to do, for which he is only paid in cash."

"And he was hired to hack the voting system?"

"No." She put an arm around his shoulder and leaned into his ear. "Let people think we're making out, I don't care. No one else can hear what I have to say."

Bryan tried to pretend like he hadn't imagined her whispering things in his ear for totally different reasons, but having her so close was distracting. "Whatever you say."

"The friend of the friend of the friend wasn't hired to hack the votes, Bryan. This person—and I don't know who it is—was hired to hack the Candidate Cams."

"Um—the what?" He couldn't help it, having Joanne whisper in his ear was turning him on, and it was really hard to follow what she was saying about the show with all the blood flowing away from his brain.

"The Candidate Cams," she hissed a little louder. "Everyone knows the NSA is spending all its time and resources on the voting itself. Yeah, the feeds from the cameras are secure, but they're not monitored as carefully."

Just then, the waiter appeared with their plates, and she slid away from him. He wasn't hungry for food at the moment, but he picked up a fork and feigned interest in his meal, hoping the server would leave in a hurry. After he did, Bryan watched him disappear into the kitchen again before saying anything.

He had to focus. Joanne was the kind of woman who was more impressed by a guy with critical thinking skills than well-defined pecs. At least, that was what she always said, although she wound up dating that lunkhead Cliff....

Forget that and think about the problem at hand if you want to impress her. "What you're saying... that's almost worse than a problem with the voting process itself."

"That's right," she said around a mouthful of lettuce.

"I mean, those cameras are there so the American people can see what the candidates do twenty-four seven... if they're being hacked, it might" —he leaned forward and whispered— "affect how people vote."

"Exactly." She speared a cherry tomato and popped it in her mouth.

He sat back. "Do you remember in season two of *Sing Your Heart Out,* our graphics guy screwed up a couple contestants' phone numbers for the vote? And we had to re-air the entire show the next night, then give the results the next week? Same thing in season three, when there was a glitch with the audio and you couldn't hear one of the contestants' singing for about four seconds? Again, we had to re-air the whole episode and let people vote *again.*"

"And that was *Sing Your Heart Out,* not a presidential election."

He shook his head, hoping to get the blood flowing back up there. "But we can't just... re-air all the candidate cams. I mean, we already voted four people off, three of whom get another shot—what a mess. But wait—how much of the footage was even hacked? Which of the candidates is behind it?"

She leaned over and said in a low voice, "I told you—all of them. The friend of the friend of the friend figured out how to hack the Candidate Cams, offered the service to all ten candidates, and they all paid the hacker off."

"So... they could all be making each other look bad?"

She shook her head. "I don't think so. Theoretically, yes, but nothing really interesting has happened on the Candidate Cams, so I'm guessing they're mostly just paying to keep whatever stuff they don't want people to know about *off* their feeds."

"How do you know it's true? I mean, maybe your friend's friend's friend is just bragging about something he *wishes* he could do."

She shrugged. "I don't know for sure, but it sounds like something every hacker in America would love to accomplish. Anyway, I thought we could investigate. You know, walk in on the candidates in the middle of the night or something? See if what we're getting on the feeds matches what they're actually doing?"

Bryan groaned. "You mean tonight, don't you?"

"We should *start* tonight." She stabbed a cucumber with her fork. "We may have to keep popping up unexpectedly in case we don't happen to walk in on something scandalous. After all, the feeds are fine most of the time. You obviously couldn't have a fake feed going all the time or someone would notice it didn't match up."

"How does that work?"

"Supposedly, the candidate can signal the hacker when he or she wants the feed replaced with something innocuous—like video from earlier when the candidate was just sleeping or writing a speech or something. When the candidate is finished with whatever thing they're doing in secret, they signal, and the hacker replaces the real feed."

"What's the signal?"

She shrugged. "My friend doesn't know. I would guess something innocent-looking—tugging on an earlobe, coughing a certain number of times, who knows."

He waved his hand in the air, and the server magically appeared. There was probably an overhead camera in the dining room. No wonder Joanne was so paranoid about being overheard.

"Could I get a cup of coffee?" he asked the waiter. "I've got a long night ahead of me at work."

28

THE SECURITY GUARDS AT the "White House" were obviously surprised to see Bryan and Joanne, but Bryan explained they were doing a new segment where he woke the candidates up in the middle of the night and fired questions at them.

The guard who'd given their IDs a passing glance laughed. "I love that idea. Hard to lie when you're still half asleep."

She buzzed them through and the gate opened.

Inside, Bryan and Joanne alerted the nighttime assistant producer of their new segment, never mentioning Shanda knew nothing about it, although Bryan didn't think she would mind. He had also read the rules of the show, and while America had to vote for official challenges, they did not have to vote every time a show host or correspondent wanted to interview candidates.

He and Joanne collected mics and tablets, while the producer, a skinny guy in a rock band t-shirt who was slumped over the control room desk napping when they walked in, scrambled to find a photographer "for additional angles," which was how Bryan explained his request. No need to explain the dozen or so cameras in each Lincoln Bedroom might or might not be working.

"Where should we go first?" he asked Joanne as they walked down the hall where all the bedrooms were located. A Goth-looking girl with a diamond stud in each nostril and unnaturally black hair trailed behind them with a tiny video camera, rubbing sleep from her eyes. She smeared black eyeliner all over face, and Bryan briefly contemplated telling her, then remembered she wasn't going to be in front of the camera, anyway.

"Like I said, we need to talk to all the candidates," Joanne said. "We can start anywhere."

Bryan paused at the first freshly-painted, gold-knockered door on the right. "Okay, whose room is this?"

Joanne consulted her tablet, which showed multiple camera feeds. With a flick of her fingers, she minimized them, then pulled up a diagram.

"Ah, this is Mr. Chump's room."

"I hope we're not interrupting Mr. Chump in the middle of something personal," Bryan said. Not that it would matter, since his Candidate Cam was ostensibly available for public viewing 24/7, but he had to act like he cared about the candidates' privacy or **#insensitiveseafoam** would trend again. He also had to pretend to have no idea the cameras might have been hacked.

Joanne took the hint and tapped the screen to pull up Chump's camera. "Looks like he's sound asleep."

"Well, let's wake him up." Bryan opened the door without knocking and was greeted with semi-darkness, the only light a dim glow around one of the ceiling corner cameras that shed just enough light for halfway decent video. He flipped on a switch set in an intricately carved panel and flooded the room with florescent lighting. To his disappointment, Chump actually was asleep in his bed. Alone. Not even his supermodel wife was with him.

He rolled over and opened one eye. "The hell is it?"

"Mr. Chump? We're doing a new pop-up interview segment where we present candidates with the kind of emergency they might face in the middle of the night at the real White House." Bryan was surprised at how easily he formulated and spit out the lie. Maybe he'd picked up some skills from the candidates. "Now, listen carefully. North Korea has just tested a nuclear missile, in direct violation of a nuclear test ban treaty we have with them and many other countries. What are you going to do?"

Chump raked a hand through his orangey hair. Bryan always wondered if the guy didn't know he was supposed to wear that little paper cap when he got a spray tan.

"You have only thirty seconds to decide, and you've already used ten," Joanne said.

"Well, ah—I need more—you know—information. Uh, how big of a missile? Was anyone hurt?"

"No, it was just a test. We don't know exactly how big it was yet...." Bryan wracked his brain. He didn't even know what nuclear explosions were measured in. Kilowatts? "Um, but it's definitely in violation of our test ban treaty. Now, do you want to try to call North Korea's president to discuss—"

"No, I don't." Chump slammed his hand down on the bedside table. "We can't appear weak by trying to reason with that pigheaded jerk. We already know he hates democracy. Can't even watch a movie without getting his poor feelings hurt. No, we have to nuke him back."

"You want to nuke North Korea? Like, a military target?" Joanne asked.

Chump shook his head. "No, we're going drop a nuke on their whiny cry-baby president. Just take out him and his mansion. We'll get one of those, you know, targeted nukes, right? Blow the Wii controller right out of his hand. There'll be a mushroom cloud of Cheetos!"

With that, he erupted into raucous laughter.

Bryan had a flashback of the toothpick-chewing redneck who also wanted to nuke North Korea, China, and every other country he didn't like. There was definitely a reason that guy didn't make it onto the show—but Chump? He still couldn't figure out how the guy had made it this far.

"So, what if North Korea nukes us back?" he asked.

Chump stopped guffawing just long enough to gape at Bryan like he was a moron. "So what? They've got a bunker under the White House. I'll be fine."

Joanne stared at Chump like she wasn't sure what the hell he was doing here either. "And... the rest of the country?"

Chump went to adjust his cufflinks, noticed he was wearing silk pajamas instead of a suit, and crossed his arms instead. "If I'm in a bunker under the White House, the rest of our country will be in good hands."

"Okay, thanks for your time, Mr. Chump," Bryan said.

29

THAT WAS INTERESTING, BUT not, you know, groundbreaking," Joanne said carefully as they went to the next room. Although they were being recorded in the control room, only scenes including one or more of the candidates would be shown to the audience. However, Shanda and any number of people in production might hear their conversation.

Bryan shrugged. "Hey, we're going to talk to all these people, right? Who knows what we'll find out? Who's next?"

"Governor Buckshaw."

Buckshaw was with two aides, preparing for the next day's face off. Everyone involved was fully clothed, although Buckshaw's belly hung over his belt by an inch or two.

"What would I do if North Korea broke the nuclear test-ban treaty? Well, I'd test a few nukes too... right off the coast of North Korea. Wouldn't hit any civilian targets. Just a very small nuke, so not too much fallout, you know. Wouldn't want that blowing back on us."

Haverty wanted a face-to-face meeting with the Korean leader, Ronda Harper wanted to discuss the problem with the UN, Morganstern planned to cut off trade with North Korea and embargo their products—"hit 'em where it hurts, in the wallet"—and Sara Finnegan wanted to hack the North Korean president and blast his secrets to the world. No one was found in a compromising position.

"Well, Bob Brumley is the last one." Joanne sighed. "Then we can go home and get some sleep."

Brumley's feed showed he was doing just that, and Bryan continued his routine of barging in without knocking.

The first thing that surprised him was the brightness of the room. Unlike in most of the sleeping contestants' rooms, all the lights were on. Brumley wasn't lying on the bed under his Alabama State blanket, as he was on the video feed. Instead, he was sitting on the edge of the bed, getting a blowjob from what looked to Bryan like a long-haired, broad-shouldered, topless woman. He could only see her from the back, and had no idea who she was.

"Oh my God!" Brumley yelled at the sight of Bryan and Joanne.

"Congressman, is this a bad time?" Joanne asked in her most pleasant, practiced interviewing voice.

"I... uh...." He looked down. "Um, you can knock that off for now, okay?"

The woman leaned back and Brumley abruptly stuffed himself back in his pants and zipped his fly. "What the hell are you doing in my room? You can't show this on television, it's indecent and pornographic to show me, ah, en-gaged in this activity with my... er, wife."

"Oh, this is your wife?" Bryan gestured to the still-kneeling woman, who looked much taller and more muscular than the photos he'd seen of Mrs. Brumley. In fact, her build looked very masculine, and he couldn't see her face. "Ma'am, would you turn around please?"

Brumley's face turned red. "This is an outrage. I will not have you talk to my wife that way. She never agreed to this invasion of our private life."

Bryan looked at Joanne. She silently tapped the tablet—Brumley snoozed on the screen.

He glanced back at the photographer, who panned the room with the cam-era, and nodded to the right, hoping she'd get his meaning. She gave an almost imperceptible nod and followed him as he circled around the side of the bed opposite Brumley. Joanne moved to block the door.

As soon as he rounded the bed and got a good look at the face of the hooker, Bryan's mouth dropped open. He wasn't sure what he expected Brumley's sex fantasy to look like, but this wasn't it.

The hooker was, in fact, a man, which wasn't too surprising given his build. The long hair, the beard, the crown of thorns, and the cross necklace, on the other hand, came as a bit of a shock.

"Is he dressed as *Jesus?*" Bryan couldn't think of a more delicate way to phrase it.

Joanne rushed to the couple, nearly tripping on the thick pile carpet, and positioned herself between Brumley and, well, Jesus. The younger man wiped his mouth with the back of his hand. The congressman edged toward the other end of the bed, as if he no longer wanted to be anywhere near the guy.

"It does indeed appear that the Congressman is, ah, was just receiving oral sex from a man wearing a crown of thorns, yes," Joanne said as the camera panned across the scene.

Apparently realizing there was no point in lying, the hooker finally looked toward the camera. He tugged the crown off his head, set it on the bedside table, and ran a hand through his hair.

"It's the only thing that turns him on."

At that point, the beautiful silence Bryan had been experiencing in his IFB ended abruptly.

"OHMYFUCKINGGAWD HOW DID WE MISS THIS?" Shanda screeched. *"Who was watching the feeds and slept through this? You're fired, you lazy-ass moron. Please tell me we blurred the blowjob and the FCC isn't going to slap us with a fine, because we can show death and destruction on TV all day, but if someone saw a sex act that would be the end of the fucking world. Shit, we'll deal with that later, we need to blast this to every news network right now. Bryan, Joanne, when Brumley's done explaining himself, you better get in here and tell me how you knew what was going on."*

Joanne looked at Bryan and shrugged. He nodded. "Go ahead. We're here because of your tip."

She walked around the bed to face Brumley. "Congressman, we received an anonymous tip that you were doing something out of character in your room. Would you care to explain why you were just receiving oral sex from someone who is not your wife?"

Brumley dabbed the sweat off his face with the sleeve of his flannel shirt. "The American public doesn't know this about me, but I have a porn addiction, which has caused me to do things I am deeply ashamed of. I now realize that I need to check myself into a rehab facility to deal with my issues, after which I hope my family can forgive me for the pain I've caused them."

Bryan looked at the... Jesus impersonator? "Uh, sir, did you receive any payment from the Congressman for this, um, for your services here?"

Jesus blinked. "I'm not a prostitute, if that's what you mean. I'm one of Congressman Brumley's aides, and we're in love. We've been together for six years now, although of course we had to keep our relationship a secret."

Brumley cleared his throat. "I believe my aide has misspoken. This has only happened a few times. The stress of the election, ah, caused my porn addiction. I am deeply sorry for my actions, and will make every effort to make things right with my wife, who I deeply love."

"Does that mean you're going to resign from the race?" Bryan asked.

Brumley looked over at his aide, who looked devastated by the news the congressman didn't love him, then back at the cameras. "Unfortunately, I think it does. I must now resign so I can get the help I need. But don't worry, America—I'll be back in four years to lead this country to salvation."

30

SOMEWHERE AROUND ONE A.M., Bryan lost track of time. There was Shanda, screaming about how screwed they were. There were the dark-suited, gray-faced people from the NSA. There was the gray-suited, pink-faced guy from the election committee who helped Shanda choose the three real people for tomorrow's challenge. Today's. What day was it? He hadn't slept.

Around three-thirty, the suits finally decided he knew nothing and dumped him back in the control room with Shanda and Joanne. The election guy—Carl? Clark? Cameron?—sat in a chair next to the show's director, a twitchy guy with sandy hair whose left hand never strayed from his coffee cup.

Shanda paced up and down the flat green carpet. She was barefoot now, her high heels kicked into the corner. Without them she looked shorter, but no less angry and menacing.

"We don't have much time until someone figures out the Candidate Cam wasn't accurate." She dragged her fingers through her hair, which looked a little like a starched rat's nest. "Then every second of every candidate cam vid will be called into question. Then someone will ask us to throw out all the results so far. Then—"

"Whoa, whoa, whoa, slow down there." Carl/Clark/Cam waved a hand in her direction. "Look, we talked to Brumley at length. He told us tonight was the first time he tried to use the fake signal, and we have no reason not to believe him at this point. Every other candidate has been questioned, and they all claim not to have been contacted by this hacker. We can't prove they're telling the truth, since Brumley claims he paid in cash and doesn't know the hacker's identity, but the NSA people are checking the previous feeds right now."

"So you're saying we could prove all the other Candidate Cam footage was legitimate?" Shanda stopped pacing and stared at him.

Carl/Clark/Kent/whatever shrugged. "If it was, sure."

"And if not? Will we be forced to scrap the whole election and start over?"

"I wouldn't think so." Clark/Carl/Kyle pulled out his phone and scrolled through something. "The rules say if any evidence of tampering is found in a vote, we have to retake the vote. Although that's mostly designed to prevent voting fraud, I believe it would still apply in this situation. The election committee would have to call an emergency meeting to discuss it, but I believe we would only need to repeat votes that happened after the first instance of Candidate Cam footage tampering."

"When will the NSA know, uh, Carl?" Bryan asked. He was supposed to go on the air at 8 A.M.

"It's Kurt, actually. Shouldn't take the geeks too long now that they know what they're looking for."

Shanda turned her glare to Joanne and Bryan. "How could you do this without talking to me? Do you have any idea how much of a mess you've caused?"

"We're not the one who asked his aide to dress up like Jesus and give Brumley a blowjob," Joanne said.

"And since when do you care if I interview the contestants?" Bryan rubbed his eyes. They felt like they were full of sand. "Seriously, we just uncovered a bombshell about Brumley. Social media is probably on fire, not that I've been allowed to see my phone in four hours. You could say thank you."

"Thank you?" Shanda stomped up to the metal folding chair where he was slumped. "Are you out of your mind? You" —she pointed an accusatory finger at Joanne— "received a tip that involved election fraud, and instead of coming straight to me or Kurt, you told *him*" —the finger swung back around to point at Bryan— "and then you both went off to test your theory. Had you not done that, we could have dealt with this internally and protected the show's—and the election's—image."

"You mean you could have lied about it, and not told the people they didn't receive the correct information?" Joanne arched an eyebrow at Shanda.

"Of course not." Shanda shook her head. Her hair remained resolute. "If it was just tonight, we could have removed the time stamp and showed the video later. Or explained that we caught Brumley trying to cheat, but that we stopped him, we've recovered the real video, and now you can vote knowing the truth. We wouldn't have had to publicly call into question everything that's been filmed since the show started. Do you know how many people hate the idea of doing the election this way? Do you know how many of the candidates are going to sue if they don't win, hang this thing up in the courts for months? Everyone except the one who wins, that's how many."

"This country has survived voting scandals before," Joanne said. "When I was a kid, I remember this big thing in the news about hanging chads and recounting votes in Florida. You know what came of it? Nothing. It was in the news for a while, then the guy conceded, the whole mess went away, and the country went back to normal. No biggie."

"NSA just emailed me back." Kurt studied his phone. "They've found no evidence anyone other than Brumley ever attempted to hide anything they did on the Candidate Cams. There's no merit to the anonymous source's claims this service was offered to everyone, and now that we know about it, the NSA won't let it happen again."

"See?" Joanne gave Shanda an icy stare. "All you have to do is release the story that we caught Brumley hacking the signal, and immediately we went in with another camera to give the viewers the *real* story. We haven't voted since then, so the voter experience hasn't been compromised. In fact, Bryan and I are the real heroes, the ones who stopped this pathetic attempt at cheating with the help of our incredible security team courtesy of the NSA. It's probably the best publicity they've had since before anyone knew who the hell Edward Snowden was. Now, if you'd like me to sell that story to NNN, would you please have the NSA sleazes return my phone?"

"Fine, but that better be the leading news story on your network in five minutes," Shanda snarled, but the look of relief on her face said she liked Joanne's spin on the story. She shot Kurt a look. "Would you tell them to give her back the phone and let them both out of here?"

Bryan ran a hand through his hair, which probably looked like crap, and wished he'd thought of a brilliant way to spin the scandal. Joanne was right, though—the NSA would actually rehab their image on this one. Besides, voters would probably be more interested in Brumley cheating on his wife than trying to cheat the viewers of seeing him cheat on his wife.

A few minutes later, electronics restored, Joanne and Bryan left the control room. Bryan wanted nothing more than to hide in his dressing room and sleep until someone woke him up, which wouldn't be long. Shanda's press release would hit every news network in the world in a few seconds.

"Hey." Joanne's eyes were glued to her phone, her fingers flying across the screen.

He stopped, hand on the cold metal knob of his dressing room door. "Yeah?"

"We did good work tonight." She stopped closer to him and he smelled her hairspray again. "Don't say anything about this now, but I know of a really good exposé we can do after the show is over."

"Huh?" He was much too tired to guess at what the hell she meant.

"Just something to think about. The spin on this story is great right now, but what if the NSA had found evidence more than one Candidate Cam was hacked from, say, the first day of the show. Would they have wanted to find that evidence?"

With that, she walked away, eyes never leaving the phone.

31

BRYAN SPENT THE NEXT several hours doing interviews with real journalists, tabloid reporters, and even some influential bloggers and vloggers. The "cheating scandal" was everywhere by seven a.m., hashed out on morning talk shows by nine, and old news by eleven.

Joanne kept her word and spun the story as *candidate tries to cheat and fails hilariously* and the other news networks followed her lead. Bryan was amazed at how easy it was to do the same.

"We have the best and brightest from the NSA working to protect the process," he read from the teleprompter during an interview with one of the NNN anchors, a dour-faced man in a pinstriped suit. "If there's even a rumor of something untoward going on, they investigate immediately and thoroughly. When they noticed an anomaly in the transmission from Congressman Brumley's Cam, they looked into it on their end while letting us know to check on all the candidates with another camera."

"So if anyone else had tried something like this, he or she would have been caught?" Pinstripe asked.

"Absolutely," Bryan said. "That's why this election process is so much better than the previous one. It was harder to identify when politicians were lying or hiding things. Voter fraud was rampant. Our aim with this show is to give the American voters the transparency in their government that they demand."

In reality, the pundits and journalists and talk show hosts didn't spend all that much time on the process or the possibility of someone succeeding at cheating. Instead, the big story was Brumley, and the most shared comments hashtagged to the show were about his preferences for cheating-on-spouse material.

Bob Brumley gives whole new meaning to the phrase 'Jesus Freak'!
#americanpresident #no

Did you get a good look before they blurred the congressman's joystick? I hate to say it, but **#ronaldwasright** *about Brumley and his small hands...*

Brumley is so religious, he can only get off with our lord and savior.
#americanpresident #americanweirdo #hypocrite

So I guess Brumley needs to join the military so he can twirl his gun around like a baton now? **#americanpresident**

I always pictured a Brumley sex scandal involving a nun's habit or a shepherd, but I guess this works. **#americanpresident #byebyebrumley**

Bryan didn't get to the set and the remaining candidates until the show started at seven, at which point he was required to read a long speech about how further attempts at cheating would not be tolerated.

"The NSA is now assigning twice as many people to monitor each of you," he said. "If you attempt to trick the Candidate Cams or cheat in any other way, you will be immediately disqualified.

"Now, who wants to hear about the next assignment?"

The candidates bobbed their heads.

"I'm eager to get to work fixing this country's problems," Chump said. "The biggest one is that I'm not president yet. When I—"

"Okay, let's meet the three new contestants, and welcome back the bottom three from yesterday's show," Bryan said before Chump could get wound up.

Clarice, Kevin, and Evan joined the six remaining candidates and everyone awkwardly shook hands. Chump wrinkled his nose like he was being forced to compete for the presidency against his housekeeper and gardener. Ronda Harper thanked Kevin for his hard work in the difficult job of customer service. Buckshaw assured Evan he would no longer be out of work once President Buckshaw introduced new legislation to get everyone on unemployment a low-paying job. Everyone told Clarice how much they admired teachers.

"I suppose that's why you keep voting to reduce funding for education," she said. "Because you admire us so much you think we can work miracles."

"I voted to increase teacher pay four times, but the rest of Congress did not." Ronda Harper looked pointedly at Phil Foster.

"You also voted to make us teach a ridiculous, one-size-fits-all curriculum that actually didn't make sense to a single student," Clarice said. "I mean, do you estimate all the numbers in the congressional budget or do you do the exact calculations? Based on what I saw at the beginning of the show, I'd say it's the latter. I hope none of my students grow up to serve in Congress."

Kevin snorted. "Actually, I think your second-graders could do a better job than Congress right now, despite the limitations of your curriculum."

The audience erupted into laughter.

"Well, let's move on to our next competition." Bryan led the three new contestants downstage, while the other six stayed seated on the couches. "Each of our three new candidates was going to go head to head with one of the bottom three. But as you all know, Congressman Bob Brumley left the competition early this morning, so we will ask the person with the next-lowest number of votes to join our new contestants, and that person is...." He gave the drumroll a few seconds, just like on *Sing Your Heart Out.* "Phil Foster, will you please join us?"

Foster blinked like a deer in the headlights, apparently unaware he was only one place away from leaving the show the day before. After a moment, he straightened his suit jacket and walked to the front of the stage, sweating under the bright lights.

"Mr. Fuller and Mr. Morganstern, we'll need you as well." Bryan waited for the final two to join them.

"Now, let's see what America has in store for everyone today. Remember, these challenges were chosen by the voting public via social media polls." He turned to face the green screen that towered over all three stages, stretching from the ceiling to the floor. A monitor beneath the nearest camera, just visible out of the corner of his eye, showed him what the audience saw. Shanda wanted him to look as "genuinely surprised as the contestants, just like when you walked in on Bob Brumley last night."

Fortunately, America's selection was somewhat less shocking than the sight of Brumley getting a blowjob from Jesus. "Okay, it looks like America wants to see the three new candidates and the three lowest-ranking candidates go up against each other in a drinking game."

"A drinking game?" Foster blinked. "This can't possibly be legal...."

"The law says challenges are decided *By the People, For the People.* You're all certainly old enough to drink legally, and your physicals reveal no medical conditions that prevent you from imbibing." Bryan tried not to appear as excited as he actually was. Most people became significantly worse liars when drunk, and they were about to get six presidential candidates trashed.

"I was in a sorority in college. I can drink any one of you guys under the table," Clarice said.

Evan bobbed his cue-ball head. "I *majored* in drinking in college. Sign me up!"

Kevin rolled a shoulder toward the lowest-ranking candidates. "I work in customer service, so I'm a regular drinker as well."

Fuller scratched his beard. "I'm more into pot, but I'm down with a nice imported beer or two."

"I'd like a single-malt whiskey, if we get a choice," Morganstern said.

"I'm going to ask you six to join me in the White House 'Dining Room' while the other candidates wait here on stage," Bryan said. "We'll be right back after this break, folks. You don't want to miss this."

32

THE "WHITE HOUSE DINING Room" was really too nice of a place for this, but there was nothing to be done about it. Bryan seated the contestants in tall, cushy chairs upholstered with cream-colored silk. The long walnut table could have accommodated twenty people comfortably.

"Artie has randomly matched up Kevin, Evan, and Clarice with a bottom three contestant." Bryan sat at the head of the table and read off his tablet. "Congressman Foster, you'll be directly to my right, across from Evan. Mr. Fuller, you'll be next to him, across from Kevin. Mr. Morganstern, you'll be on the other side of Mr. Fuller, opposite Clarice."

Once everyone was seated, he explained the rules. "Each of you will be provided a bottle of whiskey and a shot glass. I will ask each pair a question, and each person will be allowed thirty seconds to answer, and thirty seconds for a rebuttal to the other person's answer. Our attentive and creative audience has suggested common catchphrases they hate in political speeches, and we've selected the most liked/shared/retweeted of those, which you should now see on your screens at home. Whenever someone says one of these phrases, all the candidates will be required to take a shot.

"Don't worry, you guys don't have to remember all of them. I'll let you know if one of the key phrases has been uttered." Actually, Shanda would screech it in his ear, and he'd repeat it to the contestants. Whatever. "Any questions?"

"Do we have to wait until someone says one of those phrases to start drinking?" Fuller asked.

Poor guy really didn't understand the contest at all.

"I don't see anything in the rules that says he has to," Shanda said. "Artie agrees. It's not like starting drinking before the other candidates gives him a competitive advantage."

"You can all start drinking whenever you want," Bryan said. "You only have to take a drink when I tell you to. Any more questions? No? Okay, let's get started. Congressman Foster and Evan, you're up first. Evan won the coin toss during the break, so he will get to answer first."

"I can't wait." Evan eyed the bottle of Wild Turkey, the official whiskey sponsor of *American President*.

"Evan, when you're president, how will you keep us all safe from terrorism?"

"That's a good question." Evan scratched his shiny, bald head. It shone brighter than Chump's unnaturally white teeth under the bright lights. "Depends on the type of terrorism, I guess. If it's a group operating on some type of religious extremism, that's easy. Just have the voice of their god speak to them."

"The fuck did he just say?" It was getting to be Shanda's favorite phrase.

Bryan blinked "Am I understanding you correctly? You'd, um, negotiate with God?"

"Oh, no, that's not what I said." Evan rolled his eyes. "I said I'd arrange to have the voice of whoever they think is God speak to them. I mean, they're all taking orders from a human being who *claims* to speak for God, right? Why can't two play that game? Only we could do it better. Surely there's a way to get a big, booming voice in the sky. Flying sound system, hidden by a cloud or something? The Air Force could do it, I know they could. And then—"

"Time," Shanda said, and a buzzer sounded.

"Mr. Foster, uh, how do you respond to that?" Bryan asked.

Foster shook his head. "A preposterous plan. It'll never work, and it's offensive to basically all religious people everywhere. Not to mention, it doesn't solve the problem of non-religious terrorist groups."

"Can I respond to that?" Evan asked.

"Go for it," Shanda said, and Bryan nodded.

"It's not offensive. Religious extremist groups are always run by someone who perverts the word of whatever god the followers believe in for personal gain. That may be offensive to some people, but they do it for money and power, so why shouldn't we do it in the name of stopping terrorism and saving lives?

"As for non-religious extremist leaders, they also want money and power. They just go about getting those things in a different way. I say we pay their followers off, and the leaders will be left with nothing. Terrorist group disbanded."

"Do you hear this?" Foster waved a hand at Evan. "He wants us to negotiate with terrorists, give them a payoff to leave us alone."

"Not the terrorists, their followers. Without followers, the leaders won't be very dangerous," Evan said.

"So what would you do about the problem, Congressman?" Bryan asked.

"I'd appeal to the UN to send peacekeeping forces into the areas where known terrorist groups are headquartered, and work with the leaders of those countries to reduce the root causes of terrorism like poverty and lack of personal freedoms."

A dinging noise filled the room. "Whoa, he said one of the phrases" — Bryan consulted his tablet— "two of them, actually, 'appeal to the UN,' and 'reduce the root causes of terrorism.' Any variation on those themes requires a drink, so everyone take two shots and we'll move on to the next question."

The candidates knocked back their shots. Bryan wanted to join them, but Shanda had told him earlier the host had to stay sober. Lot of fun he was going to have at this drinking game.

"Mr. Fuller, you won the coin toss so you'll go first. Let's say that you're president and you have to nominate a new Supreme Court Justice. Who would you nominate and why?"

"Wow. That's a solid question, man." Fuller blinked, rubbed the side of his face a couple times, then poured himself another shot. "It would have to be someone who supports marijuana legalization, obviously. Wouldn't want my new law to be overturned by someone, like, legislating from the bench. I'd find a pro-marijuana judge, that's what I'd do." He chugged the shot as the buzzer sounded.

"I'm afraid 'legislating from the bench' is another tired phrase." Bryan nodded to the bottle, but Fuller was already pouring his next shot.

Bryan looked at his tablet. Only another fifteen minutes to go. "Kevin, who would you nominate?"

Kevin nodded and scratched his armpit through his Budweiser t-shirt. "Judge Judy. I'm serious, she's fair, she's reasonable, she doesn't put up with anyone's bullshit, and she knows the law. I can't think of a better person to be on the Supreme Court. She'd cut through so much crap and save the court so much time, it could probably hear more cases in a year."

"Would you like to respond?" Bryan asked Fuller.

He narrowed his eyes at the whiskey bottle. In celebration of its sponsorship, Wild Turkey had placed one of the top ten candidates' heads on each bottle. The one in front of Fuller held Ronda Harper's smiling face. "How does Judge Judy feel about legalization of marijuana? If she's in favor of it, I agree with him."

No dinging for that one, so Bryan moved on to the last set of contestants. "Okay, Clarice and Mr. Morganstern. Clarice, you won the coin toss so you'll go first. As you both know, our country is currently in an economic tailspin, and arguably has been to varying degrees since the turn of the century. As president, what would you do to restore us to economic prosperity?"

Clarice nodded, her face serious. "I've given that a lot of thought, and I would create jobs and economic opportunities by making sure the government spends money in the right places. No more tax breaks for big corporations. Instead, we'd use that money to improve education and fund scientific research of genuine importance—not delving into the sex lives of quail, or something pointless like that, but research with potential benefits, like advancing our technological prowess or medical knowledge. We'll also form a governmental agency dedicated to lowering the cost of producing all types of products here in this country."

Bryan looked at the time. Five more minutes. "Mr. Morganstern, your response, please?"

Morganstern folded his arms over his chest, the diamond cufflinks sparkling almost as much as Evan's bald head. "Ridiculous. Tax breaks for large corporations lead to more jobs, which leads to more spending, which leads to a stronger economy. After Cheatham lobbied Congress for legislation that saved us ten million a year in taxes, we were able to add thousands of new jobs at our bank."

DINGDINGDINGDINGDING

"Time to take a drink," Bryan announced needlessly. "'Tax breaks for large corporations lead to more jobs' is another phrase viewers are ready to retire."

Clarice poured a shot and knocked it back, licking the last of it from the corner of her mouth. She must have learned that trick at the sorority house. "So how many of those jobs were full-time and paid more than minimum wage?"

"Let them debate, we have a few minutes," Shanda said in Bryan's ear.

Morganstern swallowed his shot and frowned at her. "I don't have that data at hand right at the moment, but generally we hire for both full-time and part-time positions to give opportunities to people with varying work schedules."

"I studied this example on your campaign page, and then I fact-checked it. Most of those positions were part-time teller jobs, with no benefits, and paid only minimum wage." Clarice stared him down. "Also, thousands of full-time tellers who had been with the company for years and making considerably more, plus benefits, were let go a few months prior to that hiring frenzy."

Morganstern shrugged. "In business, sometimes you have to lay people off. That was probably before we received that helpful tax break, which led us to hire new help."

"For far less than you were paying the *old* help." Clarice traced her finger around the rim of the shot glass.

"Again, I was never personally involved in hiring and firing decisions as the CEO of that bank. You'd have to ask someone in HR about those specific numbers. To answer the question, I would fix our economy by providing more tax breaks for businesses like Cheatham Bank."

Time for the last round, then the vote. Finally. "Okay, this last question in our final round is for all the contestants. We'll start back with Congressman Foster and Evan. What is the biggest lie you've ever told? Evan, you're up first."

Evan shoved his glasses up on his nose and snickered. "Wow, I have to pick just one? Oh, gosh, well, when I was in college, I told a girl I invented Twitter in an effort to impress her pants off."

"And how did that work?" Bryan was pretty sure he knew the answer.

The unemployed comic shook his head. "Terrible. She yelled at me, 'You did not, everybody knows Mark Zuckerberg invented Twitter, you moron!'"

The audience guffawed.

"Congressman Foster?" Bryan wished he was home on his couch, watching this on his 60-inch TV. If he was, the whole thing might actually be amusing.

Foster wrinkled his brow. "In the first grade, I stole a pencil from a class-mate and lied when he called me on it. I said I'd brought it from home, and he just wanted it because it was a cooler color than his. The teacher believed me and sent him to the principal's office. I felt so guilty, I vowed never to tell another lie again, and I never have."

And if you believe that, I have a bridge in Brooklyn to sell you. "Mr. Morganstern, your answer?"

Morganstern shrugged. "I don't recall."

"You, ah, have to answer," Bryan said.

"I did. My answer is I don't recall." Morganstern folded his arms over his chest. "I was probably drunk at the time, so why would I remember?"

Looked like the banker could hold his liquor. Great. "Okay, what's the big-gest lie you can remember telling?"

Morganstern scrunched up his face, stared at the ceiling, and scratched the back of his head. He looked very much like a guy trying to appear to be deep in thought. "Well, I guess it was when I said that I'd slow our economic decline if elected president."

Bryan nearly choked on the sip of water he'd chosen to take at that unfortu-nate moment. "Ah... You *admit* you're not planning to improve the economy?"

The banker shook his head, his face stony. "The truth is, I'm going to do more than just slow our economic decline, I'm going to make our economy boom again. My campaign promise undersold what I plan to do, and since I went to an Ivy League school and have purchased the most refined words, I should have chosen better. What I'm really going to do is make our economy a magnificent and majestic tribute to human government."

At that point, Evan did what Bryan had been dying to do since Morganstern opened his mouth—he burst out laughing.

"I'm sorry, that's just...." He doubled over, his shoulders shaking with laughter. "It's just... it's just the biggest load of bullshit I've ever heard."

"And it's still steaming." Kevin had tears rolling down his face from laughing so hard.

"Bigger than that pile you shoveled in Iowa, huh?" Clarice elbowed Foster, who didn't even crack a smile.

Would the viewers vote for someone without a sense of humor? Morganstern and Foster were the only ones not laughing. Fuller, of course, howled the loudest, slapping his thigh and sloppily pouring another drink. Might as well let him go next.

"Your answer, Mr. Fuller?"

"I lied the firsh day of kindergarten when the teacher asked my name and I told her it was George Ca-looney and I lied in fourth grade when I told this girl I rilly liked that the li'l boy she rilly liked had cooties. Cooties, yesh, I said he cooties becaush—"

"I just need the biggest lie," Bryan said, before he could get to middle school.

"I dunno." Fuller twirled the shot glass between his fingers. "I bought some Girl Scout cookies once, and I told the girls I was buying them for a friend when they were really for me becaush I had the munchieses...."

"Kevin, your answer?"

"In my interview for this show, I said I'd be a better president than any of these people, but the truth is, I think my dog would be a better president," Kevin said.

"We've only got a minute left, and this is a bust," Shanda said in Bryan's ear. *"These people aren't drunk enough to tell the truth."*

"Clarice?" Bryan prompted.

She folded her arms and leaned back in her chair, lips pursed in concentration. "When they came out with the new curriculum requirements, I had all these parents ask me things like, 'Is this really going to help my child learn?' or 'My child is struggling with this new system, isn't the old way better?' The truth was that they were right, the new curriculum was bad for almost every kid in that class, but if I told them that, I'd have lost my job.

"I loved teaching, and as bad as the new curriculum was, I knew that I would at least try to help the kids muddle their way through it, so I lied. I told those parents it would be fine, and when it wasn't, then sometimes I explained things the old way when I was sure no one was looking. When the school board asked how the students were doing with the new system, I lied and said they were doing fine, because I was afraid the next teacher wouldn't make the effort to help the kids learn in a way that made sense to them. I lied to help my students, and I don't regret it."

"Well, our time is up, unfortunately," Bryan said. "The audience is now free to vote for the person among these six who you feel should continue in this competition. At the end of *American President: Aftermath,* we'll announce the person moving on in the competition, and explain the next assignment for our new top six. Stay tuned, you won't want to miss this."

Not surprisingly, *American President: Aftermath* ended with Fuller, Foster, and Morganstern being sent home permanently. Evan also scored poorly, but Clarice beat Kevin by a small margin. Although the results for the top ten had been announced in no particular order, Shanda wanted him to reveal the ranking for the six in the drinking game.

"As you can see, all three new contestants beat all of the bottom three from the top ten." He waved at the green screen behind him. "Viewer comments suggest the American people weren't too impressed with Evan's answers, although his bald head now has a Facebook fan page. Clarice and Kevin—it was close, a lot of people agreed with Kevin's Judge Judy nomination, but Clarice won by a small margin. You both did very well."

"I'm sending someone out with a special announcement," Shanda said in his ear.

She was what? A special announcement? She was supposed to clear the surprise stuff with him beforehand, but of course she never did. What the hell did she decide without his input now?

Two members of the National Guard walked on stage, and one of them handed Bryan an envelope.

"Thank you." He nodded at the guards, and they turned and marched off stage. "Well, ladies and gentlemen, I've been asked to read the audience a special announcement from this card. I have no idea what it says. Are you ready to find out?"

The audience roared.

"See, now you look genuinely surprised," Shanda said.

He ripped open the envelope, feeling like as much of an automaton as Artie.

"The election committee has reviewed its special circumstances rules," he read. "After meeting, they voted unanimously to uphold Rule Fifty-two, which states that when a candidate leaves voluntarily or is disqualified from the competition, he or she will be replaced by the person who would have been voted off the show by the least number of votes. Since Kevin scored higher than the other five who left the show tonight, he will be asked to stay. This means two contestants will be eliminated in the next round."

Kevin looked up from his cell phone. "I'm still in the running?"

"That's right." Bryan returned his gaze to his tight-shot camera. "Now, Clarice, Kevin, are you ready to face off against the other five contestants tomorrow?"

Clarice nodded eagerly. "Yes, I am. I can't wait to debate the topics with the greatest political minds in our country."

"Maybe after the show is over and the other contestants are gone we'll meet them," Kevin said.

33

THE REAL WHITE HOUSE had a wet bar, and so did the play White House where Bryan had spent most of his time for the past week-and-a-half. Too tired to fix his own drink when he got home, he slumped down at the bar and waved a finger at the bartender, who was on duty 24/7 and had served all the candidates at one time or another.

"The usual?" Hal asked.

Bryan bobbed his head.

"What a surprise. This place driving you to drink, too?" A voice said behind him, and he turned to look.

"Oh, hey Jeremy. Yeah, I guess it is." Bryan turned back to the bar and dropped his head onto the cool tile. Right now he was too tired to get into a conversation.

Jeremy sat on the velvet-cushioned bar stool next to him. "So did you see the latest picture that's going around social media?"

Nothing immediately came to mind and Bryan didn't feel like digging his phone out to see what had trended since the show ended and he had to greet 500 fans. "Don't tell me Brumley and Jesus had a three-way with Ronald Chump?"

"Dude, you really haven't seen it, have you?"

Bryan's head popped up. He didn't like that sound of that. "Haven't seen what, exactly?"

"This picture of you and Joanne." Jeremy slid his phone down the counter and Bryan found himself staring at photo taken in the restaurant last night, apparently around the time Joanne thought it necessary to whisper discreetly in his ear.

#americanloveinterest.

"Oh, no." Was he in trouble? Was Joanne? Shanda could fire a journalist more easily than the host of the show. "Did you happen to see Shanda's reaction? How mad was she?"

"Mad?" Jeremy's face did that elastic stretch of surprise thing he usually reserved for people on his show who swore their fifth marriage would be forever. "Are you kidding? When I left the control room, she was ecstatic that people were talking about something other than the hacking issue. Hell, she made us all promise to retweet your shipper nickname, Bry-anne, so that would trend, too."

"My shipper *what?*"

"Oh, I forgot, you don't know because you don't host a dating show. Don't, it's depressing. Some people audition every year and the show lead never chooses them." Jeremy paused as the barkeep delivered their drinks. He took a sip of beer then picked up his phone and tapped the screen. "Anyway, shipper nicknames are those cutesy combined names fans of celebrity couples come up with, you know, like Brangelina for Brad and Angelina? Oh, and Jesusley for Brumley and—"

"I get it." Bryan grabbed his beer and chugged half of it. Would Joanne be mad at him? Was she seeing someone? Was she still with Cliff? He'd been tempted to check her relationship status on social media so many times over the years, but he always stopped himself.

"I was right." Jeremy glanced around the otherwise empty bar, then narrowed his eyes at Bryan. "You do have feelings for her."

"What makes you say that?" Bryan waved at the phone. "It's one picture, and she was telling me about the anonymous tip she received, that's all."

Jeremy shrugged. "I see the way you look at her, and I know you both worked together in Oklahoma years ago. I figured you had a thing back then and she was the one who broke it off."

"It's not like that." He shook his head. "There was never a thing to break off."

"Oh, I get it. You carried a torch for her but she didn't feel the same." Jeremy sounded like he was introducing the relationship-spoiler ex on his show.

"It wasn't exactly like that, either." Bryan finished the beer and waved for another. The bartender popped one open and slid it down the corner, where Bryan snagged it. "Okay, I had a thing for her but I never told her, partly because I didn't have the nerve, and partly because she was dating this jerk, Cliff."

"I bet they're not even together anymore." Jeremy scrolled through something on his phone. "Her relationship status says single."

"Did I ask you to look that up?"

"I can't help it, I'm a professional matchmaker, and you obviously really care about Joanne. You should tell her now."

"Wow, you're really perceptive. You should host a dating show on TV."

"Haha. Seriously, why don't you tell her?"

Bryan stared down into the bottle. "It's not that simple. When I left Oklahoma... this thing happened, and she wound up really pissed at me."

"What kind of thing?"

"I don't know if you ever worked in TV news at a really small station" —he glanced at the dating show host, who shook his head— "okay then, I'll tell you what it's like. A lot of people think everyone on TV is rich, and that's bullshit. This little station we worked at barely paid reporters twenty thousand a year, and we had to spend a lot of money on clothes and haircuts—and the station didn't pick up the bill, right? So we all had roommates. I was living with Cliff and two photogs, and every month someone was *still* late with his share of the rent."

"That sucks, but what does it have to do with Joanne?"

"I'm getting to that, but first I have to explain Cliff. TV was really a good career for him, because his contract ended every two years and he could move somewhere else, which was perfect because that was about the amount of time it took him to date and piss off every woman in town."

"Sounds like a real prize." Jeremy stared at the row of tequila bottles lining the back of the bar. "Just the kind of person we would have brought on *Who Wants to Marry a Gay Millionaire* to spoil the show couple with the most social media attention. You must have been annoyed Joanne was into him instead of you."

"I know, right? But I couldn't badmouth him, or she'd think I was jealous."

"So what happened? How did she end up mad at you?"

"It was bad enough she was dating Cliff. But this place we lived in was small, and the walls were thinner than the last winner of *Supermodeling Star.*" He cringed at the memory. "Cliff's room was on the other side of mine, and he was really, really loud when he had sex. So as if it wasn't bad enough, knowing he was banging the woman I wanted to be with, I had to lie there and listen to them going at it."

"Ouch. That's rough."

"No shit. But that's not even the worst part. Like I said, Cliff was very vocal. Very, very vocal." He rubbed his temples. Why was he telling this story to Jeremy in a bar at work? Probably because he was too tired to think of that until just now. Might as well finish. "So I'm lying there, trying to block them out so I can sleep, and right in the middle of it he yells, 'Breaking news!' like four or five times. Then he stopped, so I guess that was when he climaxed."

Beer sprayed out of Jeremy's nose as he burst out laughing. "Seriously? Breaking news?"

"I know, what the fuck? And being Cliff, of course they didn't just do it once, they did it like three times, and he screamed, 'Breaking news!' all three times. They literally kept me up all night with that shit.

"So the next day, I was pretty useless at work, because I'd had no sleep. Kind of like now, but at least I don't have to write my own lines here." He rolled his eyes, hearing Shanda's voice in his head. *You're just here to look good in a five-thousand-dollar suit, not write your own script.* "But there I had to write packages, and I screwed something up. I was supposed to say that this guy in a fender-bender was cited for failure to register his car, and I know I meant to write that, but I think maybe my tablet autocorrected or something. I'm not sure what happened, but somehow, I put that he was cited for failure to register as a sex offender."

"Holy shit." Jeremy's eyes went wide. "Did he sue you?"

"No, fortunately my producer caught the mistake before anyone read it on air." He took another sip of beer. "Then she yelled at me in front of the whole newsroom—and she was right to do that. It was a huge mistake, and if it had gone on air the guy could definitely have sued us—both me personally, and the station, and only one of us could afford a good lawyer, so you know how that would have turned out. I probably would have been fired, and no one would have ever hired me for an on-air job again.

"But I was exhausted and sleep-deprived and Joanne was dating Cliff, and I was just in a really shitty mood that day, so I got into it with the producer. I yelled at her that I couldn't concentrate because I hadn't slept because Cliff likes to scream 'Breaking news' during sex and he and Joanne had sex all night long last night on the other side of a paper-thin wall. And of course I yelled all that in front of the whole newsroom, too."

Jeremy laughed. "Please tell me someone recorded that, it would totally go viral today."

"You know, despite the fact that we were in a newsroom, no one was actually recording at that particular time." He finished the second beer and pushed the bottle away. "Anyhow, I wasn't thinking about the whole newsroom hearing, and especially not Joanne, but I guess she had walked up behind me and I didn't see her. Cliff wasn't there, but I'm sure someone told him like five minutes later. We journalists are a gossipy bunch."

"Did you get fired?"

"Not really. My contract was up for renegotiation in a month anyway, and the station chose not to renew it. TV contracts are always stacked heavily in favor of the station—it's much easier for them to get out of it than the anchor, you know? But I had been sending out tapes anyway, hoping to get to a bigger station."

"And you did."

"No, not really. I couldn't ask anyone in Oklahoma for a recommendation after my outburst in the newsroom," he said. "A friend of mine who came out here to try to be an actor got me an audition for a local game show. The money was so much better and the contract was short-term, so I thought I'd just do it for a few months, save up some money, then try to get back into journalism, which was what I really wanted to do."

"But you wound up here." Jeremy waved around the bar. "I guess I did, too. Hell, I wanted to be a writer."

Bryan nodded. "Yeah, I was asked to read for a hosting gig on this singing show. Didn't think I'd get it, or that anyone would watch, but I *did* get the job, and the money was so good I couldn't pass it up. You know the rest."

"So you never thought about tracking Joanne down? I mean, she works at the NNN office here in Los Angeles."

He tried to copy Jeremy's elastic look of shock. "Are you crazy? I didn't even have a shot with her *before* I told the entire newsroom about her and Cliff's sex life. I definitely don't now."

"I don't know, I think maybe she's gotten over Cliff and realized she should have been dating you." Jeremy shoved the phone in his face again. "Bry-anne really is a cute couple name. Look, Valencia just re-tweeted Shanda's post, 'Bry-anne, totes adorbs!'"

Bryan waved it away. "Why would you say that? I mean the part about Joanne wanting to date me."

"Isn't it obvious?" Jeremy rolled his eyes. "She didn't have to let you in on that hacking tip. She could have gone right to Shanda and asked if she could interview the contestants in the middle of the night, with or without telling her about the tip. Either way, she would have gotten all the credit. Hell, if I was her, and I wanted to host this show next season, that's what I would have done."

Bryan stared at him. "She told me she auditioned for the hosting job, and seemed kind of pissed that I got it, when I'm not even a real journalist."

"See?" Jeremy looked at his phone again. "**#bry-anne** is still trending. Why don't you go track down the other half of that nickname? Actually, don't do it right now, you look like crap. Get a few hours of sleep first, then go ask her out."

Bryan shoved himself away from the counter and texted his limo driver he was ready to go. "I might just do that."

34

A S IT TURNED OUT, Joanne was out on assignment the next day, probably digging up more dirt on the candidates. Not that Bryan would have had much time to talk to her—he was busy doing interviews with people who wanted to know about the Brumley scandal, the drinking game, and the legality of letting Americans choose the challenges.

"I'm sure our founding fathers didn't mean for us to interpret the whole 'by the people, for the people' thing that literally," said a political commentator for one of the big cable networks who was interviewing Bryan by Skype. "Aren't you ever concerned you're doing the public—and the candidates—a disservice by allowing average people to jerk the candidates around like puppets?"

"I think it's essential for America to see what the candidates are really like, and you and I both know that doesn't usually happen with stump speeches and ads," Bryan said.

"But isn't this show turning into a circus? I mean, drinking games, random people popping up as new contestants—how can America take this election seriously?"

"I don't know how America took our electoral process seriously in the past." He had talking points on his laptop screen, but tried to look into the webcam instead. "We were basically voting for people based on them acting out their own dramas. We didn't even elect our president by a popular vote—we had some of those actors we elected picking our president for us. What we're trying to do here is strip away the pomp and trite campaign lines and attack ads and all those things that got in the way of the true democratic process so voters can make an informed decision for the first time ever. Also, I'd like to add that tonight you'll really get to see some honesty from the candidates, and no, I can't tell you any more than that. You'll just have to tune in."

Between interviews, he followed the show's social media action on his tablet. While there were a lot of comments about him and Joanne, there were even more about Jesusley, and a huge following for **#realpeople** *and* **#firetheprofessionals.**

Who would have thought three regular people would get more votes than three politicians? Everyone who's ever voted, that's who. **#realpeople #downwithpoliticians**

We should not only have a real person for President, we should have **#realpeople** *in Congress. Can we ban everyone who's ever run for office before?*

I don't know about these **#realpeople.** *I'd rather have an experienced liar like* **@therealRondaHarper** *dealing with other countries and directing our CIA and shit like that.*

Guys like Morganstern and Chump only appeal to the 1%. Even people like Harper who claim to support the poor are still just rich posers. I'd rather vote for someone who actually knows the struggles of the 99% any day. **#realpeople #firetheprofessionals #fireCongress**

The purpose of the By the People, For the People Act wasn't too put uneducated morrons in office, it was to give us more freedom in chosing a leader from the professionals. This **#realpeople** *movement is* **#realannoying** *and* **#realstupid.** *I'd rather vote for a* **#realAmerican** *like* **@therealRonaldChump** *than some whiny teacher who doesn't realize* *she'll have more school funding after we build the moat or some loser phone salesman who probably wants to pick my pocket for health insurance.*

These **#realpeople** *wouldn't last a day dealing with the machinations of Congress, they need to go back to the welfare line.* **#pumpedforChump**

Wow, these **#realpeople** *are talking about issues instead of bragging about their penises or pitching their ghostwritten books. It's almost like a real political debate or something.* **#firetheprofessionals**

Five seconds after Bryan reported to makeup, Shanda bounced into his dressing room, and he wondered if the makeup artists had cameras in their boxes of brushes or something. She always seemed to show up when they did.

"This Bry-Anne thing is still trending, but it's starting to slope off. What do you guys say to an on-screen kiss?" she asked without preamble.

Bryan stared at her until one of the makeup people tilted his head up and ordered him to look at the ceiling so she could stab him with an eyeliner pencil. "Are you crazy? We're not even—that picture isn't what it looks like, okay? She was telling me about her anonymous source and didn't want to be overheard."

"You definitely can't say that on air." Shanda sounded deeply disappointed.

"Why do we have to say anything about it at all? The show is about the contestants, not us, and no one is... talking about the NSA's role in stopping that pitiful attempt at hacking, right?"

Shanda cleared her throat. "That's true, they came out of this smelling like a rose, and it doesn't seem like anyone else is concerned about the integrity of the results so far. All right, you two don't have to address it if you don't want to, but don't specifically say you're not dating either, okay?"

Bryan nodded, causing the eyeliner pencil to jab into the corner of his eye. "Ouch. Don't worry, I know how to be coy with the press. I used to be the press, Shanda."

"You're right. I'm sorry. I forgot you used to be a real reporter."

He gritted his teeth, still blinking the kohl liner out of one eye. "You didn't ask Joanne about this ridiculous kiss idea, did you?"

"No, I wanted to talk to you first since I know you better than Joanne. I didn't want to sound like your pimp or something."

"Thank you." For once he meant it.

35

WELCOME TO THE NEXT round of *American President.* I'm your host, Bryan Seafoam, and tonight we will interrogate—I mean, get to know the top six candidates." Bryan tried not to wince at the corny dialogue, although to be fair, Shanda wasn't really joking about the interrogation part. "Candidates, will you please join me on stage?"

He was already seated in a chair between the two couches, and the contestants filed in, three from stage right and three from stage left.

Ronald Chump waved at the audience, chin pointed up in the air, his face set in its usual self-satisfied smirk. Senator Haverty had his shirtsleeves rolled up, ostensibly for the difficult task of waving with both hands. Sara Finnegan stayed in her usual stiff pose, her hair never moving as she shook hands and waved at the audience. Her gold cross necklace was twice as big as usual, probably an attempt to swing Brumley's former supporters to her camp. Ronda Harper wore her usual pantsuit and grin, and spouted the usual nonsense about how happy she was to dialogue with the other candidates. Milton Buckshaw looked pained as he grinned, and Bryan wondered if he was sucking in his gut. Probably.

Clarice was the only candidate who acted like a real human being, probably because she was. She waved a few times, but mostly looked around the stage and at the monitors and cameras, the way people often did when they weren't used to being on air. Kevin looked like a deer in the headlights. Would people rather vote for someone genuine than someone slick?

Who knew, with these voters? After all, a significant percentage had voted for a guy who wanted to bring sweatshop labor to America, for crap's sake.

"Welcome back, all six of you. As you may have heard, tonight we're going to talk to each of you about the plans you have for this country," Bryan read off the prompter. "But first, there's a little catch we haven't told you about. You may have had a preview if you watched last night's drinking game competition. Of course the idea was to get you drunk so you'd be more truthful. However, many of the contestants who are no longer with us were nonetheless skilled at holding their liquor, so tonight we're going to *really* play hardball. You're all going to be hooked up to a polygraph machine, so we'll have a better idea if you're telling the truth."

Ronald Chump was the first to react. "This is unconstitutional!"

"I hate to say it, but I'm inclined to agree," Sara Finnegan said.

"Those things aren't admissible in a court of law." Ronda Harper waved a hand at Bryan.

"Our founding fathers didn't say anything about polygraphing candidates," Buckshaw groused.

"Well, everybody already knows about my twenty mistresses, so this is a waste of time," Haverty said. "And please, don't ask me which of them is my favorite."

Clarice shrugged. "I don't care. Hook me up."

"Me, too," Kevin said.

"We've consulted with a team of lawyers and officials from the election committee," Bryan said. "They all agreed that a polygraph is in accordance with the By the People, For the People Act, if it's what the voting public wants—and it is. Now, if you'll all follow me please."

He led them downstairs to the makeshift interrogation room, which was really an unused basement with multiple small rooms, all recently soundproofed. Each one was large enough to hold a table, the polygraph equipment, and a polygraph technician.

Bryan stood in front of the row of doors and faced the candidates, most of whom looked terrified. *Deer in the headlights* didn't even cover most of their expressions. Deer being beamed up into a spaceship maybe? Deer learning Ronald Chump was considered a serious candidate for president? Hell, even a deer could see that was a bad idea.

"You've stared them down long enough, get on with it," Shanda barked in his ear. *"The audience only wants to watch the candidates fidget for so long."*

"In a moment, I will show each of you to a room, where you will be hooked up to a polygraph," Bryan said. "The show's director will go back and forth between contestants, but all six of the feeds will be streaming live on the show's website, and will be archived so viewers can watch them later.

"My correspondents and I will go from room to room, asking questions. Viewers are encouraged to suggest additional queries at any point during the process. You may take breaks to eat, stretch your legs, or use the restroom, but otherwise we will continue until eleven Eastern Time, when we will take a break and resume tomorrow morning at eight a.m. At that point, we'll continue until seven tomorrow night, when the audience will be allowed to vote. Any questions?"

"Aren't polygraphs sometimes wrong?" Ronda Harper asked. "That's why they're not admissible in a court of law."

"It's true polygraphs are not always accurate, but this isn't a court of law and no one is on trial here." Bryan waved at the row of doors. "It's up to the audience to decide if you are really lying or not, but that's how it's been since the show started. The only difference is now you have an additional tool to help you decide, America. Now, let's get started."

He ushered the candidates into their assigned rooms, then pitched to a package on the science of how polygraphs worked while the technicians hooked up the wires.

Bryan started with Ronald Chump. The multi-gazillionaire—or whatever he was, Bryan couldn't even remember anymore—was attached to so many wires it looked like someone was trying to get a direct line into his bank account. He made an effort not to smirk at the thought.

Beside Chump, the polygraph machine sat, no bigger than a printer. Above it was a tablet mounted to the wall, which would flash *Lying* or *Truthful* after each answer.

"Now Mr. Chump, tell me, what will be your first official action if you're sworn in as president?" Mine will be moving to Canada, he didn't add.

Chump cleared his throat, lifted his chin, and looked directly into the camera. "I plan to put my face on the hundred dollar bill instead of Franklin's."

TRUE, the tablet flashed.

Bryan blinked. Of all the answers he'd expected from Chump, that wasn't one of them. He glanced at his teleprompter, which helpfully said, *Artie researching.*

"Ah, Mr. Chump, I'm not sure if the president has the authority to do that, but let's say that you did. Do you really think that's the most important issue facing our country today?"

"The most important issue facing us today is the economy, and I am the only candidate who can fix it. Therefore, my face should be on the bill."

"But shouldn't your first act be to fix the economy, and then worry about changing the bills later?"

"Simply having my face on the hundred will inspire confidence in our economy and encourage more spending."

Bryan looked at the tablet. He had to hand it Chump, the guy hadn't told a lie yet.

He left Chump and moved on to Sara Finnegan, who looked bored and inconvenienced. Her gray blazer jacket hung over the back of her chair—she'd had to take if off to make room for the blood pressure cuff. The humongous gold cross around her neck was shoved to the side, but still there.

"If you're elected president, what will be your first official act?" he asked her.

"I'm going to introduce a job creation bill offering financial incentives to companies who increase the amount of products they produce here in this country," she said.

The tablet blinked *TRUE.*

"You mean you're going to give a large tax break to large corporations?"

Finnegan cleared her throat. "Only after they've hired more American workers. It won't be a blind handout to *all* big corporations. If they want the tax break, they have to hire here at home."

TRUE.

Something tickled the back of Bryan's mind. What was his brain trying to tell him? It had something to do with screaming children, the smell of french fries, and an early death from heart disease, and a "Bite me" t-shirt—that was it. The guy in the *Byte Me* shirt said something about creating new jobs, but not getting full-time work or benefits....

"So, Ms. Finnegan, tell me more about this plan. Would companies have to hire for full-time positions only? Would they get a tax break even if they only hired for minimum wage jobs?"

She shrugged. "Any job creation is a good thing."

INCONCLUSIVE.

"Is it? Do you think people who want full-time skilled work but can only find part-time, minimum wage jobs are putting a lot of money back into the economy? Or are they using a lot of government benefits, something you said you wanted to reduce?"

"Careful," Shanda said in his ear.

"Because I used to run a business, I know that sometimes saving money by hiring part-time workers at low wages enables the company to grow to a point where more full-time jobs can be added."

INCONCLUSIVE.

"Is that what you did in your many years at Hewitt Computers?" Bryan asked. "Can you name a time when you added full-time jobs after receiving a tax break, or hiring more part-time workers to save money?"

"That's difficult to say, because a business that size is complicated...."

FALSE.

"Yes or no, Ms. Finnegan, was there ever a time when you saved money by hiring part-time, minimum wage workers, and then used the increased profits to hire more full-time workers?"

"Yes, I believe there was."

FALSE.

"When was that?"

"I don't remember the exact date. A few years ago, maybe."

FALSE.

"Thank you, Ms. Finnegan."

He went to the next cubicle, where Buckshaw sat, strapped to the machine. "Governor Buckshaw, if you are elected president, what will be your first official act?"

Buckshaw smiled. "I'm going to fix our unemployment numbers. First, we'll encourage employers like that fast food restaurant where I worked to sign up for a job bank at their state's unemployment office. Applicants will be required to apply for and be turned down for those jobs before receiving benefits. Second, I'll pass a law to stop people like that young man I met at the burger place from hogging all the work opportunities. I'll set limits on how many jobs one person can have, so there are enough for other people."

TRUE.

"So if a person can't survive on one minimum wage job, or two, or whatever you're going to set the limit at, you'd prefer they seek government assistance to getting an additional job?" Bryan asked.

"Of course not. We need to trim the fat from all those entitlement programs, too." Buckshaw folded his hands over his ample stomach. "People just need to learn to live within their means. Or they can pursue higher education—anyone making minimum wage should qualify for federal student loans."

TRUE.

"Which the government earns interest on," Bryan pointed out. "In some cases, from the day the loan is made."

"Why shouldn't the federal government earn interest for financing America's future? Anyway, we'll use that money to provide tax breaks for the companies that join the unemployment-required job bank."

INCONCLUSIVE.

"So you'll earmark all interest earned on students loans for companies that join your job bank?"

"Well, *all* interest is a lot of money, but I'll try to include a line earmarking, say, twenty or thirty percent for that purpose, yes."

FALSE.

"Maybe as low as fifteen percent, depending on the expense of the program...."

INCONCLUSIVE.

"Thank you, Governor."

His next stop was Ronda Harper's cubicle. She wore a blue pantsuit and a mess of wires that, combined with her angry glare, made her look like a suicide bomber. "If you're elected president, what you will be your first official act?"

"Try not to sound so robotic every time you repeat that," Shanda groused in his ear.

"After my time at the coffee shop, I realize that our minimum wage should be raised, so I will introduce a bill to do just that," she said. "Then I'll incentivize companies to provide health insurance to part-time employees who work more than fifteen hours a week, by offering a stimulus package to those that do so."

TRUE.

"A stimulus package?" Bryan scratched his head, feigning confusion. "Do you mean a tax break for large companies?"

"Large *and* small. All size companies can benefit from providing benefits." She chuckled at her own bad pun.

INCONCLUSIVE.

"So you're going to help low-wage workers by giving tax breaks to the large companies that employ them for low wages?"

"Like I said, I'm going to raise the minimum wage."

"By how much?"

"At least a dollar. Maybe two."

FALSE.

Harper's eyes drifted to the tablet, then quickly flicked back to the camera. "But fifty cents is probably the most I can get Congress to accept."

INCONCLUSIVE.

"Thank you, Congresswoman Harper."

He moved on to Kevin's cubicle. The customer service rep looked at the polygraph machine, then the tablet, then Bryan with a look bordering on disgust. "This is necessary because no one gets to be president without lying, isn't it?"

Bryan shrugged. "It does seem to be a prerequisite. If you're elected, what will be your first official act?"

Kevin ran a hand across his sweaty brow. "I don't know. The more I sit here and watch the original contestants—they're all such lying sleazebags, who obviously care only about themselves, not the American people. I don't know how to lead a country of people who would consider them front-runners."

TRUE.

"And anything I would try to do would be useless." He ran his hands through his hair, his face contorted with panic. "Because Congress is filled with the same sort of self-centered morons."

"Then what would you do?" Bryan asked. "I just need some idea of your first official act as president."

Kevin nodded. "You know what this contest is? It's a sham, Bryan. It's a distraction, to get the public's attention while the five hundred thirty-five members of Congress rob us blind and screw us over every day. I guess I have to say that my first official act as president would be resigning, and since that would be a waste of everyone's time, I'm dropping out of this race right now."

TRUE.

"You're what?" Bryan stared at Kevin, waiting for the punchline, but there wasn't one. The customer service rep ripped off the wires, tossed them aside, stood up, and walked out the door.

Bryan chased after him. "Are you sure about this?"

"Yes." Kevin paused at the stairs and turned to face Bryan—and the cameras. His face was no longer twisted with panic—instead, he looked almost as peaceful as Bob Fuller did after he stepped outside to smoke "a cigarette." "I'm getting my stuff and going home. At least the morons I deal with in my job don't have the kind of power Congress does. That scares the hell out of me, and it should scare you too, America."

"He didn't have a chance, anyway," Shanda said in Bryan's ear.

The last contestant was Clarice, who looked far less uncomfortable with the polygraph machine than the other candidates.

"Ms. Greenforest, if you're elected, what will be your first official act?"

"I'm going to overhaul and restructure Congress," she said. "First of all, we need term limits for Congresspeople. There are term limits for the office of president, because we don't want any one person to stay in a powerful office for an unlimited amount of time, right? But in many ways, Congress has more power than the president. And yet, there are no term limits for Congress."

TRUE.

"She just came up with this watching Kevin," Shanda mumbled.

"What are you suggesting, only two terms, like the presidency?" Bryan asked.

Clarice shook her head. "Three terms might be okay for Congress. We just don't want anyone spending forty years there, something that routinely happens today. Or we could limit the number of consecutive terms. Maybe two terms, then you have to wait four or eight years before running again."

TRUE.

"How will you get Congress to vote for that?"

"That's the million-dollar question." She looked past him, directly into the camera, and folded her hands on the table in front of her in a presidential pose. In the few short days she'd been on the show, she'd learned a lot from the other candidates. "I guess it's really up to America. If Congress votes against term limits, and my fellow Americans disagree with that decision, then the obvious answer is to solve the problem yourself, America. Don't vote for anyone who voted against term limits for Congress. You'll basically be applying your own term limits."

TRUE.

Bryan tried to think of a hard-hitting question to ask, but nothing came to mind. Greenforest had no voting record to attack, and her answer was truthful, according to the polygraph.

"How will that help the American people?" was the best he could manage.

"That ties into the second part of my plan—getting rid of the SuperPACS and special interest groups and lobbyists who control much of Congress," she said. "Term limits won't completely solve the problem, but it will reduce it. SuperPACS and special interests will have to learn how to manipulate someone new every eight years. Some of their long-term supporters might be replaced by people who are less easily bought."

TRUE.

Senator Haverty had the most interesting answer. "I'll reform health care again, and I'll make it work for the people this time—and it won't cost the taxpayers any extra money."

TRUE.

"And how will you do that, Senator?"

"Almost seventy-five percent of all healthcare spending is on chronic conditions like heart disease, diabetes, cancer. Do you know how much of that is preventable?"

"No." Bryan glanced at his tablet. *CALCULATING* flashed on the screen.

"The World Health Organization estimates that if all risks factors for chronic disease were eliminated—things like lack of exercise and poor diet—we could prevent about eighty percent of heart disease, stroke, and Type Two diabetes, and about forty percent of all cancers."

TRUE.

Artie's research agreed. "That would certainly put a dent in our healthcare spending. So how will you eliminate all these risk factors? Are you going to propose a junk food tax or a tax credit for joining a gym or something?"

"Those are interesting ideas, but I'm going to start a little closer to home, by setting a good example for my fellow Americans." Haverty went to roll up his sleeves, stopped when he saw the blood pressure cuff on his right arm, and turned all his attention to the left. "When I'm president and I want to brief the press, I won't use a podium—I'll speak from a treadmill, at least when I'm at the White House or somewhere that it's feasible to do so."

TRUE.

"All state dinners at the White House will be low-calorie, low sodium, and include fresh vegetables."

TRUE.

"And I'm not going to stop there. I'm going to propose a bill to motivate Americans in the only way they understand—through their pocketbooks."

TRUE.

Bryan blinked. "You're going to *pay* people to get healthy?"

"No, I'm going to reward people for staying healthy. Do you know what happens when you pay for health insurance, and you don't get sick and go to the doctor?"

"Uh...." He looked at the tablet for help. *RECALCULATING.* "Tell us what happens, Senator."

"Nothing. That's right, I said 'Nothing.' You just pay a bunch of money for nothing. Who gets inspired by that? No one." Haverty thumped a hand on the table for emphasis. "Under my new plan, insurance companies will be required to pay back five to fifteen percent of premiums for each quarter that the insured doesn't use their insurance. They still get to keep most of the money, which they can use for the insured who do need care. The longer people go without getting sick, the higher the percentage goes. So your first quarter you get five percent back, the next six, and so on."

TRUE.

"Ask him how this works better than—" Shanda stopped talking when Bryan launched into the next question, which he'd thought of without her help.

"Why do you think this plan will work better than a soda or junk food tax?"

Haverty waved his hand around the room. "Look at obesity rates in this country. Every time we tax junk food or soda or take it out of schools, they go up even more. People don't like the government telling them what to do. They like getting extra money though. Car insurance companies have successfully used money-back programs for years. You know why? Because people have fewer accidents when they get a check every six months they don't have an accident."

TRUE.

"So does this mean you're giving up Oreos?" Bryan asked. The senator had been famously photographed eating his favorite cookie on a few occasions, once while Willard was giving a particularly boring speech to Congress about tax reform.

Haverty's smile looked a little strained. "I've definitely cut back."

INCONCLUSIVE.

"I also use the treadmill almost every day to stay in shape."

FALSE.

"Well, every day that my schedule allows."

INCONCLUSIVE.

Morganstern was last, and he blathered on about an incredibly boring but apparently true economic recovery plan, every other sentence of which involved *corporate tax relief.*

"So you're going to give big businesses tax breaks, too, like Sara Finnegan suggested?" Bryan asked.

Morganstern shrugged. "Tax breaks create jobs. Who cares if they're only part-time jobs? Would you rather have a part-time job or no job at all?"

TRUE.

Bryan thanked the banker and moved out into the hallway for his pitch to the commercial break. "And there you have it, answers to our first question. We'll be back later with suggested questions from the audience, but up next, Artie will provide statistics on the candidates' suggested first official acts. It's all coming up right after this break."

36

AFTER THE FIRST ROUND of questions, Bryan took a break and went to the Green Room for a snack and a shot of espresso. Shanda followed him, grabbing two chocolate-frosted donuts from the nearest box and immediately stuffing half of one into her mouth.

"Ohmygod, these responshes fur getting sofal medium er great," she said around a mouthful of food. At least that was what it sounded like.

Bryan grabbed a granola bar and sat on the buttery leather couch, tablet in the other hand. "These are some great questions. 'How many bribes have you accepted?' 'Ask everyone but Haverty how many mistresses they really have.' 'Ask the teacher about sex-ed in schools.' 'I want to know what Buckshaw's response to Haverty's healthcare plan is. It's a good thing we didn't get rid of pay for governors, because he won't be getting any money back from *his* insurance company!'"

"We have so many questions from viewers, I'm glad we have a whole day for this segment." Shanda stuffed the second half of the donut in her mouth. "You wanna ash tug quests but dun be too comfaffive."

"Combative?" Bryan tried to understand her mush-mouthed instructions.

"Yesh." She chewed a couple times, then swallowed. "Remember, you're not here to antagonize anyone."

"I'm here to ask the questions the American people want answered, and some of those are a little combative. And you know what? They should be. America doesn't want me lobbing softball questions at these people, and I don't want to do that either." Bryan took a sip of his espresso. "Have our ratings gone down after I asked a hard question? Did people quit watching in droves? No. Even when they thought I was too hard on a candidate, they kept watching. In some cases, more people tuned in, probably due to chatter on social media."

"That's true, which is why the networks aren't pressuring me to get rid of you," Shanda said as calmly as if she was discussing the weather. "But think about your career, Bryan. After this show is over, what do you do for the next four years? You're never going to get a job at a real news network, no matter how hardcore you get now. If the audience opinion of you goes down, it may be hard to get another hosting job, too. It's your career, just think about it."

Bryan chewed his granola bar, which suddenly felt like sawdust in his mouth. Was she right? Would he ever stand a chance of being a real journalist again? Was he doing nothing but relegating himself to a lifetime of being washed up in Hollywood, or worse, the punch line of a bad joke?

Shanda brushed some crumbs off her tweed pants and stood up. "Don't take too long. You need to get back in there and start on those viewer questions."

As she left, Joanne entered, a big smile on her face. She watched Shanda leave, bouncing impatiently on her toes, then hurried over to the couch and sat next to Bryan.

"I'm glad she's gone. I wanted to talk to you," she said in a low voice.

Bryan swallowed, his mouth dry. He ran his tongue over his teeth, hoping to dislodge any pesky pieces of granola. "Is it about that photo? I'm really sorry, I wanted to talk to you about it, but you were on assignment, and you know how the media is—"

"Oh no, of course not." She tapped him on the arm, and he got a whiff of her hairspray again. "I know Shanda was behind it. Probably has everybody followed and releases any picture that looks remotely like someone might be getting it on with someone else. Anyway, we're used to that sort of thing in this business, right? In a few days, everyone will forget about it. It's not like one of us is an aide dressed as Jesus or something, right?"

"Right." He shook his head. "That's one they won't forget any time soon."

"Anyway, that's not what I wanted to talk to you about." She leaned closer to him. "This is probably going to make for another picture that hits social media, but I don't care. I have a big lead, and I need to talk to you about it."

"Not more hacking?" he whispered.

She shook her head, and more hairspray scent wafted his way. "No. Bigger than that. *Much* bigger."

"Crap, where can we go to talk in private?" he asked quietly.

"Nowhere around here. Why don't we meet after the show tonight?"

He nodded. "Okay. You want to go to a restaurant again?"

"Yes, but a different one this time. I'll text you the address."

"Okay."

She got up and headed for the door. "Let's get back to grilling the candidates."

37

THE NEXT ROUND OF questioning was more brutal and gave the candidates less opportunity to give fluff answers. Bryan would grill three candidates while Joanne interviewed the other three.

He didn't waste time with small talk or preamble—the last thing he wanted to do was put these people at ease. "Governor Buckshaw, since you've been in public office, first as a state senator and then as governor, have you ever accepted a bribe?"

The governor's eyes went wide. "Accepted a bribe? Of course not. I would never...." He glanced over at the tablet.

FALSE.

"Are you sure about that, Governor?"

"That machine can't prove anything." Buckshaw folded his arms over his chest. "They're not always accurate, that's why they're not admissible in court."

"So, you're saying again that you have never accepted a bribe since becoming a public official?"

"Yes, that's right, I have not."

FALSE.

"Have you ever agreed to vote a certain way, in exchange for a favor, if not money?"

"No, I would never do that."

FALSE.

Buckshaw dabbed his face with a handkerchief bearing the flag of Texas. "Look, sometimes in a state senate, you agree to vote one way on one thing so that others will vote your way on another issue, but I would *only* do so if I believed it was in the best interest of the people of my state, you have to understand that."

"Is that the only situation in which you've ever let someone influence your vote or another action you might have taken in an official capacity, in exchange for some benefit to you?"

Buckshaw shrugged. His chin wobbled. "Look, in politics, you sometimes have to make deals to get a law passed. Sometimes the benefits to the people outweigh the minor favor you might do for someone. But I never did anything illegal, and I never did any favors that I didn't think were in the best interest of the people of my state."

FALSE.

"You never accepted a bribe, or any kind of favor that only benefited you personally, in exchange for voting a certain way or taking a certain official action?" Bryan pressed.

"No." Buckshaw slammed his fist on the table for emphasis. The table wobbled.

FALSE.

"And that machine is false." He pointed a hand at the polygraph, whirring away. His upper arm wobbled. "Those things are not always accurate, and this is an extremely stressful situation for every one of us candidates. How you can expect that thing to be accurate is beyond me, and I hope the American people understand that."

Bryan moved on to the next cubicle. "Senator Haverty, since becoming a public official, have you ever accepted a bribe?"

Haverty frowned, scratched his head, and appeared to give the matter considerable thought. "Accepted a bribe? No, I can't say that I have."

INCONCLUSIVE.

Bryan studied the senator. He didn't get the impression the guy was lying, exactly, but he was definitely not being fully honest, either. What was similar to accepting a bribe but not... oh.

"Have you ever bribed someone else, or been extorted successfully, Senator?"

The senator's charismatic smile disappeared faster than a campaign promise on Inauguration Day.

"Well, I...." He glanced over at the tablet, shook his head, and stared down at the table. "Yes, I have."

TRUE.

"Under what circumstances?"

"Several years ago, someone got pictures of me and one of my mistresses. I don't know who it was. I never knew. I paid them off, and they didn't ask for any more money—nor did they ask for any favors in a job-related sense." He rubbed a hand across his face. "That's why I publicly named all my mistresses when I decided to run for president. I knew that I had to get ahead of it. I'm not proud of what I did, but it was a personal matter and it didn't affect my work, other than allowing me to continue to do my job for the great people of my state."

INCONCLUSIVE.

"Was that the only time?" Bryan pressed.

Haverty sighed. "My wife threatened to tell the world about my affairs if I didn't buy her a winter home in Florida. I think she has a boyfriend there. We now have an understanding, and again, since I publicly named all my mistresses already, that is no longer an issue."

TRUE.

Bryan waited a few seconds, carefully constructing his next question. "At any point since you became a senator, have you been extorted or pressured in any way to vote a certain way, or use your position as senator to make something happen for someone else?"

Haverty stared into space for a moment, apparently trying to remember. "Honestly, no. I really can't say that I have."

TRUE.

"I find it hard to believe no one else in Senate found out about your many affairs and tried to blackmail you with that information," Bryan said.

Haverty burst out laughing. "Well, you don't understand how Congress works, son. Sure, other people knew. Some of them were my enemies and could have had a field day. But the thing is, I know how to play this game too, and I made sure to have just as much dirty laundry on all of them. Mutually assured destruction, you see."

TRUE.

Bryan's next and last victim was Ronald Chump, who couldn't remember if he'd ever accepted a bribe in his long and illustrious career.

INCONCLUSIVE the tablet blinked.

Bryan frowned. "How do you not remember if you've ever accepted a bribe or offered a bribe or not, Mr. Chump?"

The trillionaire shrugged. "I've had a long and illustrious career in business. I don't remember every deal, every agreement. Sometimes you don't know what you agreed to until after you did it, you know?"

INCONCLUSIVE.

"Are you saying you might have accepted a bribe?"

Chump cleared his throat. "I'm saying this country has bigger problems than anything I might have done to make a deal go through so thousands of people could keep their jobs."

FALSE.

"What kind of bribe did you accept or give to make a deal go through, Mr. Chump?"

Chump shrugged. "You don't understand business, kid. In other countries, sometimes bribery is the only way to get things done. The entire government is corrupt. You don't bribe, you don't build a factory there, you understand?"

"So you bribed some foreign officials so you could build a factory in another country and provide jobs there, instead of here in the US?"

"I tried to bribe—er, I mean, lobby—Congress to make the laws easier on companies here, but they just took the money and kept passing legislation to hurt large corporations like mine." Chump stared directly into his camera. "That's why I need to be president, so I can make America safe for capitalism again. I promise I'll get rid of all those restrictive laws about forty-hour work-weeks and overtime pay and safe working conditions for sensitive whiners. I'll make it possible to build in this country, without having to bribe anyone."

TRUE.

"Thank you, Mr. Chump."

38

JOANNE'S CANDIDATES WERE SOMEWHAT less interesting when asked the bribery question. Greenforest said no, and the polygraph blinked *TRUE*. Sara Finnegan declared she'd never accepted or given a bribe, and her tablet flashed *FALSE,* which she claimed was also false. Harper's polygraph was inconclusive, which people on social media took to mean she was an especially gifted liar, but not quite good enough to fool the machine.

The correspondents helped with most of *Aftermath*, providing background pieces on the candidates. At the end, Bryan announced Sara Finnegan had been eliminated. She blamed unfair tax laws for making her former company, and thus herself, look bad, but thanked her supporters and promised to return in four years. Because Kevin had left voluntarily, only one person was eliminated.

After several hours of handshaking and thanking women who threw their panties at him without giving the impression he wanted to sleep with them—that was harder than any tap-dancing a politician had to do, he was sure of it—Bryan managed to escape and told his limo driver to take the long way to the address Joanne gave him.

It wasn't hard to figure out why she thought the restaurant would be private. It was run-down, with a hanging gutter and a neon sign blinking *God Foo* because some of the letters were out and hadn't been replaced. Across the street, a dumpy motel offered hourly rates. Bryan told the driver to tool around the neighborhood and come back when he texted. He didn't want to draw attention to himself here.

Surprisingly, the place looked a little better inside. There were plants all over the place, some with long green leaves dripping onto the tables. He didn't see any bugs or rats though, and everything appeared clean.

Joanne sat at a table in a corner, below an ancient stained-glass windowpane and a hanging flower pot that appeared to be weeping flowers onto the table.

He sat across from her and leaned over the checkered tablecloth. "I guess you're right. No one's going to look for us here."

She winked as the waiter appeared. He did a double take when he saw Bryan, but quickly pulled his face into something resembling professionalism and looked away. "What can I get you tonight?"

Since she'd been here before, Bryan looked at Joanne. "What's good here?"

"I like the spaghetti, with lots of garlic bread."

"I guess I'll have the same," he said.

The waiter nodded, took their menus, and drifted off, sneaking one last glance at Bryan.

"Do you think he's going to take our picture and tweet it?" he asked Joanne.

She shrugged. "Probably not. I think he knows who I am, but he's never nabbed a picture of me. Anyway, at least there aren't any ceiling cameras here, and no one will overhear our conversation."

"So what's this big lead you wanted to tell me about? Which contestant is it about?"

She leaned over the table. "It's not about a contestant. Think bigger."

He wracked his brain. "The current president?"

"Who has more power than the president?"

"Uh...." He had no idea. "The First Lady?"

"That's not what I mean either. I'm talking about Congress."

"Of course." He leaned in closer, smelling the hairspray again. It was too bad they couldn't sit close together here, like they did at that swanky Beverly Hills restaurant. "Uh, which Congressperson does it involve?"

"All of them."

"All of them are... doing what?"

The waiter reappeared with their food, and they both leaned back as he set the steaming dishes down. To Bryan's surprise, the food smelled wonderful, and tasted even better, although the sight of all that tomato sauce reminded him of the ketchup disaster at the fast food restaurant. Fortunately there were no other patrons, so the possibility of a tomato grenade from a five-year-old wasn't something he had to worry about.

As soon as the waiter had disappeared back into the kitchen, Bryan leaned over again, steam from the plate of noodles melting what was left of his makeup.

"Well, what's Congress doing?"

Joanne slid her plate to the side so she could prop her elbows on the table and lean forward. "There's a rumor that Foster and Willard are stirring something up now that they're back with the rest of Congress."

"What are they stirring up?"

"The rumor says they're going to wait until after the finale next week, when we name the new president, and then...." She paused, looked around the restaurant to be sure no one was nearby, then said in a stage whisper, "They're going to try to repeal the By the People, For the People Act and declare the new presidency unconstitutional."

He grabbed a napkin and dabbed sweat off his forehead. "Can they do that?"

"I questioned a few legal experts—very quietly—today, and they all said the same thing. If Congress passes an amendment, they can repeal it with another amendment if they have the votes, like with Prohibition. As for whether they could apply those changes to someone who had just been elected—that's more of a gray area, and would probably wind up in court for a while."

"Jesus. Another Bush and Gore situation." Bryan shook his head. "Not what the country needs right now, and a disaster for anyone who wants our government to actually be directed by the people, and not special interest groups or SuperPACs."

"Exactly."

"Are they going to do it only if a certain person wins?"

"That I don't know. There are different versions of the rumor. I think the worst scenario would be the one where a real person like Clarice Greenforest wins, instead of a career politician. But they might still do it if Buckshaw or Harper gets in. Probably depends how hated the person is in Washington. Or it may be that so many people hate the process and want to go back to how things were that they'll try to oust anyone."

"And your source is someone reliable?"

She nodded. "I've known him a long time."

She smiled a little when she said it, and Bryan got the distinct impression she knew the guy very well. "Is this a tip from... someone you're seeing?"

"Of course not," she said so fast he knew she was lying.

"It is, isn't it? I mean, I know it's none of my business, but it kind of affects the future of the country, so...."

She shook her head and looked up at the hanging plant. "We had a thing a few years ago, but we've just been friends ever since. It was just a fling, nothing serious."

"Who is he?"

"I can't tell you that."

"You don't trust me?"

She met his gaze again. "I remember you telling an entire newsroom full of people about my sex life."

"I'm sorry." He reached for her hand. She reluctantly let him take it. "I mean it. I've wanted to apologize for years."

"Then why didn't you? My personal email is the same. I'm on every social network there is, why didn't you ever send me a message?"

He sighed. "Mostly because I was embarrassed. And the reason I did it... I was exhausted from not sleeping and fed up with Cliff and I really wanted to hurt him, not you. If I hadn't been so sleep-deprived, it might have occurred to me to leave your name out of it, but I didn't, and for that I'm really sorry."

Her lips curved upward. "If it hadn't been so humiliating to me at the time,

I probably would have found it funny. Cliff was such a womanizer. He really did have it coming."

Bryan leaned back, relieved. "Seriously. To be honest, I always thought you were too good for him."

"And you were right." She picked up her fork and twirled spaghetti around it. "It didn't take me long to figure it out. We weren't together for very long after you left. He dumped me for some college intern named Tina who misspelled half the copy she wrote."

Bryan shook his head. "I wonder what ever happened to him? He's probably still bouncing from station to station every few years."

"Last I heard, he was getting married and moving to Indonesia with his new wife to teach English."

"What?" Bryan almost choked on his noodles. "He got married?"

"Yeah, a friend of mine is friends with him and I saw her comment on the post, congratulating him. Apparently he finally found the woman who made him want to settle down. For now, anyway. I give it six months." She took a bite, chewed, and swallowed. "Well, reminiscing is fun, but what are we going to do about the show if, you know, the rumor turns out to be true?"

"The show will be over by then, but I hate to think of it all being for nothing." Bryan stuffed some spaghetti in his mouth, chewed, and thought about it. "What I've heard from people, through this whole contest, is how much big businesses and special interests are controlling Congress—and our laws. It doesn't seem to matter if we elect Republicans or Democrats, they're all being bought. This new election process was a chance to start taking back control, if only in a small way. I thought the hope was that Congress would eventually be elected like this, too. If they repeal By the People, For the People, that would be a step backward for everyone."

She drummed her fingernails on the tablecloth. "I know. The Electoral College just voted how the big money wanted them to vote. But what can we do?"

"I don't know. Seriously. We're not politicians. I don't know if there's anything we *can* do."

"I'll let you know if I hear anything else."

"Okay." He stared at the neon light filtering through the stained glass. "Maybe we can think of something."

39

THE NEXT DAY'S INTERROGATIONS started with Bryan addressing a variety of concerns that had been tossed around on social media overnight and earlier that morning.

"I understand some of you feel the polygraph is inhumane," he read off the prompter as he stood in the hallway of cubicles. "I'd like to remind you the candidates are free to refuse if they don't want to continue in the competition. Also, we felt it was necessary to point out many of the proposed suggestions with the most likes and shares actually were rejected because they were too harsh."

He turned to the green screen behind him, and glanced at the TV off to the side. Shanda popped up one of the most popular suggestions from the previous night. "Bert in Philadelphia suggested if the polygraph suggests deception, we should proceed to waterboard that candidate until we get the truth out of him or her. Millions of people liked, shared, and retweeted this idea.

"Yes, it's true, this show is here to give you a government By the People, For the People, but we have *laws* in this country. The Eighth Amendment, for example, which prohibits cruel and unusual punishment, although none of our candidates are prisoners or criminals... that we know of. Anyway, our insurance company would never let us waterboard anyone, and we're renting this building, so if we get water stains on the floor we'll never get our deposit back.

"I've also been asked to remind you the candidates are given frequent breaks to eat, use the restroom, or check how they're trending on social media. Now that we've cleared that up, let's continue with the interviews. First I'll ask some more general queries of all the candidates, then we're going to have live Skype sessions with some viewers whose questions were selected based on popularity. Each of those viewers will interview a particular candidate."

The first question for all contestants was, "What is your worst quality?"

"I don't have one," Ronald Chump said without hesitation.

TRUE, the tablet confirmed.

"Okay, which is the least of all your fabulous qualities?" Bryan no longer cared how sarcastic he sounded. The guy was clearly a narcissist, and what he really needed was a room in a mental hospital, not one at 1600 Pennsylvania.

Chump's brow furrowed in deep concentration. "That's a tough one, young man. I really don't know."

"Well, you're going to have to pick one."

Chump stroked his chin, smoothed the thing on his head that was supposed to be hair, and finally nodded. "I'd have to say it's that I'm generous to a fault."

TRUE.

Bryan had to bite the inside of his cheek to keep from laughing. "Can you elaborate on that?"

Chump nodded, chin tilted up in its usual pose. "Yes. I'm one of the richest men in the world, and I could do anything. But I choose to spend my time getting elected so I can make this country a better place."

INCONCLUSIVE.

"Are you sure making our country a better place is your only motivation?"

"Absolutely."

FALSE.

Chump frowned at the tablet. "That thing is wrong. Now listen to me, I am what's best for America!"

TRUE.

"Okay, the polygraph believes you're telling the truth about that. But is doing what's best for America the *only* reason you want to be president?" Bryan pressed.

"Yes, it is."

FALSE.

"These tests are crap." Chump folded his arms. "After I'm elected, I'm going to send them all to Mexico with my bill for the moat."

Ronda Harper said her worst quality was "getting too wrapped up in the issues and forgetting about the people," although she added she only cared about the issues in the first place because she cared so *much* about the American people.

"I've learned to remind myself constantly of why I'm doing this," she said. "I want to help every American, rich or poor, to pursue the life that will make him or her happy."

INCONCLUSIVE.

"Are there other reasons you want to be president?"

"There are a lot of things I want to improve, Bryan. But they're all important to me because they involve enriching the lives of my fellow Americans."

FALSE.

"And you're sure there are no personal reasons you want to be president?"

"Well, I confess I would feel deep personal fulfillment if I was able to change lives for the better."

FALSE.

Bryan gritted his teeth and continued to grin. How did people watch this crap and not throw their TVs out the window? "And that's the only personal reason you have?"

"Yes."

FALSE.

"Thank you, Congresswoman."

"My biggest flaw is having such a big heart and caring too much," Haverty said, his expression serious. "That's why I've had so many mistresses. I really loved all of them."

FALSE.

"Okay, some of them."

INCONCLUSIVE.

"My biggest flaw is working so hard for the people of my state—and this whole country—that I sometimes forget to take care of myself," Buckshaw said. "But don't worry, when I'm elected president, I'll make my health a priority, so I can accomplish all the great things I want to do for this country. For that reason, I'm going to brief the press from a treadmill, too."

FALSE.

"Well, not every day, but definitely my first press briefing."

TRUE.

"My biggest flaw is I sometimes doubt myself," Greenforest said, without consideration. "I know I have good solutions for this country, and I know I could do a better job than these rich, entitled, stuffed suits I'm going up against, but sometimes I don't know if I can do it, you know? I don't know if I can beat five other people who are so rich and powerful. Even if I do, I'm not sure I can ever get my legislation through Congress, which is controlled by *more* rich and powerful people. I'm not perfect and I can't promise I'll accomplish everything I set out to do, but I can promise no one will work harder to help the average person than me, because I *am* an average person."

TRUE.

40

THE FIRST QUESTION FROM the Skype session went to Ronald Chump. Their guest interviewer was named Charleen, a Millennial with unicorn hair who looked like she wanted to jump through her webcam and choke Chump.

Bryan understood how she felt.

"Mr. Chump, I want you to tell me why you think you'll be successful as president. You might have one successful business now, but most of your investments have ended in failure. The only reason you were able to start Chump Enterprises is because you had a huge trust fund—"

"It was only ten million dollars, that's all."

TRUE.

"But Chump Winery failed, Chump Condoms failed, Chump Pizza failed, Chump Lingerie failed, Chump Cruise Line failed. One out of six is hardly a good success rate, and many of your secondary divisions of Chump Enterprises have also failed. You've gone bankrupt multiple times. How can you say that track record is what the American people need?"

"Now let me tell you something, it's not about whether you win or lose, it's about whether your name means something in business." Chump pointed a finger at the monitor that showed Charleen. Her eyebrows pulled together, making her look like the angriest unicorn in history.

"You know why people invested in all those businesses?" the businessman continued. "Because the name Chump means something, and everyone who hears it thinks success because of the empire I've built, with only the measly ten million in my trust fund. Win or lose, people associate the name Chump with success, and I will lend that to America—at no charge, I will lend that powerful name to this country. Other nations will see us and think, 'We can't mess with America, they are the most successful country in the world.' Then they'll buy our stuff and our economy will get better."

INCONCLUSIVE.

"Some of the people you mentioned investing in those failed companies lost a lot of money which they were in less of a position to recover from than you," Charleen said. *"Are you saying you tricked them into investing by convincing them the project would be more successful than it was?"*

"Of course not. I wanted the projects to succeed, too."

INCONCLUSIVE.

"But did you know there was a better chance of failure than you let on? Did you conceal things that affected the possibility of success from your investors?"

"Of course not."

FALSE.

"So you're saying that attaching the Chump name to a project makes people think it will be successful," Bryan reiterated.

"That's right."

TRUE.

"But if so many of those projects you lent your name failed, can't our economy fail, too?"

"Not with me at the helm."

TRUE.

Charlie from Maryland, a middle-aged guy in a football jersey stained with what appeared to be nacho sauce, wanted to quiz Greenforest about her standing on the issues. *"You say you're independent, but we haven't heard years of your rhetoric like we have the other candidates, so I want to know how you feel about some issues."*

"Great, ask away," she said.

"Taxes—higher, lower, what do you want to do?"

"I believe large corporations should be taxed more. Giving them tax breaks is theoretically supposed to help create more jobs, but unless we find a way to ensure that happens, it really just gives the CEO a bigger paycheck," she said. "The average person, on the other hand, the person who makes less than six figures a year, should be allowed to keep more of his or her own money."

TRUE.

"Do you think we should spend more on social welfare programs?"

"We could do that, but I don't think they've ever helped anyone get out of poverty. Our money would be better spent improving our educational system, and providing more federal aid for students who want to go to college—but I'm not talking about loans with high interest rates that a recipient has to spend ten years paying back after graduating. I'm talking about more federal grants. Currently, the Pell Grant tops out at less than six thousand dollars for students with the highest level of need. The average state school costs more than thirty thousand dollars a year, and those universities receive federal funding. What if we reduced funding for the universities and gave that money to the students instead, so they could pay the ridiculously inflated costs the schools demand?"

TRUE.

"Couldn't that mean lower quality education?" Bryan agreed with her, but his job was to poke holes in all the candidates' plans.

"That's why we need more control over what public universities spend," she said. "If they're receiving any federal funding at all, they don't need to pay their professors forty thousand a year and their football coach four million."

Charlie nodded and took a sip from a beer can, apparently oblivious to the fact that he was on national TV with Cheetos dust smeared on his chin. *"How do you feel about abortion?"*

"I'd like for there to be as few abortions as possible, and for that reason I would never support any legislation to defund Planned Parenthood," she said. "In fact, I would support increasing its funding, making it easier for women to get safe, effective, affordable contraception. I also wouldn't support any legislation allowing employers to dodge paying for contraceptive coverage on employee health plans, and I would support funding only comprehensive sex ed programs in schools."

TRUE.

"And how do you plan to keep our jobs here, instead of overseas?" Charlie stuffed a handful of chips in his mouth, apparently expecting a lengthy answer while he chewed.

"There should be penalties for companies that produce products overseas. If they pay higher taxes, it will be less profitable to do so."

TRUE.

"So you're not in favor of doing away with labor laws, like your opponent Mr. Chump?" Bryan struggled to say it with a straight face.

She gave him the look she probably saved for students who claimed the dog ate their homework. "Of course not. We have that pesky Eighth Amendment, remember?"

Ronda Harper was interviewed by an older man in a plaid shirt named Bart. *"I want to know why you claim to help the poor, but spend all your time and effort in Congress helping big businesses instead?"*

"Well, that's not entirely true," Harper said. "I may have voted for legislation to help companies create more jobs, but I also voted for health care laws that require businesses to provide coverage for employees, so low-income workers can access less expensive health care."

INCONCLUSIVE.

Bart shook his head and sneered at her. *"You think that helped people like me? My company cut my hours back to part-time so they wouldn't have to give me benefits. I still have to pay a lot of money for insurance, and I'm making less of it now. You actually made my situation worse."*

"I'm sorry to hear that, Bart. When I'm elected president, I will propose a bill that would require companies to provide part-time workers with mandatory coverage, as well."

FALSE.

Harper's eyes flickered to the tablet, and a look of panic almost crossed her face, but she quickly turned it into a smile instead.

"What I mean is, I will consider if such a bill is feasible. If no one in Congress will vote for it, I might have to wait for a more opportune time."

INCONCLUSIVE.

"So then they just fire a bunch of us, and make everyone else work twice as hard or they get fired, too? You really don't get it, do you?" Spit flew out of Bart's mouth through the hole where one of his front teeth used to be. *"Nobody—not the Democrats like you, and not them Republicans, neither—is holding big corporations responsible, and you never will. I'm voting for Clarice Greenforest, because she's the only candidate who seems to recognize that."*

"You know, I've noticed that a lot of people complain about large corporations, but in the same breath say they don't want more health care legislation or a redistribution of wealth because it's too much like socialism," Harper said. "But the truth is, if you don't like socialism, you should stop complaining about big businesses and the things they do to stay afloat. I will try to make workplaces better for everyone when I'm elected, and after ten years in Congress, I'm in a much better position to do so than someone who's never held a public office before."

TRUE.

Buckshaw was interviewed by a younger guy named Nathan in a beer company t-shirt and sunglasses, who apparently thought being on national TV was "way cool."

"I want to say hi to my friends, Billy and Morgan and my super-awesome girlfriend Heidi, I mean she's not my girlfriend yet, but I'm hoping she'll—"

"I'm afraid we have limited time," Bryan interrupted. "Please get to your question for Governor Buckshaw."

"Right, right." Nathan nodded. *"Listen man, I've heard you talk about unemployment, and that's not right, man. How can you be so out of touch you think someone who's working three minimum-wage jobs just to barely scrape by*

is hogging all the jobs? Hasn't it occurred to you that if the minimum wage was higher, a person might be able to get by with one job? Do you think anyone likes working eighty hours a week? I have two jobs, and I'm still taking out loans to pay for school, and I'm going to be paying 'em back until I'm forty, man. I mean, I might as well be dead once I'm that old."

Buckshaw gave Nathan a paternal smile. "I'm sure you'll change your mind about that when you get a little closer to forty, my friend. But in answer to your question, I don't think raising the minimum wage would help. Companies would only charge higher prices, and you'd be right back in the same boat. You'd be better off staying in school and finishing your education."

"What if I can't get a job when I graduate?" Nathan shook his head. *"I'm terrified I'm going to be working minimum wage jobs for the rest of my life, plus paying off student loans. You don't have a solid plan for addressing that, so I'm not voting for you."*

"Of course I have a plan to create jobs," Buckshaw said. "I'm going to provide incentives for companies that register with the national job bank I'm going to create, so unemployed workers can find employment."

"But most of those are minimum-wage, unskilled jobs. That doesn't help people like my brother who have two college degrees and ask people if they want fries all day."

Buckshaw nodded. "But once more people have jobs, even a minimum wage one, more people will be able to spend money and that will allow companies to create more complex, higher paying jobs."

"Man, you're so out of touch, it's ridic." The Skype connection ended.

Linda from New York had a Bronx accent, a smoker's raspy voice, and a few questions for Haverty. *"I want to know more about your health care plan. If I go to the lady doctor, does that count?"*

Haverty cleared his throat. "Well—I'm sure regular yearly exams wouldn't count against you, no. We wouldn't want people to avoid regular preventative care, would we?"

"Well, what if I hurt myself running on the treadmill, huh? What about that? Will I still get my five percent back? Will I have to start over in three months?"

"I haven't hammered out all the details of the plan, but I'm sure that most healthy people would benefit—"

"What about if I don't go to the doctor, y'know, but I call the doctor and have him call in a prescription for something I've taken before? Like, I got this chronic constipation, and sometimes when the over-the-counter crap doesn't work, y'know, I call my doctor and he prescribes this prescription stuff, that really opens the floodgates, y'know?"

Haverty looked like he wanted to slip between the couch cushions and hide. "Like I said, I'm still working out the details of my plan, but I will definitely take your suggestions into account. Thanks so much for calling, Linda."

But Linda wasn't done yet. *"How about my boyfriend's Viagra? Does that count against his five percent discount?"*

Haverty's face turned redder than Buckshaw's after it was pelted with ketchup packets at the fast food restaurant. "I'm sure long-standing prescriptions wouldn't be an issue, thank you so much—"

"No, keep this one going," Shanda shrieked in Bryan's ear. *"This is great stuff."*

"I think we have enough time for another question or two." Bryan hoped he didn't look too happy when he said it.

Linda stuck a cigarette in her mouth and lit it.

"What about vitamins, do I get extra credit for taking those?" she asked around the cigarette.

"Uh... possibly, but, ah, I think you'd lose points for smoking," Haverty said. "However, my plan will allow smoking cessation programs for six months."

"Well, you just want to tell us poor people what to do, don't you?" She sneered at Haverty. *"Some Democrat you are. You just want a nanny state, telling people what to do with their bodies."*

"Now, I didn't say—"

"How about you, Senator? With all those mistresses, you must be at high risk for STDs. Will you be losing any points for that?"

Haverty cleared his throat. "I haven't hammered out all the details yet, but the plan is based on both risk factors and actual claims, so it is possible you could continue to smoke but receive a discount, it's just unlikely. Also, I'd like to point out that I practice safe sex, and sexual activity is considered a cardio workout."

Linda took a drag of her cigarette and narrowed her eyes at him. *"Wanna work out with me? Maybe you can add me to your stable of mistresses."*

Haverty's face turned a deeper shade of red. "I'm flattered, but, ah, my schedule is a bit full right now."

41

*A*FTERMATH **CONSISTED MOSTLY OF** the correspondents analyzing pieces of video on the contestants. Joanne interviewed a psychiatrist about Chump's intense interest in having his face on the hundred-dollar bill. The shrink said she couldn't diagnose Chump without meeting him personally, but obsessive self-interest was rarely a good thing in anyone.

Barnaby interviewed three of Haverty's mistresses and shamelessly hit on them. One got offended and told him to go back to the strip club where men of his character belonged.

Valencia spent most of her time analyzing what she thought of as the candidates' poor fashion choices. "I mean, seriously, does Ronda Harper ever wear anything but a pantsuit? And that Buckshaw guy needs to learn to dress for his shape."

Jeremy asked an economist about Buckshaw's plan to fix unemployment.

"He's suggesting we should mask the real unemployment numbers by creating low-paying jobs that will soon be replaced by machines." The economist ran a hand down his face and blinked at the camera. "I mean... some fast food places already have automated ordering stations. Five years from now, even those jobs will be gone. This plan is a disaster."

At the end of the show, Bryan waited out the usual drumroll and announced the loser of the night—Senator Haverty.

"I guess the American people just aren't ready to get fit and healthy." The senator shook his head. "People are thrilled about getting money back until you tell them they have to work for it."

After finally escaping the crowd of people, Bryan and Joanne went back to the God Foo restaurant. While they waited for their food, they both scanned social media for show mentions.

The next time we have these people hooked up to polygraphs, I want to know how much money Chump spends on his fake-ass hair. I bet it's more than the entire country spends on welfare and food stamps in a year.
#takeChumptotheDump

I know Greenforest has zero experience in politics, but that's why she's a much better candidate than all these people who have been lying to the American people, screwing us over, or paying off Congress for years.
#realpeople #firetheprofessionals #greenforestforpresident

I can't believe Haverty was voted off. At least he had a plan to lower our insanely high health care costs. What's Harper going to do about health care, force people to pay out-of-pocket when they get third-degree coffee burns while she's blathering about what a great philanthropist she is?
#Havertywasreal #HookersforHaverty

Bryan gave up on social media when the food arrived, and was glad the restaurant was deserted. With his luck, some idiot with a cell phone would get a picture of American President's host slurping spaghetti like the uncouth, small-town reporter he really was before this bizarre show happened.

"There's definitely a movement in Congress, and it looks like it's going to happen no matter who wins. A lot of people there are pissed off." Joanne paused to take a bite. "Haverty is going to be their next supporter, of course. But people on both sides of the aisle are mad. I mean, look at the top four. Ronald Chump? The guy wants to get rid of labor laws, bring sweatshops to America, and build a moat along the Mexican-American border. And he's outlasted Congresspeople who have been building toward this race for *decades*. There's not one person in Congress who doesn't hate the new system."

Suddenly all the amusement he'd been holding in all day resurfaced, and Bryan found himself laughing so hard tears came to his eyes.

"What's so damn funny?" Joanne looked around the room to see if anyone was watching.

Wiping his eyes, Bryan did the same, but the room was as devoid of people as it had been the night before. "I was just thinking…" Another fit of laughter overcame him. "This is the first truly bipartisan effort Congress has ever joined together on."

She snickered. "I hadn't thought of that."

"And all those people we sent back to Congress got beaten by a narcissistic rich guy, an out-of-touch governor who thinks broke people who work three jobs to get by are hogging all the good positions, a teacher from Ohio, and a Congresswoman who promises to help the poor and instead helps rich people get richer."

"You're right." She picked up a napkin and dabbed her mouth. "They're mad at the whole thing, but Drew says they'll be especially pissed if it's Greenforest or Chump."

"Drew?" Bryan stopped, fork halfway to his mouth. "Drew Morton? That's your ex-boyfriend?"

The smile vanished from her face. "What? No. Of course not."

"Oh my god, it *is* him." Bryan sat back, shocked.

"No, no, it's not, and I told you, my… source and me, that was such a long time ago."

Bryan yanked out his phone and googled Congressman Drew.

"There's only one current congressman whose first or last name is Drew." He pushed the phone back in his pocket, unsure why he felt so angry. It wasn't because Drew was so good-looking female fans called him Drew Drop-your-panties, even though he was supposedly happily married. It wasn't because Joanne dated him after she stopped not-dating Bryan. It wasn't because she might even still be seeing him.

It was because of all those things, and the fact she never seemed to see Bryan as anything but a friend.

The prick of long fingernails startled him back to the present, and he realized Joanne had grabbed his hand.

"Bryan, please, you can't say anything. Drew is a good guy, and I think he could be—*should* be—president one day, if he stays in Congress another four years. He and his wife—it's mostly just an arrangement for appearances, at this point. They both see other people privately."

"And you? Are you still seeing him? Is that why you're so concerned for his future in politics?"

She shook her head, springy curls bouncing everywhere. "No, I told you we had a brief fling, but it ended a long time ago. Now we're just friends who talk about the craziness of Washington, that's it. And it's not just *his* career I'm worried about."

He frowned. "What do you mean?"

She gave him her best *are-you-stupid* look. "Bryan. Think about it. If it ever gets out that I was sleeping with a source, my career is over. People will say I can't do my job without screwing a powerful man. I'll never get a source to trust me again, because no one will ever forget that I had a relationship with Drew and leaked the biggest bipartisan move in history, even if it was years later. I won't be remembered for breaking the story. I'll be remembered for having sex with a congressman. Please, you can't tell anyone."

Bryan nodded. "I understand."

And he did. What she said made sense, every bit of it. Joanne might not feel the same way about him that he felt about her, and her interest in guys like Cliff and Drew pissed him off, but he could never ruin her career.

Even if a little voice in the back of his head told him it might save his.

42

WITH ALL THE TALK about press briefings from treadmills, the voting public wanted to see all of you complete the next challenge while walking briskly on a treadmill," Bryan explained after the show began the next night. "The candidates have been told to wear appropriate clothing for exercise."

He walked across the stage and joined the four remaining contestants on the couches. Clarice Greenforest wore a blue tracksuit and a ponytail. Ronda Harper was decked out in sweatpants—it was the first time Bryan had seen her in anything but a pantsuit—and a lightweight sport jacket. Ronald Chump looked like a caricature from a bad nineties movie, with a gold sweatband holding back his mountain of hair, a tank top with a designer logo on the front, and baggy nylon pants. Buckshaw, for reasons known only to him and his stylist, wore baggy shorts under an even baggier t-shirt.

"Well, you've been hooked up to a polygraph, worked with a bulldozer" —Bryan gestured at Chump— "in a coffee shop" —he nodded at Harper— "and a fast food restaurant." He looked at Buckshaw. "And of course taught in a school. Do you think you all can handle a challenge by treadmill?"

"I can handle any challenge," Chump said.

"I teach PE two days a week," Greenforest said.

"I like to walk and talk with my supporters," Harper added.

"I promised yesterday I would get physically fit." Buckshaw flexed what he apparently thought was a pec. There might have been a muscle there, but it was lost in the jiggling flab.

Bryan led the way off the stage—security kept the audience from swarming around them—and back downstairs to the room where they had done the polygraph segment. The cubicles and desks had been cleared out and replaced with workout equipment. Four treadmills sat in the center of the room, with weight sets along one wall, a boxing ring in one corner, and a volleyball court on the left side of the room.

"First, we're going to warm up on the treadmills." Bryan gestured to the center of the room, and the candidates all climbed onto the machines. "We've pre-programmed these treadmills to give you all a variable workout, with sprints thrown in randomly to help you get in better shape. Now, as you're working out, I'm going to throw some random questions at you. Are you ready?"

The contestants nodded.

"Then you may all hit the start button now. This isn't a race, and you'll start out slowly before the *workout* throws you any curveballs, okay?"

Ronda nodded eagerly, swinging her arms like she was jogging even though her machine was barely moving. Clarice nodded, plodding along without difficulty. Ronald Chump started waving at the TV cameras like they were actual adoring fans as he walked.

Buckshaw hung onto the treadmill rails and nodded, already out of breath.

"Okay, first question." Bryan moved to the end of the row, where Clarice stood. Next to her was Ronda, to her right was Buckshaw, and Chump was at the other end. "The United States has been attacked by terrorists, plunging our country into an economic tailspin like the one that happened after 9/11. Remember that the economy was much better before 9/11 than it is today. What do you do to prevent a depression? Clarice?"

She nodded. "Aside from finding the masterminds of the attack and bringing them to justice—and not getting sidetracked with unrelated conflicts along the way—I'd devote funding to improving our security agencies, like the NSA, the FBI, and the CIA, and expand our counterterrorism units. I'd also invest in any type of technology that could make us safer and start a task force to study all previous terrorist attacks and figure out how they could have been stopped."

"Congresswoman Harper, what would you do?" Bryan asked.

"I'd start a PR campaign to help Americans learn to be more sensitive to other people's feelings and differences, so no one would feel the need to engage in terrorism and other violent attacks." She paused as the treadmill sped up and she had to *really* jog for a moment. "So many violent attacks in this world could be stopped if we all thought about the effects of our words, *Bryan*. But it's also important to keep terrorists from buying guns, so I'd propose a bill to tighten gun control as well, making it harder for terrorists to obtain weapons."

"You don't even know what kind of a terrorist attack it was," Clarice said. "What if we were bombed or something? 9/11 didn't involve any guns. How would gun control laws help with that?"

"She just wants to take away all... our... guns," gasped Chump, whose treadmill was forcing him to go at a rapid pace.

"Yes, Mr. Chump, we know you like the Second Amendment." Clarice curled her lip and shot a look at the trillionaire. "You'll keep that intact while you shred the First Amendment. Didn't you say you wanted a joystick to control the internet, turn it on and off at your whim?"

"Those... *comments* were... taken out of context," Chump puffed.

"Governor Buckshaw, what would be your response?" Bryan asked.

"Well, I'd...." Buckshaw gasped for breath as his treadmill sped up for twenty seconds, then slowed to a sedate pace. "I'd... go after... the terrorists. Wherever they are, I'd have them hunted down and brought to justice. Once America... sees that they're safe again... the economy... will improve."

"Mr. Chump, how would you handle the situation?"

"I'd... whoa, I'm speeding up." Chump grabbed the rails, his feet flying on the tread. "I'd bomb the Middle East, immediately!"

Bryan frowned. "All of it, or...?"

"They've been causing us trouble for years, and we've been tolerating it. I say we make a glass parking lot out of any area we think has terrorists. Teach them not to mess with us. Then I'd shut down the borders to keep 'em out."

"How will shutting down the borders help our economy?" Harper asked.

"Well, isn't it obvious?" Chump managed to give her an are-you-stupid look without falling off the machine, no easy feat, Bryan had to admit. "If people can't go to other countries, we'll have to buy more stuff from them, and that will expand trade."

"I don't think I've ever heard anything that illogical, and I teach seven-year-olds," Clarice said.

"I don't believe it. His estimated votes just went up," Shanda muttered in Bryan's ear. "Let's move on to the next exercise."

"All right, you can all get off the treadmills now. I think you're warmed up." Bryan waited as the candidates stopped the tread, patted sweat off their foreheads, and climbed down. Buckshaw panted like a dog standing just out of reach of a bag of treats. "Are we all ready for the next challenge?"

Everyone nodded. Buckshaw leaned on the nearest treadmill for support, but managed to bob his head up and down once. Slowly.

"Great. If you'll follow me over here to the boxing ring, we'll get you suited up for the main event." Bryan walked to the ring, and an assistant slid him a cardboard box of gloves. He opened it and turned to face the contestants. They'd all followed him but stared in horror now.

"You expect us to duke it out for the presidency?" Chump squinted at Bryan.

"This is ridiculous—completely out of bounds—and probably...." Buckshaw sucked in a breath. "Unconstitutional."

"What is this, some sort of modern-day brawn-versus-brains contest?" Clarice asked.

"This is barbaric, and the sort of thing that encourages violence," Harper said.

Bryan ground his teeth together, trying to maintain control. He could get out of here and get a real job, but he wouldn't. He didn't want to throw Joanne under the bus. Which just proved that he was almost as dumb as the average American voter.

"Your speech is on the prompter," Shanda reminded him, but he knew what he was supposed to say.

"One of you people is going to be the next commander-in-chief of our military," he said. "At some point, you will probably have to authorize the use of deadly force. You can't handle swiping at each other with gloves on? This is what America wants."

"I'm up for the challenge." Chump grabbed the first pair of gloves from the box and put them on.

Buckshaw nodded. "Me... too."

"Okay then." Clarice grabbed gloves.

Harper shrugged. "Well, I suppose I can do this in the name of winning the presidency and the greater good."

An assistant checked to make sure everyone's safety gear was on securely, then gave Bryan a thumbs-up. Chump was now bare-chested, and it looked like he might actually have hair transplants on his chest, too. Did he go around stealing the heads of troll dolls and gluing them to his chest or something?

Buckshaw opted to keep his tank top on. No one told him to take it off.

"Okay, we don't really have weight classes here, but we tried to match you up with someone close to your size," he explained. "Mr. Chump and Governor Buckshaw will be the first fight, then Ms. Greenforest and Congresswoman Harper."

Chump and Buckshaw were sent to opposite corners, and a referee—Bryan was eternally grateful he didn't have *that* job—reiterated the usual boxing rules.

"There are a couple caveats," Bryan added when the ref was done. "While you're fighting we want you to have a healthy debate about the issues. If one of you gets knocked down, you don't have to get up before we count to ten, you just have to go back to shouting campaign promises. If you fail to do so by the count of ten, we'll declare a TKO and the fight will be over. Understand?"

"Yes." Chump banged his gloves together. "Let's do this so I can make America awesome again."

"I got this." Buckshaw put his hands up.

The ref blew the whistle and the boxing match commenced.

Bryan stood off to the side with Harper and Greenforest. Harper looked mildly amused. Greenforest's eyes flickered around, like she was calculating the best way to win when it was her turn.

Chump came out swinging, but not really hitting much. Despite his size and apparent exhaustion, Buckshaw was fairly nimble on his feet, and easily danced away from Chump's punches.

"I hope your economic recovery plan is better than your boxing."

"I hope I don't knock you out, because an earthquake would put a financial strain on FEMA." Chump swung with his left fist, missed, then tried a sucker punch with his right.

"Oh, good idea, punching me in the stomach." Buckshaw dodged another shot and aimed one at Chump, barely grazing his shoulder as the businessman ducked away. "You know I have a lot of padding there, right?"

"Yeah, just like you pad your speeches with empty promises about fixing the economy, a job you couldn't even do in your own state." Chump swung again, and managed to land a hit to Buckshaw's shoulder.

The governor winced and danced to the side. Then he pointed at the monitor behind Chump. "Oh my god, did Chump Enterprises' stock really just lose twenty points?"

"What?" Chump turned to look at the monitor, which actually just carried the live show, and Buckshaw took advantage of the other candidate's distraction. He slammed his fist into Chump's jaw, and Chump went flying.

So did his hair.

"I *knew* it was a toupee," Greenforest muttered as the hairpiece sailed through the air and landed....

Right on the lens of the nearest camera, which was tilted up because the photographer was below the ring and trying to get a shot of the flying toupee. She fumbled the hairpiece off, readjusted the shot, then looked down at the wig, as if unsure what to do about it.

"Don't worry about his hair," Shanda said into the IFB. *"This is great television."*

Chump landed flat on his back and blinked up at the ceiling, the self-assured smirk temporarily wiped off his face. The ref ran up and started counting.

"That's all right, you just take it easy." Buckshaw pounded his gloves together, causing his stomach to jiggle. "Now, where was I? Oh, right, my campaign promises. I'm going to fix unemployment...."

"Nine, eight...." The ref displayed the appropriate number of fingers as he counted down.

"I...." Chump tried to sit up, stopped, and flopped back down. "My face hurts. Get me the best plastic surgeon in town."

"Seven, six...."

"That didn't sound like a campaign promise," Buckshaw said.

"Four, three...."

"No, it wasn't," Shanda said in Bryan's ear.

"One."

The ref grabbed Buckshaw's hand and raised it over his head.

"Does this mean I win the presidency?"

"Oh, no." Bryan sidestepped the paramedics rushing to assist Chump. "The audience still has to vote, but I'm sure they were impressed with your sneakiness in winning the fight. Can I have my next team, please?"

The fight between Harper and Greenforest took much longer, because neither of them was an idiot. Both women were fairly cagey and managed to dodge a lot of blows while arguing about who could better help the poor.

"I've been fighting for the lower and middle classes for thirty years." Harper swung at Greenforest, landing a jab to the shoulder.

Greenforest flinched and scooted away, aimed a punch at Harper's mouth. She missed by a hair. "You've been lining your own pockets for years, and you know it."

"You're milking this 'regular person' thing, and it's going to backfire when you get in office and no one respects you," Harper said.

"Well, at least I never made up a story about *my* car being chased off the road, when it was actually a security detail vehicle three cars back."

"They were stopping the paparazzi from chasing me off the road, and I *only* said that my car was in *danger,* which it was."

Greenforest took a jab and connected with Harper's face, but Harper saw it coming and managed to stay on her feet. "I have far more political experience than you ever will, and you'd do well to remember that."

"I know you're a Washington insider, but so does America, and I don't think they want any of you anymore." Greenforest ducked out of the way as Harper took another swing at her.

"I've worked hard to get to this point and no one will take it away from me." Harper slammed a punch into Greenforest's shoulder, distracting her just enough for the Congresswoman to aim her other fist at the teacher's face.

Greenforest hit the deck with a thud, and Harper started shouting about how she was going to tax the rich to help the poor. The ref ran over and started counting, but Greenforest was yelling about fixing education before he got to five.

"This is going nowhere," Shanda grumbled in Bryan's ear as Greenforest got to her feet and took another swing at Harper. *"We'll let them go for another minute, then tell them their time is up."*

43

BRYAN WAS HAPPY THE correspondents had most of the interviews on *Aftermath*, because he couldn't stop thinking about the train wreck that was coming the next night. On the one hand, the idea of America electing Ronald Chump president was horrifying. On the other hand, the idea of a real person like Greenforest—or Kevin or Evan, if he'd scored slightly higher—sounded better than any politician Washington had put up in Bryan's lifetime.

What would happen if he crowned a winner tomorrow, and Congress announced it was repealing By the People, For the People? It wasn't like America had time for another election. One thing was for sure—going back to the old system of cronyism and career politicians running things wasn't in the country's best interest.

At the end of the show, Bryan and the four remaining contestants gathered on the couches, and the National Guard delivered the envelope. After the usual break, during which a large pharmaceutical company pitched an antidepressant that, for some strange reason, caused suicidal thoughts as a side effect, he repeated all the this-is-the-moment bullshit, waited out the drum roll, and ripped open the envelope.

"The person leaving us tonight is... Governor Milton Buckshaw, I'm sorry but your run has come to an end."

Buckshaw's jaw dropped. "I... I... well, I'm disappointed, of course, but I'd like to take the time to thank everyone who supported me, and assure them I'll be back in four years. Also, I'd like to add that I am in talks to star on the next season of *Lose the Lard*, so you viewers may see me sooner than that."

"Thank you, Governor. Let's take a quick look at the most popular social media comments explaining why people didn't vote for you. This one had almost a million likes." Bryan turned and read off the green screen behind him. "'Not only is his unemployment plan hideous, but he also looks like he's probably going to die in office and one of the other three is going to get his job anyway. I'm sorry, but it's the truth. That unemployment plan, though—that needs to die today.'"

Buckshaw folded his hands over his ample stomach, as if trying to hide it. "I did receive a physical before coming on this show, you know, and just yesterday I vowed to lose weight and improve my health. I still intend to do that. In fact, I'll come back in four years, slim and trim and ready to win—and you can help, by voting for me on *Lose the Lard!*"

"Thank you, Governor." Bryan turned back to his tight shot. "Join us tomorrow night for the two-hour finale, after which you'll get to vote for the final time. The person who receives the most votes will be your next American President, the person with the second highest number of votes will be your next vice president, and the person in third place will be secretary of state. This is the episode you can't miss!"

Or the episode you can't watch if you're remotely sane, sober, and intelligent.

44

JOANNE DIDN'T TEXT BRYAN that she wanted to meet at the restaurant after the show, so he figured she was out working on a story. Or sleeping with Drew Drop-Your-Panties Morton. What a creep. That guy would never sit on information that could help his career for Joanne.

But Bryan would, because he was an idiot.

He went straight home and mustered up enough energy to shower before climbing into bed. He had just closed the frosted-glass shower door when the intercom dinged to let him know someone was at the gate.

"Shanda, I'm in the shower, can't we talk about whatever it is in the morning?"

"It's not Shanda, it's me, Joanne. I can't wait until you get out of the shower. Please, it's important, I have to talk to you."

Also because he was an idiot, he jumped out of the shower, grabbed a towel, and buzzed her through the gate. "I'll be down to open the door in a couple minutes."

"No problem. I'll wait."

He rubbed a towel around on his head for a minute, decided it probably wasn't going to do much good, threw on a bathrobe, and went downstairs. After disarming the alarm, he unlocked the massive oak door, pulled it open, and gestured for Joanne to come inside.

"This is a beautiful place." She looked around at the marble floor and staircase, the spacious living room, and the sliding patio doors that led out to his swimming pool and hot tub. "I guess I see why you quit journalism."

He closed the door and reset the alarm. "This was never the goal. I just wanted to make enough money that I didn't have to live with Cliff and two other roommates."

She smiled. "I know. Most of the people I went to school with are still struggling in places like that. Very few journalists ever make it to a national network like NNN."

"But you did." He waved at the living room entrance. "Let's go sit down."

They walked into the large, airy room and sat on the dark couch, chosen for Bryan by a decorator. It faced an abstract painting that looked to him like a mob scene of screaming people. The decorator called it "Modern Gothic Interpretive Wall Art," whatever the hell that was.

"Do you want a drink?"

Joanne shook her head. "No, I came here to talk. I assume this place is very private?"

"My housekeeper checks for bugs every day. The tabloids don't bother me too much, but it never hurts to be careful."

She nodded. "Okay, then. It's happening, Bryan. Drew has whipped enough votes to repeal the amendment, but they're not going to announce until after the show ends tomorrow night. They don't want the new president to be inaugurated."

"Crap. You don't want that to happen, do you?"

"Of course not." She ran a hand through her hair and the hairspray smell hit him. "But I can't leak this story, and neither can you. Please, you have to promise me. I know it would be good for your career, but if it gets out, Drew will know it's me, and he'll tell everyone it's because we had an affair. His career will be ruined at that point, and his wife already knows he cheats and doesn't care. People will forget his indiscretions and he'll come back again in a few years, but no one will ever take me seriously as a reporter again."

"Are you sure he doesn't want you to leak the story?" Bryan tried to concentrate on the problem and not the smell of Joanne and her hairspray. "I mean, why would he tell you?"

"He didn't, really. I might have looked at his phone when he left the room." She glanced away. "I had overheard his conversation and had suspicions."

"Are you still sleeping with him?" He didn't mean for it to sound as bitter as it probably did.

"No, really." She shook her head. "Look, we had a thing, and it was serious—not like with me and Cliff. But he was at a pivotal point in his career and didn't want to leave his wife, and I didn't want that anymore, so I broke it off. But I told him we could still be friends, because I knew how lonely he was."

"Lonely?" Bryan gripped the arm of the sofa so hard his knuckles turned white. "Are you kidding me? The guy has women throw their panties at him on the Capitol steps!"

"Sex partners and people you can talk to aren't the same thing, and I think you know that." She gestured around the room. "How many people can you really talk to?"

"Not many."

"I've never gone through his phone before. I don't know why I did, it was just something about the way he asked me questions about the show the last time we had dinner—I knew something was up. I no longer trusted him, and I was right."

"So he wasn't the guy who gave you the hacker tip?" Bryan asked.

"No, that was a genuine source. Nothing to do with Drew."

"Tell me again why you can't burn this guy who wouldn't leave his wife for you?" Anger and sleep deprivation combined to make Bryan's filter suddenly ineffective. "I've never understood why you went for dopes who didn't appreciate you, Joanne. First Cliff, and now this shmuck."

"He's not a shmuck, and he's not using me," she snapped. "I told you he's just a friend now, but if I break the story, or if you do, he'll know, and we have no proof. They'll call off the whole thing and he'll paint me as a liar. If someone outs him, says it was a real plan, he'll make sure everyone knows we slept together, and he'll probably claim it happened recently."

"What would it take to get proof?" Something tugged at the back of Bryan's brain, something a professor had told him once about the many ways to use a lead....

"I could get the emails off his phone—maybe, big maybe—if he happened to walk out of the room again and leave it. No guarantees." She shook her head. "He'd know it was me though, the minute I announced it, or you did. Not hard to figure out. We might be friends, but I've seen him blow friends out of the water for messing with him and his career goals. The guy wants nothing more than to be president in four years."

"No wonder he doesn't have many friends." Bryan stared at the dark rectangle of his big screen TV. "Do you still have feelings for him?"

"No." She sighed. "I guess maybe once I thought if he left his wife and I was still around... but no, I realize now it isn't going to happen. In fact, I think he's just using me to find out what the media does or doesn't have. And it's really none of your business what I do in my personal life."

"You're right. I was never part of it."

"Because you never wanted to be."

"I—*what?*" He stared at her. "What are you talking about? I wanted to ask you out so many times, but you were always with Cliff."

"Really?" She sat up and leaned closer. "You never said anything."

"Because you were with Cliff."

She rolled her eyes. "So? We were having a good time, I wasn't serious about him. I kind of had a crush on you, but you left while I was still with Cliff, and I didn't think you were interested in me anyway."

"Well, I was. I *am.*" It felt good to finally say it, even if she was just going to reject him again.

"I was hoping you'd say that." She leaned closer and nuzzled his neck. "Let's forget about the show for a while, huh?"

"Yeah...." He turned and kissed her. "Show? What show?"

She giggled and pulled open the robe. "I'd rather throw my panties at you than Drew any day."

"You can throw your panties at me any time you want."

She climbed onto his lap and untied the robe's belt. For a minute, he wondered if maybe he'd fallen asleep in the limo and this was just a really awesome wet dream. If so, please don't let my phone or my alarm or Shanda or anything wake me up until it's over....

Wrapping her legs around his waist, she slipped her hand inside the robe. "You won't tell anyone about the Act being repealed, right? I can trust you?"

"Oh, yeah, baby, whatever you say." His eyes popped open. Wait, what did he just agree to? Well, of course he wouldn't tell anyone, he cared way too much about Joanne, but why did she just ask him that again?

"That's good." She arched her back and flopped back on the couch, tugging him down on top of her with her legs. Not in as good shape as she apparently was, he landed face-down in her cleavage. Maybe not having time to work out was a good thing. "Everyone will know after the election, anyway."

Know about what?

It didn't matter. He could figure it out later.

And he did, as she was putting her clothes back on. "Where are you going? Don't you want to stay the night?"

"I do, but I have an assignment early in the morning, and I can't get ready here. I don't have my clothes or makeup or all my hair stuff."

"Right." That made sense. He knew it did. He knew exactly how much hairspray Joanne used to lug to work every day in a tote bag from Goodwill.

He also knew that bag went with her *everywhere*.

"Did you just sleep with me to get me to be quiet?" That also probably sounded more bitter than it really was.

"What?" She stopped, hand on the boob she was shoving into a bra cup. "Did you really just say that?"

Bryan sat up and yanked his robe back on. Suddenly the room felt cold and forbidding. "I told you I wasn't going to tell anybody before, and I meant it."

"You think that's why I slept with you?" She abandoned the bra for the time being and grabbed a shoe.

Which she threw at him.

"What? I have to wonder about these things." Why was he yelling? He wasn't sure. "You never wanted me before, this whole thing seems like a dream, I'm not Drew Drop-your-panties, Congress is plotting to undo an election, I don't know, I'm having a hard time taking anything at face value right now."

She reached behind her back and hooked the bra without bothering to stuff her boobs into the cups right. One of them oozed over the top like a busted can of biscuits. Probably not something he should mention right now.

"I can't believe you." She stomped over to the couch, grabbed the shoe she tossed, and put it on her foot. "Yeah, you're right, I chased after a lot of guys who weren't really the sticking around kind. Truthfully, I wasn't either. I wanted to focus on my career and not get tied up in someone else's dream and lose sight of mine and spend the rest of my life at a shitty station in Oklahoma with three viewers because that's where my husband is, because I saw that happen to a lot of my friends."

"What made you think I wanted to stay in Nowhereville? Why didn't you even ask me?"

"It's not that I thought you wanted to stay there, it's just that... well, to be perfectly honest, I didn't think you were good enough for national television, okay?" She grabbed her dress, yanked it over her head, and zipped it up. "But now I finally have the job I want at NNN, and I'm tired of the fast talkers and the married guys, and I think something more might be nice. Then I started working with you again, and I remembered how much I liked you. Back in Oklahoma, I liked you so much I didn't want to date you because I was afraid you'd distract me from my goals. That's why I never seemed interested."

Bryan groaned. How did he manage to screw this up so badly? "Joanne, wait, I'm sorry."

His only answer was the sound of the front door slamming.

45

THE NEXT DAY DRAGGED by. He didn't see Joanne, and she didn't answer any of his calls or texts. He spent most of his time doing interviews, pushing the show, talking about how exciting the election process was, and basically shoveling more shit than Joe Foster at the pig farm.

Every time he looked at the clock, he knew the opportunity to act on what he'd learned about Drew Morton's plan was slipping away. Once the winner was announced, there would be nothing he could do to stop Congress from making a mockery of—what? Wasn't this show a mockery of the election process anyway? Maybe Morton would do the country a favor.

But that wasn't true. Surely the voters would come to their senses and elect someone other than Ronald Chump. Anyway, the SuperPACs, the lobbyists, and Congress had far more power than the president, except in certain situations outlined in the Act....

Could one of them be the solution if a halfway sane president was elected?

At noon, he checked his phone for the millionth time. Nothing. Instead of texting Joanne again, he sent a message to Jeremy.

Meet me in the Green Room. Need a favor.

The two-hour spectacular that night was surprisingly uneventful. There were no more silly challenges or hoops for the contestants to jump through. The first hour was mostly recapping the highlights of the earlier episodes. Then they ran the correspondents' packages on each finalist's "journey to the fake White House." The whole thing was maudlin and ridiculous and he was once again reminded that exposing bullshit was the job he wanted, not helping create it.

In a few more hours, maybe he could make that dream a reality.

The second hour, they brought back the top ten contestants who had been voted off, plus Evan and Kevin, and he asked each of them the usual trite questions about their future plans. They all claimed they wanted to run again— except Evan, who announced he'd found a job as a standup comedian, and Bob Fuller, who said he'd rather spend his time reading poetry to California redwood trees. Haverty, Willard, and Foster gave no indication they were in on Drew Morton's plan, but instead rambled about continuing to work for the American people in Congress.

For the last segment of the show, the top three candidates were allowed to give fifteen-minute stump speeches proclaiming themselves the best candidates. Harper and Chump spewed the same shit they'd been saying since the first day.

Harper was going to play Robin Hood, taking from the rich and giving to the poor. "I'll put those old cronies where they belong—out to pasture. America will no longer be run by lobbyists and big business. I'm going to help small business owners by giving them the same tax breaks."

Which wouldn't make nearly the same difference to a business making fifty thousand a year as it would to one making fifty million a year, but Bryan wasn't supposed to ask questions at this point.

Chump was going to make America awesome again, by sticking nukes all over the borders, introducing sweat shop labor to the American economy, and, of course, building his moat. "And don't you worry about illegal immigrants swimming across it. I have a plan to stop that, too. You know how all those oversensitive whiners keep crying for SeaWorld to let their killer whales go? Well, I'm going to buy them off the park and put them in my moat. You try to swim across it, you might be whale food."

The only one who said anything original, in the last fifteen minutes of voting, was Clarice Greenforest.

"I've developed a plan for restructuring Congress, and I know exactly what I'm going to do," she said. "I've been rereading the Constitution, and taking into consideration that it was written when there was no internet, when voting for candidates online would have been a foreign concept. It says we have senators and representatives who are elected every two and six years, because it made no sense to have more frequent elections back then. You couldn't just vote by phone, you had to go stand in line and write on a paper ballot, and those ballots had to be counted.

"Today, everything is different, and Congress should be different, too. Our founding fathers didn't want big businesses and special interest groups running our country. So I propose to restructure Congress like this—Every time they hold a vote on something, immediately afterward, we have another vote on whether we want to keep those people in Congress. Anyone in the country can vote to remove his or her senator or representative, and if a high enough percentage of voters do so, then the congressperson is out and his or her state elects someone new. All congressional proceedings will be broadcast live in a method similar to the Candidate Cams, with the exception of matters involving national security. This allows the people to participate in the process, and stops SuperPACS and special interest groups from controlling Congress, and by extension, our laws. It doesn't matter if you own a senator if his people toss him out for voting your way, does it? This is the only way to take back our country, America, and I am the only candidate who will do it."

The next commercial break felt like it took an hour, although it was only six minutes—slightly longer than the average break, because so many sponsors wanted their ads to appear right before the winner was announced. While an ad for Come Closer Condoms rolled, Ronald Chump pulled a piece of paper from his pocket and studied it intently, mumbling under his breath. Bryan leaned over and stole a look—it said *MY ACCEPTANCE SPEECH.*

"I'm relieved you were smart enough to elect me," Chump read in a low voice, hunched over his page. "In my first official act as President, I would like to change the motto on the dollar bill from 'In God We Trust' to 'Chump Change'...."

Bryan turned his attention to Ronda Harper, who was studying her tablet. He could only see half the screen, but that was enough to know she was looking at a Twitter poll called, "Should we remove the word 'faithfully' from the oath of office because it might offend non-religious voters?" Below was a second poll, "Should we remove the words 'protect and defend' from the oath of office because it might offend other countries?"

Clarice Greenforest looked from one side of the audience to the other, clasping and unclasping her hands. Finally she stuffed them in her pockets. Her seven-year-old daughter tugged on her sleeve.

"Mommy, if you lose, do we still get to eat cake at the party? I'm hungry."

Greenforest smiled. "We will definitely eat cake no matter what happens."

After the final commercial, Bryan went through the motions of reiterating how important the moment was, and the audience erupted in cheers. *If I was watching this at home, I'd be groaning listening to this crap one more time.* Finally, he got to the last drum roll.

Bryan wasn't at all surprised when he ripped open the envelope and announced that Ronald Chump would be Secretary of State, Congresswoman Harper Vice President, and Clarice Greenforest of Ohio would be President of the United States.

After the acceptance speeches, they flowed directly into the inauguration special, with the Bible, and the spouses and kids, and a million red, white, and blue balloons raining down on the stage. Joanne was off to the side with the other correspondents. She caught his eye, then looked away. She didn't look mad anymore.

She didn't know what he was about to do.

Ronald Chump attempted to steal the spotlight by vowing to make a trip to Mexico and demand its president to build the moat for the US. Shanda cut off his mic and the National Guard appeared and moved him out of center stage.

"Pitch to break now," Shanda yelled.

Bryan looked directly into the camera. He was either about to commit career suicide or... who knew what else he might be about to do?

"We have some important messages from our sponsors," he said. "But they'll have to wait because I have some breaking news to tell you. Senator Haverty, will you please join me?"

"WHAT THE FUCK ARE YOU DOING?" Shanda screamed.

Haverty nodded and hurried to stand next to Bryan. He had a tablet in one hand.

"Just minutes ago, in our last break, Senator Haverty informed me of a grave crisis taking place in Congress right now, as we speak," Bryan said. "It can't wait until later for reasons that will soon become clear to you. Senator, please share with the audience the video you just sent me."

Off to the the side, Joanne's eyebrows disappeared under her hairline. Her face was somewhere between angry and intrigued.

Senator Haverty held up the tablet and gestured for the camera to zoom in. "I emailed this to the control room just now, but I don't know if they've had a chance to get it ready to air, so I hope you can see okay," he said. "Hopefully our mics will pick up the audio."

It would sound like crap, but people could probably understand it.

"Did you know about this, what are we doing, ohmygod Bryan I'm going to kill you," Shanda screamed.

Haverty hit play. "This video was taken a few hours ago," he explained. "I pretended to go along so I could get video evidence of this disgusting power play."

The video showed a meeting of twenty or so senators and representatives, including Haverty, Foster, and Willard, and led by none other than Drew Morton. They sat in a dark room lined with books and small statues and piles of paper, probably someone's office.

"This farce of an election has gone far enough," Morton said. "The only reason we passed the By the People, For the People Act was to show America they weren't smart enough to make their own decisions—that's why we need SuperPACs and special interest groups to steer America in the right direction, am I right?"

The group cheered.

"But we've let this nonsense go on long enough. I mean, Ronald Chump? And that moron made it to the top three. Now do you see why it's up to the leaders of big businesses and special interest groups to steer Congress? We can't trust America to make good decisions. Now let's go introduce the bill to repeal By the People, For the People, and get this thing over with before the first glass of champagne is poured, huh?"

"Ohmygod, we just got a press release from Congress," Shanda shouted in his ear. *"They're saying they... they've called an emergency session and passed the Fair Election Act, to overturn the current election results, on the grounds that the By the People, For the People Act is unconstitutional."*

Joanne mouthed thank-you from her seat on the couches, where she was going to interview the winner, and flashed Bryan a smile.

"I've just been told the Act, also known as the Twenty-Eighth Amendment, has been declared unconstitutional by Congress," he explained to the audience. "The Fair Election Act they've just passed in an emergency session states election policy will revert to the plan specified in the Twelfth Amendment, which laid out our previous Electoral College system."

Greenforest frowned. "I can veto that bill."

"Of course you can, although Congress assures us it has the two-thirds majority to override your veto. As for the rest, our legal team is on it," Bryan read off the bubble of information Artie popped up on his tablet. "Given that this deals with brand-new legislation, and the fact Congress's attempted bill calls into question the constitutionality of said legislation, most likely this thing will take forever to resolve, and probably make its way to the Supreme Court. However, I believe you will remain president until that happens. I do have a suggestion though—as a member of the voting public, I can at any point make suggestions to candidates, and to the president, too."

"What are you doing?" Shanda screamed.

He reached behind him and turned off his IFB. If he needed something, he could turn it back on, or just ask Artie on his tablet.

Joanne got up from the couch and joined the group on center stage, apparently deciding the winner interview wasn't happening any time soon, and whatever was going down right now was more newsworthy.

"What is it?" Greenforest gave Bryan a wary look. Couldn't blame her. Look at what Congress had just done.

"I did some reading, and as the current president, you can restructure Congress as described in your campaign plan right now by issuing an executive order—if three-quarters of the voting public agrees. You see, there's another interesting thing in the Twenty-Eighth Amendment. For years, there was a lot of controversy surrounding executive orders and what the president did or did not have the authority to do on his or her own. To settle that issue, the By the People, For the People Act includes a clause that says an executive order made by the president will stand, even if Congress opposes it—but only if a three-quarters majority of American voters supports that executive order. As the sitting president, you can issue one right now and call for a vote. I think the public just expressed their desire to do things this way by voting in record numbers this year."

"Preposterous! It doesn't really say that," Chump said.

"Have you read the Twenty-eighth Amendment, also known as the By the People, For the People Act?" Bryan already knew the answer.

Chump folded his arms over his chest. "I have the best team of lawyers."

"Well, why don't we ask the contestants from Congress?" Bryan waved at the rest of the top ten. "You all read the whole thing, every word, before you voted for it, right?"

Crickets again.

"Did any of you read it?" Bryan pressed, glad he'd turned off his IFB and didn't have to hear Shanda's undoubtedly unpleasant reaction.

Bob Fuller shrugged. Sara Finnegan pulled out her cell phone and tapped on the screen, probably googling the Act.

Buckshaw stuffed his hands in his pockets. "I'm not in Congress, and I was busy solving the unemployment problem in Texas, as you'll recall."

"Of course I read through it," Haverty said. "But, you know, it's a very long bill. Obviously I didn't memorize every word...."

"I was absent when they voted on that bill, because I was working to help the farmers of my state, and I'd proudly do so again," Foster said.

"I don't recall." Willard straightened his tie.

"I read it," Joanne said. "In fact, we had a lot of fun with the Act at NNN. Our assignments editor had us print the entire thing. Did you know it fills four five-inch binders? Duplexed, I might add. The language was very dry, but that was a huge story. We brought in a team of legal experts to help us understand anything that seemed ambiguous. I assure you, the clause is exactly as Bryan described it."

Greenforest nodded. "Of course it is. I may not be in Congress, but I read the Act so I could explain our new election system to my students."

Chump rolled his eyes at her. "Why would Congress vote for a clause like that? Wouldn't it limit their power?"

"I read that bill, and I voted for it because the likelihood of the voting public coming to a three-quarters majority was so small as to be meaningless." Harper must have thought it was safe to speak up now that she had confirmation of what the Act said. "Under our old election system, voters couldn't even agree on the candidate to nominate within their own party. Supporters of each candidate spent more time attacking each other than the other party. We'll never have a majority popular vote, and I'm sure the other members of Congress understood that when they voted."

Bryan shrugged. "On most issues, I imagine you would be right. However, it seems to me that the voters agree on one thing—they prefer the new election system. Also, through the course of this show, we've learned almost everybody is frustrated with Congress as a whole, and the large corporations and Super-PACs that control Congress."

"So if President Greenforest makes an executive order to restructure Congress, and the majority of voters agree, there's no legal recourse?" Joanne asked.

"I'm sure Congress has a team of lawyers waiting to fight that, of course," he said. "Again, this is new legislation and there aren't any other cases to provide a legal precedent, so it's hard to know for sure. Most of the legal experts I've talked to think it's unlikely Congress will win a legal battle if the president gets the votes. But if they do and the restructuring gets canceled—well, America, you can still vote these crooks out in two years, and I recommend you do just that."

Harper stepped up beside Greenforest. "I will support your executive order in any way I can, Madam President."

"So will I. I need to keep my position so I can get Mexico to build that wall. Besides" —Chump leaned over and elbowed Bryan, then pointed at the new president and vice president— "when these two girls get in a cat fight and kill each other, guess who gets to be president?"

Bryan blinked. "The Speaker of the House?"

Chump shook his head. "Of course not! The Secretary of State is next in line."

"That's not how—" Bryan started, but the new president cut him off.

"I'm sure Secretary Chump can familiarize himself with how things work later." She smiled but her eyes shot daggers at Chump, a trick she'd picked up after only a few days of hanging around with politicians. "My fourth-grade class at home could explain it, I'm sure."

"Personally, I'd like to hear why Mr. Chump assumes the president and vice president are going to, and I quote, 'Get in a cat fight and kill each other,'" Joanne said.

"You're clearly trying to write a hit piece about me." Chump folded his arms and turned his back on her. "Madam Prez, listen, you have to help me introduce a bill so we can sue all the journalists who write horribly negative stories about me."

"Not now." The new president shot him a look that probably used to silence her classroom, and Chump apparently decided to save his suggestions for later.

Greenforest smoothed her gray pantsuit, which was slightly threadbare and looked like it had been bought off-the-rack a decade ago, maybe for a job interview. She looked over at her husband, who wore a *Greenforest for Prez* t-shirt and a look that said, *what the fuck just happened?* and her daughter, who was playing a game on her tablet. Finally she turned her attention back to the cameras.

"I am going to issue that executive order to reorganize Congress right now," she said. "And I'd like to let the voting public know that my order and a call for a vote on it will be online shortly. I would appreciate your votes."

46

"WAIT UP," JOANNE YELLED as Bryan was about to get into his limo. He paused as she ran up to him.

"Are you fired yet?" she asked.

He laughed. "I don't know. They don't need anyone to host this show for four more years, but I know Shanda isn't too happy. She threatened to sic the network's lawyers on me, but I'm trending almost as high as Greenforest right now, so I guess not, at least for now."

"My boss from NNN called," she said. "He says they want to go into production on a new show to cover everything Congress does, at least until the amendment stuff gets straightened out. Off the record, the show's lawyers don't think it will. Congress is much too afraid of the voting public to try to pull off another coup, and I've even heard talk they could be accused of treason, although, being Congress-people, it's unlikely they will ever be charged."

"Sounds like an interesting show. I hope they're letting you host it. That's the job for you." He sighed. "I'm sorry about last night, I really am. That wasn't like me. I've just gotten so used to machinations with these people." He waved at the fake White House.

She nodded. "I know. And thank you for finding a way to out Morton without involving me. How did you get Haverty to do it?"

"I asked Jeremy to make a deal with him for me. He got a meeting with the Senator by asking to interview him about whether he'd pursue his health care initiative in the Senate. Anyway, Haverty got to take credit for turning in the dishonest congressional members, so he'll be a shoe-in if he runs again in four years. He'll be the guy who cleaned out Congress, the only honest person in, well, Congress. And Jeremy gets to write Haverty's biography, so he can do something other than host banal reality shows."

"About that." She put a hand on his shoulder. "I am going to be hosting that new show on NNN, but I told them I'd like a co-host, if you're available. You should be covering real news and exposing bullshit, not shoveling it. What do you say? Do you want to work together again?"

He smiled. "I'd like that. Just promise me I never have to be nice to Ronald Chump again."

"The first time he's a guest I'm going to annihilate him. You can jump in any time you like."

V.R. CRAFT DREW ON her extensive experience at being underemployed, watching too much TV, and dealing with compulsive liars when she wrote *Fail to the Chief,* a book about politicians competing in the ultimate reality show. She wrote it in a month after being outsourced from the only job that had paid her like she was not a kindergarten dropout.

Craft paid too much for a college diploma that loses value every day—only to be underemployed in multiple retail jobs—and that was just one of the many issues she wanted to address in this book. So she dedicated herself to writing a comedy about the world's biggest circus, er, caucus, otherwise known as the presidential election.

V.R.'s skill set includes sarcasm, satire, and snark. If those things were valued by employers, she'd be rich, but they're not so please buy her book.

For the past several years, she has written for the local *Gridiron Show,* which roasts local and national celebrities and events, and maintains a blog called *Sharable Sarcasm.* She has been published on *The Satirist,* and has been writing for *Humor Outcasts* since September of 2016. Other books to date include *Stupid Humans, Trust Pill,* and *Stupider Humans.*

www.ingramcontent.com/pod-product-compliance
Lightning Source LLC
Chambersburg PA
CBHW050404260626
47156CB00003B/864